WICKED KNIGHT

KNIGHT'S RIDGE EMPIRE #1

TRACY LORRAINE

Editing by Pinpoint Editing

Proofreading by Sisters Get Lit.erary

Photography by Wander Aguiar

NOTE

Author's Note

The Knight's Ridge Empire series is set in London, UK. Other than Stella, all characters speak British English, so spelling and grammar may be a little different.

Stella moved from Rosewood High at the end of her junior year. She is going back a year in Knight's Ridge sixth form and starting as a year 12/lower sixth student. The boys are all in year 13/upper sixth, the US equivalent of senior year.

WARNING

This book contains content that might offend you!

Do not keep reading if you do not like...
-Dub/non-con
-Bullying
-Knife and blood play
-Mutilation
-Humiliation
-Somnophilia
-Sexual violence
-Exhibitionism/voyeurism
-And probably some other questionable things I've forgotten.

Enjoy!

CHAPTER ONE

Stella

"Looks like you're up next," an unfamiliar voice says from a little farther down the hallway.

I glance up. Our eyes connect for a beat, and I recognize the pained look within them. I'm sure she's just endured the same speech I'm about to get.

I can only assume it's her first day too. Although I have a suspicion that might be where our similarities end.

Where I'm light, she's dark. Her almost black hair is twisted up into a messy updo, her makeup is heavy, and she's even managed to ditch the required school shoes for a pair of biker boots.

That little bit of defiance makes a smile twitch at my lips. Maybe we have more in common than I first thought.

As she makes her way down the hall, I glance back as the woman waiting for me appears in the entrance to her office.

I met Miss Hill, Knight's Ridge's Student Welfare Director, a few weeks ago when Dad and I came to look around and finalize everything for my attending here.

"Thank you," I whisper, slipping into her office. Lowering my purse to the floor, I drop into the chair in front of her desk, waiting for her to join me.

She sits, brushing a strand of hair out of her face and looking more than just a little flustered. *How badly had that previous meeting gone?*

"How's your first day going?"

I blow out a breath and quickly run the events of the morning through my head.

Well, I turned up and walked straight into the boy I screwed in a graveyard a few days ago. Only, he was not pleased to see me, and the first words out of his mouth were a threat.

I was forced to sit through the 'this is the first day of the rest of your life' bullshit speech from Mr. Davenport, our Head of Sixth here at Knight's Ridge College.

And I've had homeroom and two classes, both of which seemed to include the British versions of the cheer bitches of my past—vapid, spiteful girls who openly turned their noses up at me the second I walked into the room.

I guess my only saving grace was that I didn't have any classes with him.

I push all that to the side and force a smile onto my lips.

"It's been great," I lie, twisting the hem of my blue and white tartan skirt around my finger.

"Well, you sure do have experience with first days at school."

I laugh, because it's either that or I push the chair out behind me and leave as fast as I entered.

I don't need anyone relaying my past. I'm more than aware of just how many schools I've attended over the years. Of how many new starts I've had. Of how many groups of bitchy girls have made it more than clear on day one that I don't belong, how many teachers I've met, classes I've started and never finished, how many boys I've fooled around with knowing I'd be gone only days later and never thought about again.

"There's a whole load of new firsts here for me, though." I pull at the tie around my neck and scowl.

"I'm sure you'll be used to it in no time," she says softly.

I like Miss Hill. I did from the first moment she introduced herself to me. Unlike some patronising teachers I've met over the years, she seems... normal. Down-to-earth. I also don't get the impression that she's Knight's Ridge born and bred like I'm sure some of the staff are. She seems a little more... worldly, and I respect that.

"I guess that all depends on whether I get the chance or not."

"Your father seemed pretty adamant that you'll get to spend two years here."

"I can only go on past experiences. I think seven months was the longest time we've ever spent anywhere."

"That must be exhausting. You deserve to be able to settle here, Stella."

"Yeah. As I said, we'll see."

Silence falls over us for a beat before she slides a copy of my schedule across the desk ready for us to discuss.

"How have your classes been?"

"Great."

"I know you've only had two so far, but if you feel

anything needs to change, if you've made a mistake, it's better to speak up sooner."

"I'm confident in my choices, Miss Hill," I assure her.

"Okay. Well, in our last meeting you talked about your love of cheerleading and gymnastics. As promised, I've spoken to Miss Peterson about you joining the gymnastics squad. They train on Tuesdays and Thursdays after school. She also got this for you... I know a number of her girls attend classes."

Miss Hill slides over a folder with UKCA printed across the front.

"Thank you. I appreciate it, but I've already signed up to a local club. I'm starting Wednesday night."

"That's great. I'm so glad you can continue with something you love."

"Yeah," I mumble, more than ready to get out of here and figure this place out first-hand.

Thankfully, the bell rings out through the old building we're sitting in, signalling the start of lunch.

"I guess I should let you go and find some food. Our sixth form restaurant is great, I'm sure you'll enjoy it."

The fact that she calls it a restaurant makes my brows rise. I'm used to old cafeterias with equally as old and tasteless food.

"If you need anything, my door is always open. I know starting here is going to come with some challenges, but I'm confident you're going to thrive."

"Thank you," I say as sincerely as possible, before grabbing my purse from the floor and heading for the door.

"Do you need directions?" she offers.

"I'm sure I can figure it out," I say, taking off down the hallway.

I was given a chaperone first thing this morning to help me find my way around, seeing as almost all the other kids have spent their entire school lives in Knight's Ridge, but I quickly blew off the goodie two shoes, who looked about ready to explode with excitement over the fact that she'd been chosen for the role. I almost felt bad when her bottom lip wobbled after I told her that her services wouldn't be needed. I had a map, courtesy of my previous visit to Miss Hill's office. And after all, schools aren't exactly that hard to navigate. It's almost a hobby of mine at this point.

The scent of garlic and cheese is enough to lead me in the direction of the restaurant. I walk down the hallways of the old stone building most of the sixth form is situated in, taking in the pristine paint and the artwork on the walls and wonder just how the hell I ended up here.

Where are the old, damaged lockers? The graffiti? The kids having fights in the dark corners where no one's watching... or worse.

Other students pass me, each one dressed the same as the other.

The girls in their hideous tartan skirts—the length of said skirt telling me all I need to know about their social standing—boys in their badly fitting grey pants, and everyone in the same tie and navy blazer.

It's bizarre. And it's going to take some time to get used to, I'm sure.

The second I step into the restaurant, though, everything begins to look a little more normal—the building with its high vaulted ceilings aside. There are kids queuing for food and others sitting around the huge array of tables.

It takes me no more than five seconds to work everyone out.

There are the IT nerds, the artists, the science geeks, the student body council, the girls who are too shy to look at a boy, and the boys who are horny but too terrified to even risk looking at a pair of tits in case they shoot their load in their pants. And then, right at the back of the vast hall, is Knight's Ridge royalty.

Unlike the rest of the room, these guys are sitting atop the tables and one of them has a speaker set-up, filling the room with obnoxious hip-hop.

I spot a couple of the girls from my classes. All of them seem to be wiggling about in the guys' laps, staring up at them as if they're something special.

The second I get a look at their faces, I realize they really fucking aren't. They're just the same pig-headed, arrogant assholes that seem to think they control everything.

They're hot. Sure. But they all know it, too.

My teeth grind and my fingers curl as my eyes search for *him*.

The douchebag from the graveyard who thought threatening me this morning was the best way to reintroduce himself.

Fucking asshole. There's no way he's not a part of that crowd.

When I finally locate him, the anger that was stirring in my stomach explodes at the sight of him pinning the girl who I assume is the ringleader of the bitch crew against the restaurant wall.

Her golden hair is pulled back into the sleekest ponytail I think I've ever seen, and her face—even from this distance—is flawless. Thankfully, I can't see her body, but I know from previous experience that she's got the curves of a fucking goddess.

If I had the energy to feel anything about her when our eyes locked as I walked into my English lit class earlier, then I'd have hated her. But like most cheer bitches from my past, I paid her little mind before holding my head high and dropping into an empty chair, all the while feeling her laser beams of hate burning into my back.

To girls like her, any new female is a threat.

Well, I've had a taste of what she's currently grinding up against, and while it might have been fun, after the less than friendly reception I received only a few hours ago, she's more than welcome to him.

I have no desire to get in the middle of whatever they've got going on.

Ripping my eyes from the 'it' crowd, I find the short line waiting for food and head over.

My stomach growls, and when I get a look at what's on offer, I realize that it's not just the smell that's that much better than my previous schools, but it actually looks edible as well.

With a tray full of food, I walk toward the tables, scanning for the closest viable option.

There's no way I'm joining any of the geek tables.

What I really need is an empty one. I'd much prefer to sit alone than pretend I care about whatever the people around me are talking about.

Finally, my eyes land on an almost empty table, and when I recognize the one person sitting at it, I know it's where I'm meant to be.

"Hey, do you mind?" I ask, nodding toward the empty side of the bench.

She glances up, her eyes assessing me for a beat before one of her shoulders lifts in a shrug and she looks back down as if I'm already boring her.

"Sure."

Lowering my tray, I take a seat.

"Your first day too?" I ask, although I'm not sure why the words fall from my lips. It's not like she's giving off 'hey, I'm friendly, talk to me' vibes.

It takes her a second, but she finally drags her attention from her cell and toward me.

Her eyes narrow as she looks me over. I know why. I'm sure I don't look anything like the kind of people she's usually friends with.

"Y-yeah. Is it that obvious?"

Copying her move, I shrug. "Just that you were coming out of Miss Hill's office, and now you're sitting here alone."

Shooting a quick glance over her shoulder, she mutters, "Not really my kind of people."

"Tell me about it," I agree, spearing a piece of pasta with my fork and popping it into my mouth.

Oh my God, I inwardly groan when the flavors of the ragu hit me. This really isn't one of the school cafeterias of my past.

"You American?" she asks with a sigh, sounding utterly bored by our riveting conversation.

"What gave me away?" I joke. "I'm Stella, by the way," I add when she doesn't look like she's going to reply.

"Emmie. What do you have this afternoon?"

"Math. You?"

"Art."

I nod as she looks back down at her cell and begins scrolling.

Okay then, maybe my first impression that we were going to have absolutely nothing in common was correct.

Ensuring we're really not going to have any more conversation, Emmie pulls her AirPods from her bag and shoves them into her ears.

I get it. The music booming from the back of the room isn't really doing it for me either.

Without meaning to, I look in the direction of the speaker.

But I regret it almost immediately when I lock onto a pair of dark, angry eyes.

I suck in a sharp breath as something crackles between us, but I don't back down.

I'm Stella fucking Doukas. And if I've learned anything over the years, it's that the worst thing to do—especially on the first day in a new school—is to look weak.

CHAPTER TWO

Sebastian

"What's wro—ugh, really, Seb?" Teagan whines when she follows my stare and finds what—or who's—caught my attention. "She's hardly your type." Teag rolls her eyes so hard, I swear it must hurt. I hope it fucking does. My teeth grind as I push her away from me. "What?"

Taking a step closer to her, I stare down at her, my expression hard. "Don't pretend you know anything about me, Teag." Her lips part to argue, but I cut her off. "All you know is how hard I can make you come. Don't think there's any more here than that."

Her lips twist in irritation, but she clearly gets my warning because she keeps her mouth shut.

Stepping past her, I rejoin the guys at the table, who take one look at my face and push away the girls who were pawing all over them.

Usually, I allow it. Hell, I more than allow it, especially if it ends up with us in that little storage room a little down from the restaurant, but not today. Today, I want to wrap my hands around someone's fucking throat and squeeze the life out of her... and as much as Teagan might get on my tits, she's not the one I'm interested in.

"You gonna tell us what the fuck is going on yet?" Theo barks, his jaw tics in frustration.

I get it. I've been like a bear with a sore head since the second I learned just whom I'd fucked in that graveyard only a few nights ago.

I was still fucking furious when I turned up at his doorstep and demanded alcohol no less than an hour after she walked away from me.

He assumed it was because of the date. He called Alex and the three of us got wasted, raising a glass or ten to those I've lost. But little did they know, that was only the tip of the iceberg.

Alex shoots a look toward Stella and my fists clench, a move that doesn't go unnoticed by anyone around the table.

"You know we've got your back, man. But you're gonna need to give us a fucking clue here," Nico says, sounding weirdly concerned for once in his life. Motherfucker usually doesn't give two shits about anything.

Clearly just as shocked by his concern, his cousin, Theo, turns his eyes from me to him.

"What?" he barks. "Would you rather he kill someone?"

Theo's lips part to say something, but Toby beats him to it.

"Leave him be. If Seb don't wanna talk then he don't

have to. Hell knows I don't share my secrets with you twisted motherfuckers," he mutters with a smirk.

Reaching over, I squeeze his shoulder.

"See, why can't you all be more like Tobes? Let me drown in my own misery."

Movement across the restaurant catches my eye, and my heart jumps into my throat as I watch her pick up her tray, dump the contents and head for the exit.

Nice try, Doukas.

"Her pussy must have been really fucking good," Alex concludes, making Nico and Theo snort a laugh.

"Fuck this. I'm out."

Abandoning what's left of my lunch on the table, I leave them behind without a second thought, following her like a fucking junkie needing a fresh hit.

Their concerned stares burn into my back, but I don't give a fuck about them. The only thing I can think about is her. About the fact that she and her fucking cunt of a father dared showed their faces in London, let alone start here.

Knight's Ridge is our empire. Not his. And it's certainly not hers.

Most kids in this place give me a wide berth on the best of days, but with the current scowl on my face, everyone damn near jumps out of my way as I trail after her.

She's completely oblivious to the fact that she's got a stalker as she turns the corner, her ass swaying, her short tartan skirt that I'm sure is meant to be demure riding a little too high on her thighs with every step she takes.

Tugging up the hood on the hoodie I shouldn't be wearing, I continue after her.

A few kids glance between us with concern etched

onto their faces, but not one of them would be brave enough to get in the way of my intentions.

The only ones who'd risk it are still sitting in the restaurant, completely oblivious as to what my issue is with this girl. I've not so much as breathed her name to them, because the second Theo hears it, he's going to know, and he's going to be standing right behind me as I take exactly what I'm owed from this girl.

But as much as I might appreciate his support, right now, I want her all to myself.

She slips into the girls' bathroom without so much as looking over her shoulder.

She seemed pretty perceptive that night in the graveyard, but it seems that maybe she's let her guard down.

Silly, silly girl.

The second I step into the toilets behind her, the three girls doing their makeup at the basins turn to me, their eyes wide and fear covering their faces. Another who walks out of one of the stalls actually yelps.

But none of their reactions stop Stella as she closes the cubicle door behind her, forcing me to wait.

Without saying a word, I shoot a look over my shoulder to the exit, and the girls stop what they were doing and all but run.

It seems luck is on my side that this room was filled with nerds who are terrified of us and not Teag and her friends who'd want to try to jump my bones the second I walked in.

The door slams behind the last one and I set about making sure we're alone, swinging each door open to ensure there's no innocent little girl hiding.

Once I know that no one's about to jump to her

rescue, I rest my ass back on the basin and fold my arms across my chest.

"Didn't think you were a hider, Hellion," I growl after a few silent seconds.

"And I didn't have you down as someone who wants to listen to me pee, *asshole*."

The corner of my lip twitches before I remember that nothing about this girl is meant to amuse me.

I hate her.

Hate. Her.

After a few seconds, she lets out a frustrated sigh before clothing starts rustling and she flushes the toilet.

The moment she pulls the door open and reveals herself, my breath catches in my throat.

I try to slam down my reaction before she notices, but if the way her eyes narrow tells me anything, it's that I was right about her perception skills.

She knew I was following her, yet she thought it was a good idea to lead me in here.

I keep my eyes on her face as she moves toward me.

I could only make out the basics of her features in the moonlight that night, but I knew it was her the second she stepped out of her car.

No other girl I've ever come across would drive a matte black Porsche 911. Weirdly, and even more annoyingly, my first thought was that it suited her. Suited us.

Her white blonde hair is hanging smoothly around her shoulders, almost like a curtain, and her makeup has been applied so perfectly she'd give Teag and her girls a run for their money.

Her curves, that I still vividly remember having

pressed up against me as I pinned her to the tree, are mouth-watering under her uniform.

"Finished?" she asks with a scowl on her face as she steps up beside me and reaches for the soap and then the tap to wash her hands.

"We haven't even started yet, Hellion," I warn, but she doesn't so much as flinch at my cold tone.

"Was there something you actually wanted?" She turns her back on me and pulls a paper towel from the dispenser to dry her hands.

Using her moment of distraction, I close the space between us, forcing her front against the cold, tiled wall before her.

Fighting my groan as her arse presses against my cock, which is interested in way more than proving how much we hate her, I remind myself of the reality.

She doesn't scream. She doesn't fight me. She doesn't react in any way as I press harder against her.

"You shouldn't be here," I snarl quietly.

"Yet here I am anyway."

Her nostrils flare as she sucks in a breath.

"Why? Why are you here?"

"Why are *you* here?" she parrots.

"This is my fucking school, Doukas. My fucking empire."

Despite the fact that she's at my mercy, her only reaction to my statement is to throw her head back and laugh like what I just said was the funniest thing she's ever heard.

In my moment of confusion, I make a mistake. A fatal fucking mistake, because my grip on her lessens, allowing her just half a second to move, and she fucking takes it.

My eyes widen and she faces me a beat before she

moves. Pain erupts between my legs and her hands press against my chest, pushing me back to the opposite wall.

My eyes water and my balls feel like they just fucking exploded as I bend over, cupping them.

"Do you remember what I said to you that night?" she asks, her shoes clicking against the tiled floor as she walks over to me.

Unable to stand, I drop to my knees. The only part I'm able to see of her is her blurred calves.

Lowering down to her haunches, she looks me dead in the eyes, her light blues shining with excitement and achievement.

"Do not underestimate me, *asshole*."

Not giving me another second of her time, she stands and marches away.

"What the fuck do you think you're doing? Let me the hell in," a female voice barks from outside the door the second Stella pulls it open.

"I think your boy might need some assistance," Stella says as other footsteps filter through the room.

"What the fuck?" Theo barks, standing over me and drilling holes into the top of my head as Alex reaches for my arm to pull me up.

"It's nothing," I grunt, the pain once again overtaking my body as I try to stand.

"Fuck off. Who is she?"

I look between my two best friends. I should confess, but also… I want to keep her all to myself to play with right now.

"Not here," I seethe.

"We'll find out," Alex warns.

"I don't doubt it. But right now, what I really need is ice."

"Let's get the fuck out of here."

"You wanna skip on the first day?" I ask, my brows lifting at Theo's suggestion. It's something we're more likely to hear from Alex or Nico. Theo is never one to skip. "We've not got training tonight, so no one will miss us."

He's got a point.

"Let's go," I mutter, more than happy to leave Stella to navigate Knight's Ridge alone for the afternoon, wondering if I'm going to pop back up again at any moment.

"I've got weed," Alex announces. "It's good shit. Maybe it'll loosen you up a little."

When we get to the door, as expected, I find Nico and Toby guarding the entrance, scaring off any girls who might look like they want to enter.

"Those two are going to be fucking trouble, man," Nico says to Theo, nodding toward the end of the corridor just before two girls disappear around the corner.

My teeth grind at the sight of her light hair and the sway in her step.

Turning up here was a bad idea. But what she just did was really fucking stupid.

And I'm going to make sure she regrets it.

CHAPTER THREE

Stella

The second I step from the bathroom, I come face to face with Emmie once again.

"Just let me in," she snaps, looking between the two guys guarding the door with her hands on her hips and a fierce expression on her face.

"No," one of the guys damn near growls, taking a step toward her.

But at no point does she cower down.

"Come on, Em. These assholes aren't worth it."

"You got that right," she scoffs, looking at the guy who moved closer to her up and down as if he's nothing more than a piece of shit on her shoe.

I knew there was a reason I liked her.

Backing away from him, she acquiesces and walks beside me—although backwards, as she continues to hold his eyes.

"Any idea where other bathrooms are?" I ask once we're out of earshot, and she finally spins, walking beside me as if the two goons aren't burning holes in our backs.

"No fucking idea. But it's got to be easier than fighting them idiots."

"You noticed that too, huh?"

I know the second *he* appears from the bathroom. A shiver of awareness races down my spine. But I refuse to allow him to know that his stare alone affects me, and I continue around the corner without so much as glancing over my shoulder.

Pulling the map from my pocket, I run my eyes over it.

"Next to the girls' locker rooms."

"I know where they are," Emmie announces, picking up speed.

I don't bother telling her that I don't actually need the bathroom. I just trail along behind her, my body moving on autopilot while my head is still back with *him*.

What the hell is his issue?

We had one night. One hot night, sure. But what is he expecting me to do?

Is the blonde from the restaurant his girlfriend and he's worried I'm about to announce his misdemeanour in the graveyard to her?

Is he that ashamed of our time together?

I remember vividly how he reacted to me that night. He might have regrets, but he wanted that as much as I did.

I figure he's got some other reason that only he's aware of. Or, and probably more likely, he's just a cunt.

Following Emmie into the bathroom, I move toward

the sinks, or more specifically the mirrors, while she disappears toward an open stall.

Just like the rest of Knight's Ridge, the bathrooms are nothing like I've experienced in a school before. They look like something you might find in a hotel, not a place for kids. Okay, insanely wealthy and stuck-up kids, but still.

I've only taken two steps forward when someone's eyes catch mine in the mirror.

"Give me strength," I mutter to myself, but not hiding the words as they fall from my lips.

"Who are you?" the blonde who was trying to climb *him* like a tree not so long ago demands, spinning on her heels and placing her hands on her hips as she narrows her eyes at me.

"Clearly not your new best friend," I quip, ignoring her and lowering my purse to the counter so I can dig out my lip gloss.

A frustrated growl rumbles in the back of her throat.

"Your boyfriend sure seemed interested, though. You saw him looking, right?"

I shouldn't bait her, I know that. But winding these bitches up is just too easy sometimes.

"I don't know who you are, but let's get one thing clear," she spits as I twist the top of my gloss and set about topping up my red lips. "Seb is mine. I've got plans for the two of us this year. Plans that don't involve skanks like you."

My brows lift, but I don't rise to it.

Seb... Sebastian. I let his name roll around in my head for a second or two. Annoyingly it suits him.

The image of his dark eyes burning into my mine as

his cock moved inside me only days ago hits me, but I fight the smirk that wants to erupt on my face.

"Thanks for the heads up. But I think we should probably let Seb make his own decisions, don't you?"

Dropping the tube back into my purse, I smack my lips together and turn to her.

My eyes track down her body for a beat, my nose curling up in disgust.

"Not that there's really a decision to make here."

When I turn away from her, I find Emmie has appeared from the stall and is standing behind me, watching our interaction with curiosity.

"You're right. There's no way he'd want your skanky, American arse."

A smile tugs at the corners of my lips at her attempt to cut me down.

"Girl, you really need to work on your insults. I would've thought after the thousands of pounds your parents have thrown at your education,"—I throw my hands up to indicate our surroundings—"you'd be a little more intelligent. When you're ready for a real argument, come find me." With a wink in her direction, I flick my hair over my shoulder and march from the bathroom, once again with my head held high and a satisfied buzz flowing through my veins.

"Okay, so I have no idea who that bitch was, but that was fucking awesome," Emmie says a few seconds later, catching up with me.

"Thanks."

"Who's Seb?" she asks curiously as we continue walking. Honestly, I've got no idea where we're going, and quite frankly, as long as I don't bump into Seb and his crew of douchebags or that bitch, I really don't care.

"No one of any importance."

"He clearly is to her."

"She's more than welcome to him in her quest to climb the social ladder. I have zero interest in all that bullshit."

"Same," Emmie agrees as we emerge from the building to find the sun shining.

"I thought it always rained in England," I muse as we walk toward an empty bench.

"I'm sure you'll experience plenty, don't worry."

Only five minutes after we sit down, the bell rings for our afternoon classes.

With simultaneous sighs, we get back up and grab our bags.

"It can only get better, right?" Emmie asks me when we're almost at the door.

"Oh, I don't know. I've had quite an entertaining day."

"Gotta love a good bitch fight," she mutters.

"Hmm... there's a thought," I whisper as I imagine dragging her to the ground by her hair. "There's always lunch tomorrow."

Emmie's still chuckling to herself when we part ways to head to our different classes.

I scan the room the second I step into my math class, but I'm not sure if I'm disappointed or relieved when I don't spot the blonde.

I find myself a seat and get my things out as the rest of the room begins to fill with students.

I know the second I have eyes on me. My entire side burns with awareness, and after squaring my shoulders ready to face whoever it is that's so interested in me, I look over.

Two girls stand blocking the doorway, much to the irritation of the students trying to get into the room.

I vaguely recognize them as the blonde's friends and roll my eyes when they continue to glower at me.

"Girls, please. You're both in the way," an exasperated sounding teacher sighs, stepping up behind them.

My eyes widen when he appears over one of their shoulders. He doesn't look old enough to be teaching, and shit, he's hot.

Both of them practically fall over themselves to get out of his way and allow him into his own classroom.

"Sorry, Mr. Wicks," they both sing, unashamedly batting their eyelashes at him.

Good God.

"Right, well. When you're all ready, shall we get started?" he asks the rest of the room once he finally manages to get inside.

Turning my attention to where he situates himself at the front of the room, I put the scowling girls out of my mind, along with the arrogant douchecanoes, and focus on what I'm here for.

Something catches my eye as I pull up to the house. The first obvious thing is that Dad's car isn't here, but that's no great shock. He's hardly ever here. The second thing is the dark lump in front of the door.

I stare at it as I pull my car to a stop but quickly kill the engine and get out.

"Oh, ew," I mutter when I step up to it and find it's a dead bird.

Stepping around it, I push the front door open to

discover Calvin, our head of security, waiting for me in gym shorts and a tank.

"For real?" I ask, knowing exactly what that look means.

"For real, Baby D. Go get changed. Your dad wants you ready for dinner in two hours."

"Ah, so he's going to grace me with his presence tonight, then?"

Calvin quirks a brow at me.

"Twice in one day. It's almost like he's feeling guilty for the school he's enrolled me in," I mutter, kicking my shoes off and heading for the stairs.

"Good first day then?" he quips.

"Fantastic. Can't wait to go back."

"You started a fight, didn't you?"

I can't help but laugh as I climb the stairs.

"You know me so well, Cal."

He groans before shouting. "I'll meet you in the basement. You can unleash some of that anger."

I might give him shit, but working out with Cal is one of my favorite things to do.

"By the way, there's a dead bird outside by the front door," I shout back before slipping into my room and closing the door.

He's been our head of security for years, for as long as I can remember. Over the years I think I've probably spent more time with him than I have my dad. It makes me sad that he's given up all his time to protect us—from what, God only knows—when he could have had a family of his own to care about, but he's never given me even a hint that he wants any of that, and I don't feel it's my place to ask. So I allow him to train me in whatever martial art he feels like each time he gets me into our home gym, and I let out a little of the aggression I seem to always carry around with me.

Between him, gymnastics, cheer, and cutting down whatever bitch decides to have a go at me, I've found a way to channel my inner badass bitch. Mostly.

Happily, I rip off my school uniform. I throw my shirt in the laundry and hang the rest up, ready for what I'm sure will be an interesting second day at Knight's Ridge College. The first has certainly been eventful.

I pull on a pair of shorts, a sports bra and tank before heading back down to find my sneakers and then Calvin, who's more than likely already warming up in the basement.

I discover I'm right, long before I get down the stairs, because the rhythmic sound of his feet hitting the treadmill finds its way up to me.

"Right, where do you want me?" I say the second I walk into our state-of-the-art home gym.

Just like all the other houses we've lived in, I know Calvin had a hand in designing it, but it's by far the most extensive one we've had when it comes to equipment. It does make Dad's promise of this being it for us ring a little more true. But even still, I'll take it with a grain of salt.

"Warm up then kick-boxing."

A smile curls at my lips as I imagine going to town on both Seb and his blonde hussy.

"Sounds like a plan, boss."

By the time he's finished with me, I'm covered in sweat, my makeup from the day is leaking down my face, and my hair's stuck to the back of my neck, but my muscles ache in the most delicious way as I drag my weak, exhausted body back up the stairs to shower, ready for dinner.

Dad is waiting for me in the kitchen with Angie when I finally emerge almost an hour later.

"Hey, sweetheart," he says, a wide smile curling at his lips. "Did you have a good day?"

"Oh, you know. Same shit, different place."

"Stella," he warns, his voice low and dangerous. Only it doesn't scare me like it does most other people.

"What? She started it," I argue.

"You're right. Some things never change."

"You trained me to be a fighter. What did you expect?"

"Just... please don't get kicked out of that place. You have no idea how hard it was to get you in last minute."

"Have I ever been kicked out of the bazillion other schools you've sent me to?" I ask, lifting a brow.

"Smartarse," he mutters, turning to Angie. "How long?"

"About ten. If you want to go and take a seat, I'll bring it through."

"You're too good to us, Angie," he says softly, smiling at her.

I watch the two of them. For years I've wondered if there's ever been anything there.

Much like Calvin, Angie has been with us for as long as I can remember and seemingly more than happy to play house with us instead of having her own.

She's a little older than Dad, but only by a few years. She's so lovely and still has a banging body, so I wouldn't put it past either Dad or Calvin having a go at her. Assuming she's into men, of course.

I follow Dad into the dining room and he shrugs off his black suit jacket and hangs it over the back of his chair.

The room, just like all the others, is about as modern

as interior design comes. All our houses have been the same, although our one in Rosewood was by far the sleekest. This one has just an edge of homeliness about it, thanks to some of the older features of the building.

The walls are all a stark white and each piece of furniture is black. It's not exactly my style, but Dad seems to love it, and he's the one paying for it.

"So seriously, how was your first day?" he asks once we're both seated.

"It was fine. Classes were great, teachers were good. It's a fantastic school." *Shame about the other students.* "What about you? How's work?" I ask, hoping, like always, that he'll open up and actually tell me something useful.

"Yeah. Good," he says, his expression hardening, telling me that's all I'm going to get.

"What about the other kids? Any potential friends?"

I smile at him. For someone who's clearly done very well for himself, he really is freaking clueless when it comes to me and school.

"Yeah, fingers crossed. This place will be like home in no time."

"I mean it, Stella. We're staying here. This is it for us."

"Sure."

He sighs, clearly sensing that I don't believe a word of it.

It's fine. I get it... I think.

CHAPTER FOUR

Sebastian

I fall on the sofa and slouch down, resting my head back while Theo crashes around in his kitchen.

He moved into his family's coach house after we finished school for the summer, and I quickly made myself at home in his spare bedroom, preferring to be here than in my own house.

It's the perfect place for us to hang, throw parties and do all the shit that we don't want Theo's parents seeing. Not that we're naïve enough to think that they're not aware, but it's better than being directly under their roof.

"Here," Alex says, dropping down on the other end of the sofa, his eyes boring into the side of my face.

Ripping an eye open, I find him holding a joint out for me.

"You need to chill the fuck out, man."

His words are like a red rag to a bull.

"Give me that," I demand, snatching the spliff from his fingers and placing it between my lips, waiting for him to light it.

They want answers, they're going to have to work for it.

The sound of bottles hitting the coffee table finally makes me lift my head to find Theo sliding beers over to us.

"Take a hit then tell all, motherfucker," he demands as he falls back and tips the bottle to his lips, taking a pull.

I do as he says, not because I want to follow his fucking orders, but with the joint hanging between my lips, the temptation is too strong.

"I fucked her a few days ago."

"Right?" Theo asks, a smug grin on his lips. Banging some random girl isn't exactly an unusual thing for me. I do spend most nights in the bedroom beside his, so he's more than aware. That's if we even make it that far.

"She turned up at the graveyard..." I trail off, not needing to explain to either of them what night it was or the reason I was hanging out in a deserted graveyard in the first place.

"Weird," Alex mutters.

"Yeah, although not as weird as the fact that she approached me while I was knocking cans off the wall."

"Holy shit. Does she have a death wish, or is she just fucking plain stupid?"

"Neither, it seems," I mutter, taking another hit and holding it in my lungs until it starts to burn.

The room starts to blur a little around me, making my words flow that much easier.

"She's got fucking balls of steel and is a better shot than the two of you put together."

"Fuck you, man," Alex scoffs. "You know I'm better than both of you."

"Whatever." Theo waves him off, too interested in what else I might have to say. "You gave her your gun?" he asks, his brows damn near hitting his hairline.

"I never stand down from a challenge, and she was a fucking tempting one."

"I get that, man. But your fucking gun?"

"Yeah, well, if I knew who the hell she was when she first turned up, I never would have handed it over, that's for fucking sure."

"Who is she?" Alex asks.

The two of them stare at me, waiting as if I'm about to divulge all of the Family's secrets.

"Estella Doukas."

Both their chins drop simultaneously.

"No," Theo breathes, his features hardening as realization hits him. "No, Galen wouldn't be so stupid," he says with more confidence than he should.

"Well, he apparently is, because it's her, man."

"Well, fuck me," Alex sighs, taking a hit on his own joint. "Was she good?"

"What?" I bark, utter disbelief coating my words.

"I'm assuming you fucked her in the graveyard. That's hot, dude. Was she good?"

My chin drops to tell him the truth, that she was fucking insane, but for some reason it feels wrong.

"It doesn't matter. If I knew who the fuck she was, I never would have touched her."

"That good, huh?" he mutters, reading into my words.

"Is she here with him?" Theo asks, focusing on the main issue here instead of getting distracted by how tight her fucking pussy was.

My cock swells the second that thought hits me, because fuck, it was just that fucking tight.

Reaching down, I pull at my trousers, making a little more space.

"Fuck me, you want another round too, don't you?"

"I wouldn't touch her with yours now I know she's that traitorous cunt's daughter."

"Sure," he laughs, "You keep telling yourself that."

"We need to tell my dad," Theo announces.

"No," I bark. "Not yet."

"Why the fuck not?"

"Well, for one, the boss has no clue that we know the truth about what went down. And second, you tip him off, he'll go straight after Galen and scare him off. I wanna know why he thought it was a good idea to come back, let alone bring his devil spawn with him."

"Bit harsh," Alex mutters, his voice lighter than usual. When I look over, I find he's almost smoked his entire joint and his eyes are blown wide fucking open. Motherfucker's high as a kite.

It's probably a good thing, because if he weren't high right now, he'd probably be halfway to finding where she is, ready to burn her house to the ground for even daring to come near us—me—after what her father did.

"Is it?" I ask, releasing a mouthful of smoke. "She has no right to be here. There's a reason they were banished all those years ago."

"Maybe there's more to it than we know," Theo points out. The only reason we know about the existence of Galen Doukas in the first place is because we overheard a conversation between his father, the Family's boss, and his uncle Evan, the underboss, a few years ago.

"I don't give a fuck if he shits fucking glitter. I know

all I need to know. He's going to regret coming back here, and he's going to regret bringing her even more."

Theo nods at me in agreement before reaching for the joint that's slowly burning between my fingers.

"Whatever you want, bro."

I nod in appreciation. He might not actually agree with me, but it doesn't matter, because this is how we work.

This has everything to do with me, and ultimately, it's my decision. And I know that my boys will be right behind me.

"She's fucking hot, though," Alex mutters, earning himself a dead arm when I reach over and punch him. "What? I'm just saying. I would."

"Bro, you'd fuck a tree if it had a hole," Theo barks.

All Alex does is shrug. He can't really argue.

"I need to get laid. All this talk of revenge fucks is getting me horny."

Before either of us can respond, Theo's cell dings with an alert that makes us all sit up.

"He wants us in."

Both of us look at Alex, who's smiling to himself as he stares at the wall.

"What the fuck was in his joint?"

"Dread to fucking ask, bro. We'll get him a coffee on the way. The boss will have his fucking balls otherwise."

The three of us pile into Theo's Maserati and head deeper into the city where the boss is waiting for us.

The street we pull up on is lined with clubs, bars, and most importantly, The Empire, the Cirillo casino and hotel.

"So we're assuming this is Nico's doing, then?" Alex mutters from the back, sounding a little more with it.

"Nah, he wouldn't. And I doubt the boss really gives a shit that we skipped," I say. He leaves most things that happen under Knight's Ridge roof for us to deal with, including our presence.

"We can only hope. He's been in a bitch of a mood recently," Theo mutters.

"So maybe he does know about Doukas," Alex adds as we climb from the car.

"I guess we're about to find out."

Together, we make our way through reception, our shoes clicking against the black tiles beneath us.

Eyes land on us as we cut through the small crowd, and I can't help but stand a little taller.

Holding everyone's attention at school is one thing. They're all kids who don't really understand all of this outside of the gossip and the stories we fill their heads with if we need some entertainment. But the clientele here is mostly more than aware of who we are and what we do, and it earns us a different level of respect.

There's a young woman standing by the casino doors whose eyes eat up my body like she wants me for her next dessert.

A knowing smirk curls at my lips, and I'm about to sidestep the guys to go to her when a hand wraps around my upper arm.

"Work first, pussy later," Theo growls, sounding more like the heir to all this, than I'm sure he realises.

"Fine," I mutter, continuing forward to the lift.

Anyone who was heading in this direction hangs back, allowing us to climb into the car alone.

Theo unlocks the panel above the standard floor buttons, revealing an extra set before punching the code in to take us to the top floor.

The air is thick as we ride in silence. We never know what Theo's father, the boss, is going to demand of us. And after the day I've had, I'm not sure I've got the energy for it.

"Afternoon, lads," Alex's dad says when we step into the security room that leads toward the deepest part of the floor, where we'll find Theo's father waiting for us.

"All right," Alex slurs, earning himself a raised brow from his father.

"Good day at school?" He winks, telling us that he's more than aware we didn't make it through the whole day.

"Yeah, you know how it is."

"Sure do, kid, but you want to earn your place here, you gotta not be a useless drop out."

"Won't happen. I got the smarts," Alex says, tapping the side of this head.

"Sure."

"Boss is waiting." Evan's deep voice booms across the room, drowning out the whir of the computers around us and commanding everyone's attention. The only man on Earth who's scarier than him is his big brother, the boss, Damien Cirillo.

We follow the voice toward the boss's office, quickly catching up with his underboss and slipping into the room behind him.

Evan takes his place standing beside Damien, who's sitting at his massive, carved, don't-fuck-with-me mahogany desk.

Unlike the rest of the modern hotel and casino, Damien's office is old school. Framed photographs of the men who've come before us line the walls, surrounded by ornate mahogany furniture. The paintwork is a deep blood red, and the carpet gives me a fucking headache each time I come in here.

I glance over at Alex, wondering if his head is spinning from having to stand on it.

I smirk when I find his chin tilted slightly up. I get it; it's almost like the weird shapes are moving when you're sober, so I can't imagine how they must look to him right now.

Over in the corner of the room, slumped back in a chair and sipping on a glass of whisky is Charon Ariti. Toby's grandad and the boss's consigliere.

"Afternoon," Damien says, his deep voice echoing around the room.

As a kid, I remember being completely terrified by him and Evan. They're so different from how my sisters portray our father.

"Problem with school this afternoon?" he asks.

"U-uh..." Theo starts, but his father soon cuts him off.

"Whatever. I'm down on security tonight for a private function. I need the three of you ready to work—sober," he says, pointing a searing look at Alex, "by nine."

"And you couldn't have told us that on the phone?"

"You should be at school. If you're not there, then you're working." Sitting back, he slides a piece of paper toward the three of us.

My heart damn near stops in my chest when I look down at the person in the photograph.

"Estella Doukas," Boss states as I fight to keep my expression neutral. The last thing I need is him reading something on my face that I'm not ready to give away yet. "She started at Knight's Ridge today."

"And what's this got to do with us?" Theo asks, cool

and calm like ever. If I were to glance over, I know I'd find his hard mask firmly in place.

It's a mask he's inherited from his father, and his grandfather before that. It's the reason I know without having to ask that one day he'll be the one sitting in that chair, running this Family and dishing out orders.

"I need the three of you to keep an eye on her."

"We're not babysitting," I blurt out, regretting it instantly when Damien's cold, hard eyes lock on mine.

I swallow, regretting making any kind of deal out of this.

"I'm not asking you to babysit her. Stella is more than capable of looking after herself."

Don't I fucking know it. My balls ache just at the thought.

"So why do we need to look out for her?"

"You just do." Damien pins his son with a look that cuts off any argument he might have. "And needless to say, this stays between us." Ripping his gaze away, he ensures that both Alex and I hear his silent warning. *Nico and Toby are not a part of this. And Stella isn't to know.*

Great, just fucking great.

"Seeing as you've given yourselves the afternoon off. I've something else for you. Go to Marco's. He's late on payment."

"You want us to—"

"No. I want you to go there and serve as a reminder that worse is going to come should he miss his deadline."

"You got it, Boss."

Damien nods at us and Evan steps around the desk, ready to see us out.

"And I'll assume I won't be hearing any more about you three bunking off."

"You got it, old man." Theo salutes his father, much to Damien's irritation.

Theo is more than aware of the respect Damien expects from him, but he pokes the bear at every opportunity. I have no idea what he's expecting to happen. Damien has never been, and will never be, a soft and caring father. Pissing him off will only lead to pain in the long run, but Theo seems set on finding out just how painful that might be.

"Alexander," Damien calls before we step out of the room. "Don't disappoint me."

Alex nods before Evan closes the door behind us, sending us on our way.

"I didn't sign up to be a babysitter for the ball buster," Alex mutters as we pile back into the lift, ready to go and give Marco a gentle nudge in the right direction.

"Seb's got it covered, right, man?" Theo asks once the doors have closed. "He wants back in her pussy again, after all."

"No. I want to use her to get to her old man."

"Right, sure. So you won't mind if my sitting comes with a side of cock then," Alex quips.

"I dunno, she looks like she could be a handful. Maybe she'd need both of us," Theo adds, making my teeth grind at the thought of her pinned between the two of them.

"You're a pair of fucking cunts," I spit, blowing out of the lift the second the doors are open.

I don't even bother looking for the woman who was hanging around earlier in my need to get out of this fucking place.

CHAPTER FIVE

Stella

"I heard they killed a guy," someone whisper-shouts as I walk into the girls' locker rooms after school the next day, ready to try out for the gymnastics team.

I roll my eyes at the excited gossip. Seb's friend's black eye and split lip, and his and the other one's busted knuckles, are all anyone's talked about all day.

Having met them, albeit briefly, I'm not surprised they found themselves in the middle of a fight. They are conceited douchebags, after all.

They're probably in some rich boy gang, pretending to be dangerous in the hope it gets all the girls.

Idiots.

I think back to his warnings the night in the graveyard and roll my eyes. He really needs to think again if he expects me to be scared of him.

It's not until I've lowered my bag to the bench that the gossiping stops, and I know why. Their attention drills holes into my back.

I guess it stands to reason that Blonde—who I've since learned is actually called Teagan, thanks to some gossip I heard earlier about what she got up to recently behind the swimming pool with some guy—is on the gym team. I guess this is Knight's Ridge's version of the cheer squad.

Just like when I overheard it earlier, a wave of something I really don't want to acknowledge at the thought of her being with Seb rolls through me. No one's mentioned his name, but from what I've seen, he seems to be the only one that vapid bitch is interested in right now.

Reminding myself that I don't care, I suck in a calming breath and prepare to turn around.

"Are you lost?" Teagan asks, her two sidekicks standing just a little behind her with equally pissed off looks on their faces as they stare at me.

"Um... nope. I don't think I am," I say, throwing my hair over my shoulder.

"I don't think you've got what it takes to be on my team."

"Oh really?" I ask, taking a step toward her. "And why would you think that?"

"Because over here you actually have to work, not just jiggle your pom-poms for the dads in the crowd."

"Is that right?" I ask, anger burning through my veins at her assumption of me, mimicking their stances and placing my hands on my hips.

"You should probably just leave now before you embarrass yourself."

"Yeah, maybe. Or I could stay and watch you eat a piece of humble pie when I wipe the floor with you."

Not waiting for a response, I turn my back on them once again and begin getting ready.

I'm faster than them, seeing as they spend most of the next ten minutes whining like the little bitches they are and trying to intimidate me into giving up.

They are seriously barking up the wrong tree if they expect me to cower down to them.

Only a few of the quieter girls have left the locker room by the time I do, and I find them warming up while Miss Peterson—I assume—talks to them with a wide smile on her face.

"H-hi, Miss Peterson," I stutter, interrupting their conversation. "I'm—"

"Stella," she says with an even wider smile.

Okay, I like her already.

"I've done some research, and I must say, I'm impressed. I think you're going to fit right in on this team."

Yeah... or not.

While the rest of the team emerges from the locker room and begins warming up, Miss Peterson walks me around the gym, showing me all their state-of-the-art equipment, talking me through the competitions they take part in and proudly pointing out their trophies. Maybe Teagan did have a point being worried about adding new members to her team, even if she did go the wrong way about it.

"Why don't you warm up with the girls, and then you can show us what you can do. I saw on your transfer documents that floor is your favourite."

"Yeah."

"Teagan's our champion floor gymnast. A little competition will be good for her."

"Great," I say, but it's full of sarcasm that I'm sure she doesn't miss.

I join the others and come to a stop beside a light-haired girl who's stretching into splits.

"Hey," she says, a welcoming smile on her lips. "I'm Calli."

I can't stop the smile that pulls at my lips, finding someone who's not immediately seeing me as some kind of competition.

"Hi, I'm Stella."

"I'm not sure whether I should tell you that you're stupid or brave for this," she confesses, clearly having heard the altercation in the locker room.

"I guess we'll find out," I laugh, switching positions.

It turns out I'm not the only one who's here to try out for the team. A handful of other lower sixth students have turned up, all of whom Miss Peterson knows because they've been competing lower down the school. I am the only actual new person, which is why I'm the one called on to show off my skills.

Clearly Miss Peterson has done her homework as she sets the girls up on the different apparatus once two other teachers join us but keeps me, Teagan and her two shadows standing beside the sprung floor.

"Show us what you've got then, Stella," she says, her eyes shining with excitement.

Challenge accepted.

Adjusting the waistband of my shorts, I step up to the corner of the floor, feeling the eyes of every person in the room on me.

Most just want to see what I'm capable of, but there are three at least who are currently praying that I fall on my face. And it's those three sets of eyes I meet right before I take off on my series of tumbles across the mat.

I manage a solid landing just an inch inside the line, and after sucking in a deep breath, I realize that the room around me is in silence.

Glancing over at Miss Peterson, I find she's got the widest smile on her face, her hands together as if she had clapped, while the three beside her fume to the point their faces are glowing red—none quite as brightly as Teagan's.

"Your previous coach wasn't exaggerating," Miss Peterson says as Teagan mutters, "It wasn't that good."

Whatever.

I spend the next two hours ignoring the hate-filled stares they shoot across the gym and focus on losing myself in doing some of my favorite things.

Cheer has always been my number one, but gymnastics is a close second. Dad signed me up for my first class when I could barely stand and I've been addicted since. I just love that weightless feeling of flying through the air. That's the exact reason I climbed to the top of a cheer pyramid at my first opportunity.

"I've decided," Calli announces when we finally get back to the locker room after our session. "You're brave."

I laugh as I make my way toward her.

"I think I prefer that option."

"Just watch your back. You've probably already realised this, but Teagan, Lylah and Sloane are mega bitches."

"Oh really, I didn't notice," I deadpan.

Some of the girls shower and replace the image of perfection they walked into these locker rooms with. I, however, just pull a hoodie out of my bag and throw it over my shorts and sports bra, preferring to shower at home.

Campus is quiet when I emerge from the building. Thankfully, Teagan and her bitches were too busy to pay me any attention as I slipped out. Her confidence was already in tatters while we were practicing, so I don't think she had the energy to go another round with me.

There are still cars littering the parking lot. I scan the expensive models, shaking my head at the insane wealth of this place.

In the past, my Porsche has stood out like a sore thumb, but here, she blends right in. Hell, compared to some, she actually looks cheap, which really is saying something.

Voices filter down to me from the other end of the lot, and I regret looking up the second my eyes lock with a certain dark pair.

Thankfully, Seb and his loyal followers have kept their distance today, although I must admit I've been waiting for them to make their move.

I didn't get the impression that yesterday was all Seb wanted from me. And I'm sure he's not going to take the ball ache I gave him lying down. I might have got him on his knees, but I'm sure it's not somewhere he makes a habit of being.

Images flicker through my mind of another time I had him on his knees, but I lock them down almost as quickly as they erupted.

His eyes hold mine for a beat before he takes a step forward from the Aston Martin they're standing around. His face is set, anger rippling from him as his eyes track down my body.

The urge to pull my hoodie tighter around me to

cover up is strong, but there's no way I'll ever cower to this jerk, so I stand there and let him get his fill.

"Careful, *Sebastian,* anyone would think you wanted another round," I announce loudly. Something tells me he's the only one who'd care about anyone learning what happened that night. That he lowered himself to touch the new girl, or whatever it is he thinks of me that suddenly made him hate me.

His friends scoff and laugh behind him as his fists curl.

"You need to watch your back, Doukas," he seethes.

"Oh, so we're on last name terms now," I quip. "You'd better tell me yours then."

"I'm giving you nothing," he snarls, lifting his hand and pushing his wet hair from his brow.

Glancing back at the other four, I find them in a similar state. From the gossip I've heard around this place in the past two days, I can only assume they're on the soccer team—or football, as it is here. They seem to be the ones who think they own the school, and these five ooze power. Or at least think they do.

"Right, well, as fun as this little catch-up has been. I've got better things to do with my time." I drop my eyes down his body, my gaze locking on his crotch. "And I'm sure you need to go and ice your balls."

His jaw tics, his eyes narrow in warning as he steps closer.

He doesn't stop until there's only a hair between us. His heat burns into my body, but I don't so much as flinch as I'm forced to look up at him.

I don't give a shit that I'm smaller. I've already proven that I can take him down with minimal effort.

"You really think you're something, don't you?"

I shrug. "I think I'm better than you."

He moves faster than I expect, his hand wrapping around my throat a beat before my back collides with a car.

"And that would just be another mistake you've made."

I quirk a brow in an attempt to look bored by his big scary bad boy act. But I also hope that it's enough to stop him reading into how his possessive hold affects me.

The tighter his fingers get around my throat, the more my blood begins to boil. Only now, it's not with anger.

With him right in my face, his hot breath tickling over my skin and his freshly-showered scent in my nose, I can almost convince myself that we're right back in that graveyard, just two lost people searching for something in the darkness.

"Seb, put her fucking down," one of his boys barks, and everything comes crashing down around me as reality hits once more.

Leaning in closer, his lips brush my ear and I have to fight to suppress the shudder of desire that wants to rip through my body.

"I'd keep looking over your shoulder if I were you."

He moves back with his brows pulled together when all I do is laugh.

"You're all mouth, *Sebastian*." I say his name in my best posh English accent in the hope of it pissing him off.

"Am I?" he seethes, his voice so low that no one else has a chance at hearing him. "Keep trying me and you might be lucky enough to learn how wrong you are."

"Try me, asshole. I'll be waiting."

"Seb?" A sickly sweet voice pierces through the lot

and I outwardly groan, knowing who it belongs to without even looking.

"Oh, your little plaything is here. Go and give her all your bullshit. I'm sure she'll lap it right up."

His eyes hold mine, the air between us crackling as I'm sure Teagan fumes in the distance.

"At least I won't need that ice for my balls. Teag's mouth will sort me right out."

If he's waiting for a reaction after that statement then he's going to be bitterly disappointed.

"I hope she bites."

"Seb," she hisses this time, "get your hands off the rubbish."

He releases me like a good little puppy.

"Aw, so you *can* be trained," I quip, much to his irritation if the vein that bulges by his temple is anything to go by. "Good to know."

The dangerous growl that rips up his throat does weird things to my insides. Things that tell me I need to get the hell away from him right now.

Pressing my palm against his chest, I ignore just how muscular it is and force him to back up.

"You're right," I say, glancing at a shocked Teagan. "The trash really needs to keep his hands to himself."

"Oh, I wasn't talking about—"

Pushing from the car he backed me up against, I step toward her.

"Back the fuck off, Teagan. I don't want anything from you. That asshole is all yours."

I hold her shocked stare for a beat before turning my back on the lot of them and stalking toward my car.

It's not until I've got the door closed behind me that I let out the frustrated breath I was holding.

Was it too much to ask to start here and just blend in?

Apparently so.

My cell pings in my purse, and instead of just getting the fuck out of there and away from the idiots who are still loitering, I drag it out.

A smile curls at my lips when I find a call from Harley. Just seeing her name makes me smile.

Harley and Ruby were the first real friends I've made in years after vowing to never get close to anyone after my first few schools. I learned quickly that it was a waste of time and effort to make friends when I was ultimately going to be ripped away from them in the coming weeks or months. But there was something about Rosewood that allowed me to lower my walls, and I reluctantly let them both in.

Then the inevitable happened, and I had to leave them behind.

But unlike the friends that came before them, they've both kept in touch, making this whole move that little bit easier.

"Hey," I say, my voice lighter than it has been for a while. "How's it going?"

"Hey. It's good. We're just on lunch, thought I'd check in. How's the fancy new school treating you?"

Groaning, I fall back into the seat and give her a very basic rundown.

"You've been there two days and annoyed both the queen bitch and her king already. That's got to be a record, Stella, even for you."

"They're a bunch of assholes," I scoff.

"I don't doubt it."

"How's senior year treating you?" I ask with a heavy

heart. I should be there experiencing it with them, but here I am, starting over once more.

"It's great. Ruby is fucking killing it as cheer captain already."

"As if she'd do anything else." I smile, thinking of her taking charge and whipping the new squad into shape.

"And the boys? Kyle?"

I swear I hear her swoon at the mention of his name alone.

"Everyone is great. The boys are going to kill it this year, I can feel it. Ash is a great captain," she says, mentioning Ruby's boyfriend. "What about you? You managed to find a cheer club?"

"Yeah, I have. I'm going tomorrow night. I joined the gymnastics team at school, too."

"That's awesome. I'm so glad you're finding your feet."

"Yeah, although a few already want to knock me off them," I joke.

"Then they need to learn you're not one to be messed with."

"I'm biding my time. Although, there is already one boy walking around with bruised balls courtesy of my knee."

"Yes, girl," she squeals.

As I laugh at her excitement, I reach out to start my car—only the usual purr of my girl's engine doesn't erupt. Instead, a warning light flashes on my dash.

"Fuck," I bark.

"What's wrong?"

"Something's up with my car. Can I call you later?"

"I've got practice after school, so it might be late your time."

"Okay, you ring me when you're done. If I'm awake I'll answer, if I'm not then I won't."

"Sounds like a plan. Good luck with your car."

"Thanks," I mutter. Hanging up, any excitement that might have bubbled up from talking to Harley has well and truly vanished.

"Seriously?" I bark at my car when I try to start her again and get the same warning light.

Groaning, I tilt my head back and close my eyes, praying for strength.

The only good thing about all this is that Seb and his little lap dog have both left.

A yelp rips from my lips when someone knocks on my window.

With my heart in my throat and my pulse thundering through my body, I crack my eyes open and look to the side.

"Fucking hell," I mutter to myself, seeing one of Seb's boys standing slightly bent over so he can look inside my car.

Lowering the window, I snap, "What?"

His vibrant blue eyes make my breath catch as they stare into mine.

Unlike Seb's dark ones, these don't seem to hate me, which is somewhat of a relief because I'm not sure I've got the energy for any more barbed comments or scathing insults.

"You got a problem?" he asks, his smooth British accent washing over me as he glances at the glowing warning light on my dash.

"Uh... I'm fine. I'll just call recovery."

"Want company?"

My eyes narrow in confusion.

"Why?"

"Because everyone else has left," he asks, standing aside, allowing me to see the deserted parking lot aside from a black BMW that I can only assume is his.

"I'll be fine. I'm more than capable of looking after myself."

"So I heard," he deadpans. "But that's not why I'm offering."

I lift a brow, not believing a word of it.

"Can't I just be a good guy?" he asks innocently, although he doesn't look like he's taken offence to my unspoken words.

"When you're friends with the devil himself, probably not."

A smile curls at his lips.

"Don't let Seb hear you call him that, it might go to his head."

"Not possible. His ego is already bigger than belief."

"True, that. Unlock and let me in."

I hold his eyes for two more seconds, searching his ocean depths for any hint that he's playing me right now.

With a sigh, and knowing that I'm probably going to regret it, I unlock my doors and allow him to drop into my passenger seat.

His manly scent immediately assaults my senses, and I almost tell him to get the hell back out. I don't want my baby smelling like boy—or at least that's what I tell myself as my mouth begins to water.

He's the douchebag's friend. Rein it in, Stella.

"I'm Toby, by the way."

"Stella," I say, instantly regretting it when his lips curl into a smirk. "But you already knew that."

"I would usually say that news about hot new girls

spreads pretty quickly around here, but it seems you're a bit of an enigma."

Ignoring the flutter in my lower belly at his admission that he thinks I'm hot, I focus on the rest of his statement.

"Exactly how I like it."

"You sure seem good at making enemies, too."

"My favorite hobby."

He chuckles.

"Well, I can assure you, you're good at it. Not many girls happily go up against Seb or Teagan."

"Oh please. They're both conceited jerks who think the world owes them something."

He snorts a laugh but coughs in an attempt to cover it up.

"And here I was thinking you were one of his posse."

Sitting back in my passenger seat, Toby stretches out his long-ass legs, the fabric of his shorts pulling tight across his muscular thighs.

"I'd kill for him. Doesn't mean I have to agree with everything he does."

My brows rise at his blunt statement, but I think I understand. Not having all that many friends over the years, especially no lifetime ones, means I've missed out on those kinds of connections.

"Kinda like a brother, then."

"Exactly that. The five of us, we're family in all the ways that matter."

"Great, so if one of you hates me then ultimately you all do."

"I'm reserving judgement. He's not given me anything concrete to go on yet, so I'm following my gut."

"You trust me?" I ask.

"I dunno. You're just..." He looks over at me, his eyes

taking in every inch of my face. "You're different. I like it."

"You're one of only a few who haven't instantly judged me, although you did help Seb corner me in the bathroom and stop any help from entering... but I can see past that, at least until I get to know you."

"That's good of you. So are you going to ring for help or what?" He glances down at the cell that's still in my hand.

"Uh... yeah. She's fully covered, so I'm sure someone will be right out."

"She?" he asks with a smirk.

"Yeah. Why? Isn't yours?"

"Oh hell yeah. I've just never heard a girl personify their car like guys do before."

"I'm not your average girl."

"You can say that again," he mutters to himself as I lift my cell to my ear.

I'm on hold for what feels like forever as I'm forced to listen to the shitty music they play down the line before I'm finally told that all their rescue mechanics are busy and it'll be at least two hours before someone can get to me.

"This is bullshit," I snap, jamming my finger into the screen to cut off the call.

"Come on," Toby says, sitting forward and reaching for the handle, "I'll take you home."

"And leave her here?"

"Babe, this place has more CCTV than Buckingham Palace. She's gonna be safe. Plus, it's not like anyone can drive off in her."

"Fine," I sigh, unable to argue with that.

I follow him over to his car and drop down inside,

noticing the same new car smell mingled with the fresh boy that's currently lingering in mine.

"This is nice," I say, running my fingers over the red that cuts through the dash of what is obviously a custom M3.

"It was a birthday present."

"Wow, someone obviously loves you."

He grunts in agreement and quickly follows it up with, "Money isn't everything."

Looking over, I find his jaw locked and his grip on the wheel so tight his knuckles are white, so I figure it's probably not the best time to ask him to elaborate.

"You're gonna need to tell me where I'm going," Toby says after a few tense minutes.

"Oh shit, sorry." I quickly give him directions and he gives me a double take when I tell him the street. "What?"

"Expensive houses around there," he mutters, opening a bottle of Gatorade and swallowing down a few mouthfuls.

"Says the one in a custom BMW."

"Sorry, I shouldn't judge."

"It's fine. I've suffered worse."

"Teagan's a bitch."

"Ah, so it's common knowledge then. Don't tell me, her pussy is made of diamonds, which is why the guys put up with her."

The mouthful of the blue liquid he'd just poured into his mouth sprays out, covering his windshield, wheel, his hand and shorts.

"Oh shit, I'm sorry I—"

"That's the best thing I've heard all week."

"It's only Tuesday," I mutter, rummaging around in my purse for some tissues.

"I don't have high hopes for my week," he deadpans.

He's still trying to mop up Gatorade when we finally pull into my driveway.

"I'll pay to get it detailed," I offer, because the second it dries up, it's going to be a sticky mess.

"Don't worry, I've got it covered."

"Okay, well..." I hesitate, staring at the front of the house when he pulls to a stop. "Would you like to come in?"

"Uh... Y-yeah," he says, turning his mesmerising eyes and megawatt smile on me. "Sounds good."

"And I didn't even have to offer you the cake that I know will be waiting."

His eyes light up at the mention of Angie's cake.

"Just wait. Depending on what our housekeeper has made, it's better than sex."

"Who the hell have you been screwing?" he asks as we both climb out of his car.

His question tells me a lot—mostly that he has no idea what his so-called brother has been up to recently.

"No one decent, obviously," I shoot over my shoulder before letting myself inside.

The house is in silence as we step into the hall.

"Whoa, this is... modern," Toby comments as I lead him through to the kitchen.

"Yep, it's Dad's thing," I mutter, closing in on the slices of millionaire's shortbread that are sitting on the counter waiting for me.

I put a few slices on a plate before passing Toby a couple of cans of soda and telling him to follow me.

He trails me all the way up to the top floor of the house—my floor—and into my bedroom.

"Often invite boys into your room only minutes after

meeting them?" he asks as I toe my sneakers off and lower the plate to the nightstand.

"Ones who rescue me, yeah," I laugh, shrugging off my hoodie and draping it over the chair.

My skin tingles with awareness, and, when I look back, I find him standing in my doorway with his eyes locked on my ass.

"Are you okay to hang for a bit? I need to go clean up. I'm a mess."

He clears his throat, walking farther into the room.

"You look fine to me."

"I'll be five minutes. Make yourself at home."

I grab a clean set of clothes and slip into my bathroom, closing the door behind me before he can say anything else.

What the hell are you doing?

My heart slams in my chest as I rest back against the door.

I'm playing with fire, inviting one of Seb's friends here, but the wicked part of me loves it.

There's nothing more entertaining than tormenting jerks who think they're in charge.

I have the quickest shower of my life before pulling on a clean pair of booty shorts and a tank. Also probably a bad idea, but I'm in this deep, so I may as well continue.

CHAPTER SIX

Sebastian

"I'm sorry, Toby is fucking where?" I bark around a mouthful of Theo's mom's moussaka.

"Stella's," Nico repeats as if I didn't hear it clearly enough the fucking first time.

Theo and Alex both shoot me a concerned look, but I'm too fucking angry to care what they think.

"Why?" I grate out.

"Probably because he wants to fuck her," he says simply like it's the most obvious thing in the world. "I mean, she's hot and totally his type."

Out of all of us, Toby is the only one who's even remotely choosy about the girls he spends time with, and I can't deny that what Nico is saying is true. She's totally his type, which makes the fact that he's inside her house right now even fucking worse.

I don't realise the growl that fills the room that

rumbles from my throat until every set of eyes around the table burns into me.

"Something you need to confess, bro?" Nico asks, although from the look in his eyes I don't think he really needs me to confirm what he already suspects.

"Fuck this," I bark, pushing my almost empty plate away and shoving the chair out behind me so fast it crashes to the floor. "Fuck all of this." I blow out of the room like a storm and then, quickly after, the house.

The late afternoon sun warms my skin as I erupt from the back of the Cirillo mansion and march down to their insane home gym at the bottom of the garden.

As a kid, I always thought the one we had in our basement was impressive, but like most things that Damien touches, it has to be the best of the best. Only weeks after they moved into this house following the death of Theo's grandfather, he turned this into something that rivals the best gyms in the city.

I breathe in the fresh scent as I step inside, causing the automatic lights to flicker into action.

Pulling my phone from my pocket, I ignore the temptation to track Toby's to discover where she lives and instead connect to the Bluetooth so I can blast my angry workout playlist through the building.

Dragging off my t-shirt, I hit the treadmill and turn the speed up, needing to feel something other than the anger, the burning need for revenge that has taken up every one of my thoughts since I learned the truth.

Finding her has only made it worse.

The bitterness that's been festering inside me is starting to poison everything in my life.

I run until my legs ache and my lungs burn with my need for air, but fucking finally, the images of what I want to do to the cunt who ruined my life, who broke my family, abate enough to focus on something else.

I hit the stop button and slow my movements until the belt comes to a halt.

When I step off and turn around, I'm not surprised to find someone sitting on the rowing machine, waiting for me with a concerned look on his face.

"I'm fine," I say, grabbing a rolled-up towel from the shelf and wiping my sweaty face and chest.

"No, you're not. And you haven't been for a long time. But this... right now... I'm worried."

"I'll sort it out."

"No, you're fuelled by anger, and that's dangerous. You make stupid fucking decisions when you're mad."

I hold Theo's stare for a beat. I can't argue.

"It's fine."

Pulling an energy drink from the fridge, I down it in one before throwing it in the bin.

"I need to go home."

"See... stupid decisions."

"I need to see if she's still alive. And anyway, it's not as stupid as going to her. What the hell is Toby thinking?"

"I'll talk to him."

"And tell him what? You heard the boss. This is our job. Does he even know who she is?"

Theo shrugs.

My fists curl and my need to trail him, to find out the truth about why he's in her house, almost gets the better of me.

"Go home and see your mum. You know where I am if you need me."

I let out a long breath before swiping my shirt from the floor and dragging it over my head.

"Thanks, man."

Theo doesn't speak again until I'm at the doors.

"We'll make sure he pays, Seb. We'll make sure they both do."

With a nod that I'm sure he can't see, I blow out of the building and head toward my car.

My Aston purrs to life the second I press the start button, and I floor it out of the driveway, hoping that the journey will relax me somewhat.

It doesn't.

By the time I pull up at home, I can't recall any of the turnings I took or if I even stopped at any red lights. The only images in my head were of the night in the graveyard, only it wasn't me with Stella, but Toby.

"Fucking arsehole," I bark, slamming my palm down on the wheel.

My phone once again burns a hole in my pocket to find out where they both are.

Going to her house this early on is a risk. Bumping into her dad before I've figured out a plan would be really fucking stupid.

I sit there for the longest time, just staring at our silent house.

Unlike the one I just left, there is no movement inside, no sign of any kind of life. No happiness.

It's the place I grew up, but I struggle to find any attachment to it seeing as life inside is even more miserable than it looks from out here.

This isn't a family home. It's not even a home. It's a pile of bricks where a couple of people barely exist.

With a sigh, I push the door open and move toward the front door, the stones crunching loudly under my feet. It should alert anyone to my presence, but I highly doubt that the woman inside will be in any state to be expecting me.

A shudder rips through me the second I open the front door.

The house stinks. It's stale, musty and unloved.

Once upon a time, it used to be entirely different. But I've only seen evidence of that in photographs or heard my sisters talk about it. A time I don't remember. A time I barely even experienced. A time that died right alongside the heart of this home.

We might all meet here every two weeks and pretend to be a normal family, but we're far from it.

"Mum," I call, my deep voice echoing in the silence of the house.

Not getting a response, I take a step toward her favourite place and come to a stop in the doorway to prepare myself for what I might find.

Three. Two. One.

"Jesus fucking Christ," I mutter, taking in the state of the place before my eyes land on the heap of a woman who's on the old carpet between the sofa and the coffee table, surrounded by bottles and needles.

She has good times. Times when she might just be able to keep her promises about cleaning up and becoming a mother once more. But those times are always followed by this devastation.

I get it, to a point. Loss is hard.

Hell, I feel it every fucking day. I fight it every fucking day. And I didn't even know one of them.

It was hard to deal with as a kid surrounded by women and having my brothers' fathers help raise me.

But the second I learned the truth, my grief for the

man I can't remember but miss something fierce turned into this beast inside me who was hellbent on revenge.

Every step I've taken since that moment has been about making things right.

I didn't just lose my dad that day. My sisters didn't just lose their father, my mum lost her husband. Our entire family lost everything. Everything that's important.

And then to be struck again only fifteen years later.

It's cruel. Really fucking cruel.

Damien Cirillo would never have allowed us to be on the street—nor would I, which is why I demanded I be brought into the Family much younger than I'm sure he'd have liked. But there was no way I was sitting around watching everything turn to dust around me.

Stepping over everything, kicking a couple of bottles out of the way, I scoop Mum's almost weightless body into my arms and lift her from the floor.

She doesn't make a sound aside from her shallow, rattling breaths as I walk her away from the mess and turn to the stairs.

I've done this so many times now that I'm able to detach myself from the situation as I monotonously go through the steps of cleaning her up, changing her disgusting clothes and putting her into bed.

She's not made a sound the whole time, and as I sit myself on the edge of her bed and hold her cold hand in mine, everything comes rushing back with a vengeance and my heart drops into my stomach.

Pulling my phone from my pocket, I make the call I always do when she's in this state.

"Again?" the deep voice rumbles down the line.

"Yeah. Could you—"

"I'm on my way, boy," Dr. Rosi says, sympathy oozing from his voice.

"Thank you."

I left the front door unlocked earlier so he could let himself in, so I leave Mum and head to my own room.

It's filled with all my stuff, minus most of my clothes that now live in Theo's coach house, but it still doesn't feel like a place I belong.

The shelves are lined with football trophies, ones I've had to celebrate alone, mostly.

Sophia and Zoe, my older sisters, did the best they could. But they've gone and made lives for themselves now, something I can't blame them for. I don't want to be here either.

Stripping out of my clothes, I head for the shower. Turning it on as hot as it goes, I wait for the steam to billow before stepping under the burning torrent of water in the hope that the pain will distract from everything inside me.

Pressing my palms against the tiles, I hang my head, desperate to come up with a plan, something that will settle this burning need for vengeance that won't abate.

I could just look at the tracker, find the house and walk up with a gun.

But that would be too easy, too painless.

I've suffered for almost eighteen years. One bullet through the head seems too kind after everything he's put us through.

It needs to be better than that. Which is why I'm starting with his daughter.

He tried to protect her all those years ago, so I've no doubt it's his top priority these days.

Ultimately, if I break her, I ruin him. And that's exactly what I need. What I crave.

By the time I've showered and dragged on a clean set of clothes, Dr. Rosi is talking to Mum in her room—not that I think for a second that she's actually listening.

"Hey," I say, stepping into the room and finding her hooked up to some fluids.

"Hi, Seb." I hate the sadness in his voice, the pity. "Twice in as many weeks," he mutters quietly, as if I need reminding.

"Each visit is one less you're going to need to make," I whisper. We can't continue this way. Mum's body is giving up after the years of abuse. I don't need a doctor to tell me how this is going to end. I just need to turn eighteen before it happens to save all the bullshit of needing to be in someone's care.

Dr. Rosi lets out a sigh. I know what he wants to say. He wants us to try to get her into rehab again. But after all the previous failed attempts, I can't help but think we should just let her put an end to it all.

She's miserable. Has been since the day she learned she was a widow, and it's only got worse from then on.

At least back then she had young kids to keep her somewhat distracted. But now, with her girls gone and only me left—a miniature version of my father to remind her of what she lost—she's totally given up.

She knows it won't be long until I'm gone too. Hell, I practically live with Theo as it is just to get away from all this. It's only my guilt that keeps bringing me back.

"Thank you," I say, not needing to hear any kind of lecture from him.

"Anytime, Seb. You know that."

I nod as he begins packing up his stuff.

"You know the drill," he says, backing toward the door.

I do. Hell, it happens so often that even Mum will know what to do when she finally wakes, each time angrier than the last that I saved her.

"Until next time," I say, my voice cold and emotionless.

He disappears from the room and I stand there for a few minutes, just staring at her almost unrecognisable face.

I can only imagine what our father must think of her now.

My phone ringing drags me from my morose thoughts and I pull it from my pocket as I walk out of the room.

Sitting here watching her is going to achieve nothing.

I roll my eyes when I see Sophia's name on my screen.

"Hey, Sis," I say, forcing as much lightness into my tone as possible.

"Are you okay?"

"Theo called you, huh?"

"He messaged me, suggesting I check in. What's going on?"

I drop down on the top step and run my hand down my face.

"Dr. Rosi just left," I confess.

"Again?"

"Yeah. It's getting worse."

"Let us help you, Seb. Please," she begs. It's not the first time and it probably won't be the last. She wants to put Mum into a facility and for me to move in with her and her husband, Jason. It would be fine if they lived close enough for me to still attend Knight's Ridge. But they don't. And I refuse to leave the only place I have some kind of solace from the rest of my life.

It's the only place I'm not constantly reminded of how shit my life is. Although with *her* now walking the halls, my reprieve might be shorter lived than usual.

"I'm not leaving school," I argue.

"I know. You're practically living at Theo's. I'm sure Damien wouldn't mind making it more permanent."

"She won't want to be in a place like that. Why would we want to make her even more miserable?"

"She's killing herself, Seb."

"And who are we to stop her," I snap. If she really doesn't want to be here for her kids, then why should we make her?

"Seb," she sighs.

"Sophia," I echo.

"Are you going back to Theo's?" she asks, changing the subject slightly.

"I don't know." I have no idea what the hell I'm doing right now.

"You should."

"We'll see. How's Phoebe?" I ask, thinking of my niece.

"She's great. She's almost walking. It's going to happen any day now."

"Send me a video. I want to see it."

"Of course."

"You should go. I'm sure you have better things to do than talk to me."

"Seb, you know I'm right here if you need me."

"I do. But I'm good. I promise," I lie.

Right now, I'm the exact fucking opposite of good.

"Okay. Love you, little bro."

"Love you too. Give Phoebe a kiss from me."

"You could come here and give her one yourself."

"Enough, Soph," I warn.

"I know. Sorry. I'll see you Sunday, yeah?"

"You got it."

I cut the call and lean forward with my elbows on my knees, my phone hanging from my fingers.

I have no idea how long I sit there, drowning in the misery that is my life. But when my phone pings again, it scares the shit out of me.

Toby: You want me?

My brows lift at his question before the realisation dawns that Theo decided meddling with my family wasn't enough. He's gone after Toby as well.

Although, I can't deny that I'm mostly happy about this one.

My finger taps against the side of my phone for a few seconds, trying to come up with something that's going to mean he has to leave Stella.

A thought hits me and I start typing my reply, hoping it's enough to drag him away from her.

CHAPTER SEVEN

Stella

Toby: Did you manage to sort your car? Do you need a lift to school?

I can't help but smile as I stare down at his message.

He was really sweet last night. Way more than I'd ever have given him credit for, seeing as he's Seb's friend, and he seems nothing more than a straight-up jerk.

After I emerged from the bathroom, aside from the odd lingering glance, he was the perfect gentleman. I'm not sure if I was grateful or disappointed that he didn't try anything.

The last guy who touched me needs to be erased by someone else. But equally, I've made enough stupid mistakes for at least a week, so I figured it was for the best for now.

We talked about classes, about the future, and thankfully we kept away from the heavy stuff.

It was nice. Easy. And when his cell went off and put an end to our time together, I was kinda gutted that he had to leave.

I'd had a message while we were hanging out from Dad, letting me know that he wasn't going to make it home, so I was more than happy to have company while I could get it. He promised me that he'd get straight on to sorting out my car and ensuring I had a replacement by first thing this morning.

But as of yet, that hasn't materialized, and the driveway is empty aside from Calvin and Angie's cars.

I've spent most of the past hour on the phone trying to sort it out, so now not only do I not have a replacement car to get me to school, but I'm about to be very, very late. Toby's message couldn't have come at a better time.

Stella: You're a lifesaver. Thank you.

Toby: Anytime. I'll be fifteen minutes.

I blow around my room like a whirlwind, dragging on my clothes and throwing some makeup on my face. By the time I fly down the stairs just over seventeen minutes later, I'm a hot mess.

Me being late on day three is one thing, but I don't want to make Toby late too.

From the way he was talking last night, he loves school—he is in sixth form for his third year, since he restarted after changing subjects from his first—and I'd hate myself for making him miss anything when he's just trying to help me.

I blow through the kitchen, grabbing a cereal bar for breakfast as Angie watches on.

The gravel of the driveway crunches under my feet as I damn near run toward Toby's BMW, my bags flying out behind me. I've got my first cheer class after school, and I have no idea how I'm going to get there if I still don't have a car. Uber, I guess. But I've yet to try it out here.

I pull the door open, throw my bags inside and quickly follow them, falling into the passenger seat.

"Sorry, I'm late, I—" My first indication that something is wrong is that the locks engage almost the second I start speaking.

The second is the scent.

It's different from last night.

"What the actual fuck?" I bark, my eyes narrowing on the guy in the driver's seat.

"Morning, Hellion. How's it going?"

Despite the fact that I heard the locks, my fingers still twitch to reach out and try them. But I keep myself still, not wanting him to see how desperately I want to escape.

"Where's Toby?" I spit, feeling even more flustered than I was when I bolted from the house and hating that he's witnessing me being less than focused and composed.

"Fighting off the hangover from hell." A smirk twitches at his lips, and it tells me everything I need to know.

"You got him wasted so he couldn't pick me up, didn't you?"

"I didn't know he was definitely going to pick you up so... call it a lucky break."

"You're driving his car," I point out.

"Well done, Hellion. Nothing gets past you, does it?"

"You're infuriating."

His threatening smile finally emerges, as if he's actually pleased that I've noticed.

"That's the least of your worries, baby."

"Don't call me that," I hiss, folding my arms under my boobs. Despite the fact that I'm covered in my school uniform, his eyes still drop like I might have just flashed him. "Are you finished?"

He sucks his bottom lip into his mouth and drags it between his teeth as his eyes roll up to meet mine. They're darker than they were when I first climbed into the car, and it sends a wave of desire through me.

"I'm not fucking you in Toby's car," I blurt out before I can think better of it.

Seb snorts in disgust.

"I'm not interested in repeats or Toby's sloppy seconds."

"Probably a good thing, seeing as he was so much better than you," I lie. "It would be a total let down."

My insides do a little cheer when his lips press into a thin line and his teeth grind.

"So what's the plan then? You gonna lock me in here and sit outside my house all day? I don't want to burst your bubble, but someone will probably notice. If you want to abduct me, I'm sure you could be a little more creative."

His eyes hold mine for so long that I begin to wonder if he actually heard me, or if I even said the words out loud.

The second it becomes clear he got every single word is the same second I realize I've let my guard down.

His hand wraps around my throat and he pins me back into the chair.

My heart slams in my chest. I'm shit out of luck at helping myself right now.

Calvin has trained me on how to defend myself in most situations, but being in the confines of a car isn't one of them.

"What do you want from me?" I force out as his grip only gets tighter.

He smiles once more, but this time, there's no amusement in it. Only malice.

"I want to hurt you. Punish you. Ruin you. Break you," he hisses, almost as if he's actually talking to himself. "I want to make you cry, beg, plead with me for mercy despite the fact that you know it'll never come."

My head spins as I try to register his words and the seriousness behind each and every threat.

"That's some heavy shit for someone you just met."

"You have no idea who you are, do you, Doukas?"

I shake my head slightly, because I think it's more than clear that I don't have a fucking clue what he's talking about.

"Your mortal enemy, by the sounds of it," I sass. "Not that I really think you're brave enough to do anything about it."

He moves closer, his body hovering over the centre console. "You really need to watch what you say, Hellion. You really shouldn't be challenging me."

"The only one of us who's ended up hurt so far is you, as far as I'm aware. So you really should step up your efforts, big man."

His jaw tics, his fingers tightening as the sound of a car approaching fills the small space around us.

Calvin's car appears from behind the bushes as he backs out of the driveway.

"Our head of security is trained in every martial art out there. Unless you want to test that, I'd suggest you get your disgusting hands off me right now."

Sensing that I might be telling the truth, he rips his eyes from mine and looks over his shoulder just as the trunk and half the car comes into view.

With a frustrated grunt, he releases me and falls back into his seat.

Before Calvin has a chance to reverse though the gate, Seb floors the accelerator of Toby's M3 and we fly forward, the engine purring beneath us.

If I weren't so shaken by his words and his possessive grip, then I might even appreciate the sound.

Part of me expects him to take me somewhere other than school. He clearly has some less-than-desirable intentions when it comes to me, if what he keeps spitting at me is true. But to my surprise, he drives us straight to Knight's Ridge.

I'm still trying to decide if he's full of shit, or if he's biding his time, putting me on edge and ready for the perfect time to strike. If that's the case, then I hope he's aware that I'm going to be waiting for him.

Unlike yesterday, he doesn't park in either of the free spaces where I found them. Instead, he drives to the very back row, one space down from where my poor Porsche is still looking uncared for, ensuring we're under the cover of the trees, shielded from prying eyes.

"What do you want?" I bark, fed up with his games. "We've got ten minutes to homeroom."

"Homeroom?" he mocks, attempting an American accent.

"Whatever, asshole. Just let me out."

"What's it worth?"

"I'm sorry, what?" I spit, in complete disbelief that he's requesting payment of some kind to allow me out of the fucking car. Although, I'm not entirely sure why I'm surprised. It's totally douchebag jerk behavior.

"Why should I let you out? I should leave you here, let everyone think you skived."

"Wow, if that's your idea of 'ruining me' then I really don't think I have anything to worry about. I could call for help before you get across the parking lot, asshole."

He kills the engine, plunging us into silence so that only our increased breathing can be heard.

Everything instantly becomes more intense and my fingers curl around the seat beneath me, my nails digging into the soft leather.

He leans over, his scent stronger as he glares pure hatred into my eyes.

I swallow anxiously, waiting for what he's going to do next.

There's a click that startles me and makes my brows pull together as my heart thunders.

The second he moves and something cold gently presses against my thigh, I know I was right to be nervous.

Although, hell, I can't deny that his fingers wrapped around his switchblade don't look hot as hell.

"Seb," I breathe. It's meant to be a warning, but as I watch the tip of his knife trail up my thigh, scratching my skin ever so slightly and leaving light red marks, it sounds anything but.

He stops when he gets to the edge of my skirt and his eyes lift from my leg to mine.

My chest heaves as they connect. I hate that he can see exactly what the sight of his knife against my skin does to me, but I'm powerless to stop it.

"You're fucking wet for me right now, aren't you, Doukas?"

"Fuck you," I seethe, although it's pointless. We both know the truth.

"You're a fucking liar, you know that? A liar and a whore."

"And you're a jumped up, conceited prick who thinks the world owes him something just because he's pretty."

A wicked smile pulls at his lips, and I instantly realize the mistake I made.

"You think I'm pretty, Doukas?"

My teeth grind as I suppress a groan of frustration.

His eyes drop from mine in favor of my lips the second my tongue darts out to wet them, and a wave of desire rushes through me at the thought of him kissing me.

I might hate him, but damn, if the memories of how good we were together in that graveyard don't make me crave all the things I shouldn't.

His knife digs in a little deeper, making my breath catch.

Both of our gazes drop to the blade as a tiny pool of blood surrounds the tip.

Dragging the knife up, Seb swipes his thumb through the redness before lifting it to his lips and sucking it into his mouth.

His eyes darken more than I thought possible until the only thing staring back at me are the dark orbs of the devil.

"Almost as sweet as your cunt," he murmurs when he pulls his thumb free.

"You're a—"

"Careful, Hellion. Remember who has the knife."

"You really think I'm scared of you, don't you?"

"It doesn't matter if I think you are. All you need to know is that you should be."

Holding my arms out to the side, I say, "Do your worst."

A wicked smirk curls at his lips, and I focus on that. On the fact that he really thinks he's got the upper hand here just because he's the one holding the knife.

I hold his eyes as the blade begins to move once more. He inches my skirt up until he's at my panties, his own chest beginning to move at a rapid pace, his increased breaths fanning over my face.

Whatever it is he's thinking about doing with it is really getting him going.

Good.

He's going to play right into my hands.

"Seb," I moan again when the blade connects with the lace that's covering me, only this time I intend for it to make me sound like the whore he's accused me of being.

His eyes flare and his lips part as he keeps moving.

The blade cuts through the flimsy lace and digs into my skin, but I've never had a problem with pain, especially when it's going to bring me out on top.

I wait with my heart in my throat for the right moment, and I find it not a second later when he pauses and drags in a shaky breath.

Remembering everything Calvin has taught me over the years, I grip Seb's forearm with one hand, slamming it down on the centre console.

He's so fucking shocked that he releases the blade without thought.

The metal handle is warm from his grip as I wrap my fingers around it and bring it to his throat.

"Nice fucking try, asshole."

I press the blade against his skin, forcing him to sit back in his chair.

The desire in his eyes morphs into fury as realization slams into him about what just happened.

"I warned you," I breathe, getting right in his face much like he was mine not so long ago. "I'm not a fucking toy you can play with, intimidate. I am not that fucking girl, and the sooner you realize that, the better this whole thing will play out for you."

He swallows, his Adam's apple bobbing against his knife.

"Do you know what?" I ask, my own smirk playing on my lips. "You look even prettier when you're at my mercy."

"You're playing with fire," he warns.

"Oh, baby. I'm the one who ignited the motherfucking flames." His brows shoot up at my words. "Straight from hell, remember?" I say, recalling our conversation from that night. "Now, this is how it's gonna go," I tell him, pressing the blade a little harder until I begin to break the skin. "I'm going to get out of this car before I'm even fucking later for class, and you're going to let me go. But don't worry, baby," I say, my voice softening as if I actually fucking like him. "This isn't over. You might have started this war, but I'm going to be the one who ends it."

He blinks twice but never says a word.

Taking that as his agreement, I pull the knife away slightly to see what he's going to do. He stays put, his eyes burning into mine, but when I sit back he moves, unlocking the doors and allowing me to climb out from the car.

My panties are in tatters, and I make the most of the privacy he allowed us by tucking my thumbs under my skirt and letting them fall down my legs.

He watches my every move, his jaw tics and that vein at his temple pulsates.

"Oh," I say innocently, "did you want these?" I throw my panties into the car, ensuring they hit his face before falling onto his lap. "They're the last pair of mine you'll be getting into, I can assure you of that. And thanks for this," I say, holding up his knife. "It's not as pretty as my pink one, but it seems pretty sharp."

Before he manages to respond, I throw my bags over my shoulder and slam the passenger door shut.

Accomplishment washes through me as I walk away.

The wind whips around me despite the fact that the early morning sun warms my skin and my heart skips a beat when it catches my skirt. That slight panic is soon replaced with satisfaction, because I know his eyes are drilling into me and there's no way he missed it.

Spinning around, I find I'm right. His dark and dangerous eyes are fixed right on me as I lift my hand and flip him the bird, the widest smile I can manage breaking across my face.

CHAPTER EIGHT

Sebastian

My hand lifts and my fingers touch the tender patch of skin that was just under the blade of my own knife as I watch her walk away.

I'm not sure if I'm mortified that she managed to get the upper hand on me yet again, or impressed at how easily she turned the tables.

She's definitely one of us, and I'm not sure I like knowing that given the chance, she could fit right in. Hell, it seems that Toby has already embraced her into his life if the smile on his face and the way he talked about her when he got to Theo's last night were anything to go by.

The second I saw his reaction to her, I knew that dragging him away was the right thing to do.

He didn't tell us anything happened, and I was too scared to ask, but Stella sure took pleasure in announcing that he was better than me.

My fist curls at the thought of him touching her, at taking what's mine, when a gust of autumn wind blows and makes my morning a whole fucking lot better.

It's only for the briefest moment, but the sight of her bare, knickerless arse makes my cock harden even more than it already is and forces all the air out of my lungs.

"Fuuuuck," I breathe, my hand dropping from my neck in favour of the ruined scrap of lace that's in my lap.

I'm about to lift them when she suddenly turns and locks her light blue eyes on mine. They're full of achievement and joy. And when she lifts her middle finger up at me, her smile would knock me on my arse if I weren't already sitting on it.

I shake my head, my eyes narrowing in warning, but it's a fight not to let my true feelings show at this very moment.

Stella Doukas is a mystery that I might want to destroy, but hell if I'm suddenly not interested in finding out a little more about the missing mafia princess before I put an end to it all.

After all, she seems like she could be a lot of fun while she lasts.

When she finally turns around, I make my move, lifting her knickers to my nose and inhaling her scent. Just as fucking sweet as the night in the graveyard that started my addiction with my little hellion.

I decide to give myself thirty seconds to get a grip on myself, but I quickly discover that I'm not going to get that long because Theo's Maserati pulls into his space and a furious looking Toby stumbles out of the passenger seat and makes a beeline straight toward me.

"What the fuck, Seb?" he barks when he's halfway between us.

"Shouldn't have drunk so much, huh?"

My words are like fuel to his already out of control fire, and he closes the space between us with shocking speed considering his raging hangover.

My back collides with his car.

"You got me fucking wasted so you could get to her, you arsehole," he booms in my face, his spittle hitting my skin.

"Someone needed to help her, and you weren't exactly capable."

His lips twist in anger, and I brace myself for the hit that's sure to come.

Toby might not show his inner monster all that often like the rest of us, but don't think that's because it's not there. He's just better at controlling his demons.

"You're a fucking cunt for pulling that stunt, Seb," he says, seconds before the pain I was expecting blooms across my face as his fist collides with my jaw.

I'm about to retaliate when we're dragged apart.

Nico wraps his arms around Toby's chest while Theo comes to stand between us.

"Finished?"

"Barely fucking started," Toby seethes, his face reddening even more when my only response is to smirk at him over Theo's shoulder.

"Let's fucking go," Theo barks, shoving me in the direction we should be heading in.

"You don't just get to piss all over her and claim her as yours," Toby mutters.

"Oh yeah?" I ask, turning around to see him still being restrained by Nico. "Watch me, motherfucker."

"Seb," Theo hisses.

"What? I saw her first," I deadpan.

"Yeah, don't we fucking know it."

We walk in silence toward the building, and only a few minutes later Alex pulls into the car park and jogs to catch up with us.

"What's going on?" he asks, clearly sensing the tension.

"Stella fucking Doukas happened," Theo deadpans. "Toby wants her."

"Oh fuck." He glances over his shoulder. "How's that going?"

"Shut the fuck up. She's mine."

"You don't actually want her though, do you?"

"No. But I sure as fuck don't want Toby anywhere fucking near her."

"I don't think you need to worry about Toby exposing just how much of a cunt you are. Something tells me she already knows."

"Wait," Alex spits, making the two of us stop, "why are you bleeding?" he asks, glancing at my throat.

"Our princess is pretty fucking handy with a knife as well as a gun," I say as a smirk curls at my lips and my cock swells at the memory.

"Galen's fucking trained her, hasn't he?"

"Damn right he has. Maybe he's not entirely fucking stupid. He knew she was going to come up against us eventually. He's made her his personal fucking soldier," I explain.

"What the fuck is he playing at? And why the hell is the boss protecting them?" Alex murmurs the exact kind of thoughts that were running through my head as I laid in bed last night, listening to Toby snoring his arse off.

"Fucked if I know," I mutter, storming toward the building, more than ready for the distraction of class to start. Not that I really think for a second that I'm going to be able to get her out of my head. Or the fact that she's got my fucking knife. My *father's* knife.

"Seb," a high-pitched voice says the second we step into the common room. "You never called me back," Teag whines, stepping up to me and running her hands up my chest before linking them behind my neck.

"Because I didn't want to talk to you," I say. She texted at some point last night, but after all the shit I'd already dealt with, the last thing I needed was her whining in my ear about some bullshit that happened at gym practice. I already know who she'd have been moaning about, because it seems that it's not only me that Stella has made an enemy of.

And she's also the only reason I allow Teag to remain pressed against my body, because her hate-filled stare burns into my skin.

She's here somewhere, I just haven't discovered where yet.

"Seven o'clock," Theo whispers, knowing exactly what I need.

Pressing my hand against Teag's lower back to press her body tight against mine, I glance in her direction.

Exactly as I was expecting, she's glaring right at me with her curvy legs stretched out in front of her and her skirt riding high.

My teeth grind at the thought of her being bare beneath and showing every motherfucker in Knight's Ridge what she's hiding.

Sitting back in her seat, she crosses her arms across her chest, a smug smile curling up one side of her mouth.

"Mate, you're in fucking trouble," Theo mutters.

"Nothing I can't handle," I say as Teag's lips connect with my neck.

Stella's eyes flare with irritation. Ripping them from mine, she turns to the girl sitting beside her.

She's new too, but unlike Stella, who looks like an angel—a fucking lethal one, mind you—she's all dark and dangerous.

"Who's that?" Theo asks, clearly taking in the same girl as me.

"No clue. Interested?" I ask, lifting a brow.

"In the bad biker bitch? I don't fucking think so," he scoffs. But despite his words, his eyes linger a little longer than necessary.

Sure you're not.

"What happened here?" Teag asks when she finally realises I've got a cut across my throat.

"Ah, you know how it is, Teag."

Her eyes light up with excitement at the thought of what we do. It's the only fucking reason she's interested. To build her social status. I'm pretty sure she wouldn't turn any of us down for a chance at joining the Family and all the celebrity factor she thinks comes with it.

She's clueless. Clueless and fucking delusional.

Thankfully, the bell rings and she's forced to pull away from me.

"I'll see you later, yeah? I've got a free third if you wanna meet up." She wiggles her brows suggestively and my cock threatens to shrivel up at the thought alone.

Movement over her shoulder catches my eye, and when I look up, I find Toby and Nico in the doorway. Seconds later, Stella bounces up to them and looks up at Toby like he just hung the fucking moon.

"Sorry, I'm busy all day," I say, my voice cold and lacking any kind of emotion.

"O-oh." Unfortunately, she follows my line of sight and tenses when she finds Stella. "Really, Seb? She's nothing more than American trash."

"You're fucking right there," I mutter, less than gently pushing her aside and storming across the room.

I stop right beside Stella and throw my arm around her shoulder. She immediately tenses and I brace myself for impact, although to my surprise it never actually comes.

"I hope you're not giving my boy here all our dirty secrets, Hellion."

"Fuck off, Seb," she spits, earning amused snorts from both Toby and Nico.

"She loves me really, don't you, Princess?" Lowering my arm, I grab her ass and squeeze until it hurts.

"Oh yeah. I can barely contain myself around you." She rolls her eyes dramatically and steps out of my hold. "Was there something you wanted, Sebastian?" she growls.

Holding my hand out, I say, "Yeah. I think you have something that belongs to me."

"Uh... nope. I don't, so see you later," she says, her tone much softer as she addresses both Toby and Nico before disappearing out into the hallway and slipping into the mass of students making their way toward class.

"I take back what I said earlier. Eat your heart out trying with that one, Seb. She fucking hates you," Toby says.

"Huh, you noticed that too," I mutter. "Makes winning all that much sweeter. Game on, Tobes. Game fucking on."

"Jesus fucking Christ," Nico mutters, turning away from the both of us and heading toward his own class.

"Pull another stunt like that and I'll fucking end you," Toby warns, his brows pulled together, his usual bright blue eyes dark with evil intent. It's a look I'm fairly familiar with... but it's never been directed at me.

"All's fair in love and war, Toby. Didn't you learn that already?" I disappear out of the room, leaving him standing on the spot and probably planning a million ways to kill me.

Get in line, motherfucker. Something tells me that Stella is right at the very front.

CHAPTER NINE

Stella

"What's that?" Emmie asks at lunch, lowering herself to the other side of the bench.

I glance at the item I'm twisting around under the table and smile.

"Switchblade," I answer honestly.

"Should you... uh... have that in school?"

I shrug. "It's not mine. I stole it off Seb this morning."

Her brows lift. "So that was what the intense eye contact was about in the common room."

"Something like that. I'm waiting to see what he comes up with to get it back."

"Fair enough," she mutters, spearing a fry with her fork and shoving it into her mouth.

Any other girl would ask a million and one questions,

or even look a little concerned, but Emmie continues on with her day as if we're just talking about the weather.

She continues eating her lunch, although mine mostly goes untouched. I'm too up in my head after my interactions with Seb this morning.

I'm pissed at him for the stunt he played with Toby. Why they're friends, God only knows. Seb is an epic douchecanoe and Toby seems like the sweetest guy I've met for a while. Talk about opposites attracting.

My mind drifts back to being inside the car with him earlier and my thighs rub together mindlessly.

It amuses me that he probably thinks I'm walking around with my cunt on display for anyone who cares to look. I'm not, of course. The first thing I did when I got into school was slip into the bathroom and pull out the spare pair of panties I had in my cheer bag.

He's more than welcome to the pair I threw at him. Another memento of our time together.

It makes me wonder what he did with the pair he ripped off me in the graveyard. Maybe he's one of those kinky dudes who keeps the panties of all the girls he rails in the top drawer of his dresser.

I wonder how many of Teagan's he has?

My body cools instantly at the thought.

A shudder rips through me at the memory of her rubbing up against his body in the common room this morning as if she needed to mark her territory.

"Look out, incoming bitch at twelve o'clock."

"Fucking hell," I mutter, not bothering to turn to look at her approach.

Did I fucking silently summon her or something?

A shadow falls over both of us as Teagan and her puppies come to a stop at the end of our table.

Still, I keep my eyes downcast, as does Emmie, which amuses me greatly. Although Tcagan has a different opinion if her irritated scoff is anything to go by.

After long seconds, I turn to look at her, although I let it be more than known that I really don't have the energy for it.

"I'm sorry, can we help you?" I ask, sounding bored. "If you're looking for your owner, I haven't seen him since this morning."

Her face burns bright red, much to my amusement.

"Miss Peterson would like to welcome you to the gym team," she forces out between gritted teeth.

"Oh yeah?" I ask with a wide accomplished smile. It seems like my day just keeps getting better and better. "Tell her I can't wait. And if she needs a new captain at any point, I'm more than willing to step up."

Teagan's chin drops as I stand, bringing myself up to her level.

"Keep pushing me, Teagan. I dare you."

Before she has a chance to respond, I grab my tray from the table and take off toward the building.

I'd rather be doing homework than be forced to breathe the same air as that bitch.

"Okay, that was freaking awesome," a familiar voice says from behind me as I step into the building.

Glancing to my left, I find Calli, the girl from gym last night.

"Glad I could entertain you."

"I haven't seen anyone go up against Teagan since... well, it's been so long I can't even remember."

"About time she met her match, then."

"I'm pretty sure it was year eight," Calli muses as we continue walking side by side. "She took Ashleigh to the ground by her hair for kissing whomever she fancied at the time."

"Good to see she's grown up," I deadpan.

"Girls like Teagan never do, do they?" she asks.

"Hopefully I won't be around to find out."

Calli laughs as we slow down to enter the bathroom. Fingers crossed it's less dramatic than Monday's visit.

"What do you have this afternoon?" she asks.

"English language. You?"

"History."

"Sounds like fun."

"Meh, I dunno. I don't really know what I want to do. I'll probably end up following my brother's footsteps and retaking this year once I figure shit out," she confesses as she slips into one of the stalls.

"It's not a bad thing."

"Maybe not. I just wanna know when everything's meant to start making sense, you know?"

"I don't think it ever does. Just gotta go for it and hope for the best."

"Not sure I like that option."

"Life's unpredictable. Gotta roll with the punches."

"That what you're doing with Teagan?"

"Sort of. Mostly I'm just enjoying myself."

"Hey," I breathe, a wide smile playing on my lips when I walk out of my English class to find Toby leaning against the opposite wall, waiting for me. "How'd you know what class I had?"

"I have ways." He winks, pushing from the wall and falling into step beside me.

"Any news on your car?"

"Well, mine has been picked up. I had a message from my dad saying that a replacement should be at our house by the end of the day. Useful seeing as I'm here, right?"

"You want a lift to your class?" he asks, remembering that I'd told him about starting cheer tonight.

"No, it's fine. I'll just call an Uber. I've already taken up enough of your time."

"Trust me, I've got nothing better to do tonight."

"Not hanging out with the guys?" I ask, testing the water as to where he stands with Seb. He told me last night that he sees him as a brother, but there was obvious tension between the two of them this morning.

"Nah, I got homework."

"Fair enough."

Pulling out my cell, I find the Uber app and wait for it to open.

"Put that away, Stella. I'm taking you." He looks over at me, his blue eyes holding mine and cutting off any argument I might have had.

"Thank you," I say, hoping he hears just how sincere it is.

We're almost out of the building when a heavy arm lands on my shoulder. My first thought is that it's Seb, but when I turn I find another of his little gang of dickheads.

"Where we going, kids?"

"Fuck off, Alex."

"Who's got your knickers in a twist, Tobes? Still pissed at Seb? You know I had nothing to do with that, right?"

"Shut the fuck up. Haven't you got something better to do than irritate me?"

"Umm..." he thinks for a second. "Nope. I'm free as a bird."

"For fuck's sake," Toby mutters as we continue to where Seb abandoned his car this morning. "You know your car's over there, right?" He points at a black Audi across the lot.

"Yeah, but I'm not in the mood to be alone."

"You're a pain in my ass, Demios."

"He loves me really." Alex opens Toby's passenger door and waits for me to drop into the seat before he closes it again. It's way more gentlemanly than I'm expecting.

Neither of them joins me for a minute or two as they have a brief argument over the roof of the car, their voices so low I can't make them out. But when they both pile in, the tension between them is palpable.

"So where are we going, Princess?"

"She's got a cheer class in Chelsea," Toby says for me.

"Sounds great. I'm in the mood for a road trip."

Alex gets settled behind me as Toby starts the car and pulls out of the lot.

"For real?" Toby barks when some hip-hop erupts from the speakers.

"What?" Alex asks, affronted. "I'm sure Stella's down, right, girl?"

"Uh... whatever," I mutter, not really in the mood to get in the middle of the two of them.

"See, the princess loves it."

"I wouldn't go that far," I say, quietly enough that only Toby can hear, and he snorts a laugh beside me.

The journey across the city is shorter than I was expecting, and I'm soon climbing from his car and thanking Toby once again for the lift.

"You want me to swing back when you're finished?"

"No, seriously. You've done enough."

He wants to argue, I can see it in every inch of his face, but he bites it back and nods instead.

"Have fun."

"I'll do my best. Thank you."

"Anytime, Princess."

"Yeah... uh... don't let that stick. I'm not a fucking princess."

Alex's eyes meet mine before I close the door. There's something in them, but I don't hang around long enough to even attempt to figure it out.

"You have to be fucking kidding me," I say a little too loudly once I've navigated my way to the locker rooms after refusing the help of the woman at reception.

All faces turn toward me. Most look completely oblivious, apart from the one my eyes are locked on.

Teagan Weston is quickly becoming the biggest pain in my ass, and that's something considering I've got Seb after me, wanting to *ruin me* or whatever bullshit he spat at me this morning.

"You have to be joking," she screeches.

"I really, really wish I was."

"Are you literally trying to take over my life?"

I can't help but laugh. "Trust me, your life is the last thing I want."

Turning my back on her, I walk farther into the room and thankfully into someone who is much happier to see me.

"Calli?" I breathe, a genuine smile on my face.

I didn't only choose to join this squad because it's got the best reputation, but also because it's not the closest to school, and I kinda hoped I could leave all the stuck-up bitches behind. Seems I might not have been the only one to think like that.

"You should have said you were joining."

"If I knew you cheered, I would have."

"I'm so glad you're here."

I smile at her while Teagan continues to fume behind me.

I change, fully prepared for a repeat of my gymnastics try-outs the second I walk out into the gym.

Thankfully, that's not my experience at all. It turns out that our coach is fucking fierce, and she takes zero shit from her girls or any messing about.

It's perfect, and other than the lasers of hate Teagan shoots me anytime we come within a few metres of each other, nothing happens.

And to ensure it stays that way, the second we're done, I grab my stuff and get the hell out of there.

She can think I'm running if she likes, but quite frankly, I'm just fed up with looking at her face. Bitter does not look good on her.

I'm almost jogging as I exit the building, and the last thing I expect is to run into a solid body blocking the doors.

"What the hell?" I gasp, trying to catch my breath.

"Heard you might need a lift," a deep voice rumbles.

Lifting my eyes from his wide chest, I find an amused set of green ones staring down at me.

"What the hell is it with you lot? Anyone would think you're my fucking babysitters." Taking a step back, I suck in a deep breath that's not full of the scent of hot boy. "Let me save you some time... I don't want, or need, looking after by any of you. I'm more than capable of looking after myself. Just ask Seb, he's got the wounds to prove it."

"I'm more than aware, Princess."

"And what's with the dumbass nickname?"

"Shall we?" he asks, gesturing toward the street and completely ignoring everything I've just said.

"No, we shall fucking not." Marching past him, I hitch my bags up higher on my shoulder and storm out of the building. "Of fucking course," I mutter to myself when I discover it's pouring down with rain.

I look down the street in each direction, wondering which way to go as I get assaulted by what feels like ice cold droplets.

"Ready to give in yet?" a smug voice says. "The nearest tube station is about an eight-minute walk, or you could just stand here and wait for an Uber. Or, you could get in my dry fucking car and let me take you home."

"Why? Why do you want to escort me home? Teagan's in there. I'm sure she'd love a visit."

"Nah, Seb's welcome to her," he says.

Rolling my eyes, I take off toward the lot, it's the most sensible decision if I don't want to end up drenched.

"I want you to know that I'm not happy about this, and if you try anything, then I've still got this." I pull Seb's knife on him and flip it open.

His eyes widen in shock, but I soon discover it's not because I'm threatening him.

"Seb gave you his knife?" he asks as we fall into his fancy-ass Maserati.

"Oh yeah, we're like BFFs. We share everything. He's also got two pairs of my panties."

His head rears back in shock.

"Two? I know about the graveyard, Princess. But is there something else I should know?"

"Asshole," I hiss.

"It's Theo, actually. Good guess, though."

Pulling my hair down from the messy bun I threw it up in before practice, I redo it while Theo starts the car and puts the heat on—I'm assuming for my benefit, seeing as I'm not exactly wearing a lot and am now dripping in rainwater.

"So, what brings you to London?" he starts once I'm strapped in.

"Who says I haven't been here a while?"

He glances over at me and raises a brow in a 'do I look like I was born yesterday' expression.

"Fine. My dad's work. We've moved all over America. I've been to at least one new school a year before we've moved on again."

"How come you hopped across the pond this time?"

"Honestly? No idea. Dad doesn't really go into detail about what he does."

"Which is?"

"Security, I think. He made it clear that it wasn't my business a few years ago, so I keep my nose out of it and just let him do his thing."

"What about your mum? How's she feel about all the moving about?"

I stare at his profile for a beat, wondering why he's so fucking interested all of a sudden when he hasn't said a word to me before now.

Feeling my attention, he glances over.

"Just making conversation," he mutters, answering my unspoken question.

"I don't have a mom. She died when I was a baby."

"That sucks."

"It is what it is. Can't miss something you never had,

right?" I ask, resting back and staring out of the window as a very wet London passes us by.

"You'd be surprised."

Part of me wants to demand he explain, but the other part doesn't want him to know I care in any way about what he's got to say.

"So, what's the deal with you lot? In some fucked-up gang or something?"

He laughs, and I can't help but want to smile at the amusement in it.

"Or something, Princess."

"Care to explain?"

"No, not really. I'm sure you've heard the gossip," he says cryptically.

"Do I look like the kind of girl who falls for that kind of bullshit?"

"Fair enough. You're right. It's probably best you don't believe everything you hear."

"Your friends included?"

"You're not stupid, Stella. I'm sure you can work it out."

"What's Seb's deal with me?" I ask, noticing that we're beginning to get closer to home.

"Seb is... complicated."

I can't help but snort a laugh. "He seems pretty simple to me. Privileged douchebag who can't handle when he doesn't get what he wants."

"While that might be partly true, there's much more to him than meets the eye."

"Like?"

Theo stops at a red light and lifts one hand to push his hair back from his brow as he considers how to answer my question.

"Let's just say you're not the only one to lose a parent young."

"And that makes him a cruel fuck toward me because?"

"Look, I can sit here making excuses for him all night if you want me to. But if you really want answers, I'm not the person you should be talking to."

"Yet you were the one who randomly decided to give me a lift."

"You'd have preferred it if I were Seb?"

"He let me play with his knife. He was more fun," I deadpan.

"You know he's going to want that back, right?"

"Then he'd better come and get it."

Theo pulls into my driveway, and I realize for the first time that I never gave him any directions.

"Oh look. Your replacement is here," he says, nodding out the windshield.

"It's fucking red," I spit the second my eyes land on the new Porsche sitting in the driveway beside Angie's car.

"Not my favourite either," Theo mutters, pulling to a stop behind it.

"Where's Toby? Why didn't he just pick me up?" I ask before pushing the door open.

"He's working."

"Homework. Right."

"R-right," he mutters.

"Well, thanks, I guess. This whole journey was... enlightening."

"See you tomorrow, Stella. Try to stay out of trouble."

I nod at him, pretending to take his warning on board but mostly hearing it as a challenge.

"Hey, sweetie," Angie replies from the kitchen when I call for her. "The keys are in the bowl if you want to check her out."

"She's only temporary, right?"

Angie laughs, already knowing how I feel about the color.

I dump my bags on the side and swipe the key before heading back outside once I've checked that Theo's left.

The model, everything about the 911 looks to be the same as mine. Everything aside from the color.

Unlocking it, I pull the door open, and I'm about to drop into the seat when a white envelope stops me.

Picking it up, I turn it over but find it blank.

Assuming it's from the garage, I drop it onto my lap as I start the engine and sit for a few minutes, letting her purr settle me. She's not my baby, but she's close.

Resting my head back, I close my eyes and just take a moment to absorb everything.

Theo was the last person—okay maybe not the last, but he was pretty far down on my list—that I was expecting to find after cheer practice. And although he might have said quite a bit on the way here, I don't feel like I've really learned anything. Well, other than the fact that Seb's lost a parent. That sucks. I should know. But what the hell has that got to do with me?

My stomach rumbling forces me to sit back up, ready to go and find what Angie might have made for me. The sight of the envelope stops me and I quickly rip it open.

Inside is one square piece of paper, and I quickly pull it out.

I soon find out that it's not something from the garage but a photograph that makes my heart jump into my throat.

I stare down at the image. It's a little fuzzy, but it's obvious that it's Toby and me... in my room last night.

"What the actual fuck?"

My hand trembles as I stare at it. Who the hell took this? Who would care enough to take this?

Flipping the image over, I find a note scrawled across the back.

You never should have come here.

"Motherfucker," I bark, the image crinkling as my fist curls.

Fucking Sebastian.

No wonder he sent Theo to pick me up. He was busy trying to fucking play me.

CHAPTER TEN

Sebastian

"She's back home safe," Theo says, strolling into his place a little after seven.

"Great," I mutter, not even glancing up from my tablet.

"Tell me again why couldn't you pick her up yourself?"

"Because I couldn't, okay?"

"Right. You should just go over there and fuck her, get it out of your system so you can focus."

"Stellar advice there, Theo. Thanks."

"What? It's what you would usually do," he argues, resting his elbows on the counter of his kitchen and looking over at me.

"Yeah, well. This is different."

"Because she's our missing princess?"

"No, because she... because her father ki—" I cut myself off, not allowing myself to say it out loud.

"I know, Seb," he says, standing once more and pushing his hair back from his brow. "But—"

"But what, Cirillo? Tell me how I should be handling all of this."

"There's no right or wrong, but... you're not the only one who's lost people."

Silence stretches between us as I try to read into his words. The realization hits me.

"Fuck me. You're on her side."

"What? No. Never. But did you ever consider that maybe she's hurting just as much as you?"

I raise a brow at him.

"This isn't about her," I snap, jumping from the sofa and storming from the house.

"Seb, come on, man," he calls after me. But I'm done. So fucking done.

It's not as late as the last time I was here so it's still light—although barely, with the heavy rain clouds darkening the sky—as I make my way down the old bumpy paths to get to the two gravestones I usually only visit once a year. It's still raining, but nowhere near as hard as it was earlier. But everything since my previous visit here has been so fucked up that it's the only place I can think about being.

With a bottle of vodka and a joint ready to go, I lower myself to rest against the same stone I was sitting against that night.

"Everything's fucked up," I mutter in the hope that someone might just actually listen to me. "Mum's a disaster. I'm a fucking disaster." Resting my arms over my knees, I lower my brow to my arms and suck in a shaky breath. "This wasn't how it was meant to be," I whisper.

Lifting my head, I stare at the stone opposite me.

Christopher Papatonis
Loving husband and father

Grief consumes as I stare at it, pain from the fact that I have no memory of the man Sophia and Zoe talk so highly of. Mum too, when she's able to.

But that is nothing compared to the pain that rips through me when I glance over my shoulder at the stone I'm resting against.

I've got endless memories of this one, and I have no idea if that makes it any easier or just more painful, knowing what a bright light was taken from us.

Demi Papatonis.

Emotion burns up my throat as I think about her smiling face as we used to run around the garden together, causing general chaos in the house that Sophia and Zoe had no choice but to deal with, seeing as they were older and Mum had checked out even back then. If only we knew how bad it was going to get when we lost Demi as well.

There was barely a year between the two of us, and aside from the guys who've always been by my side, she was my best friend.

And then one day, she was no longer there.

Gone to be with Daddy, I remember Sophia trying to tell me, as if it would make it all better.

It fucking didn't. Nothing could ever make it better.

Tipping the bottle to my lips, I swallow down half of

it in the hope of drowning the pain. I've always failed in the past, so I have no reason to think it'll be any different tonight.

There's only ever one thing that makes the pain any better.

Losing myself in someone else.

In her.

Flipping my lighter, I suck in a deep hit, hoping that it'll magically make everything in my life right now make sense.

Time seems to stop as I sit there with the drizzle soaking through my hoodie, the sodden ground ensuring my arse is just as wet.

But I don't care. Here, I feel closer to her. To him, even though I never knew him.

"Tell me what to do," I whisper into the silence as the darkness begins to swallow me whole.

I have no idea how much time passes as I sit there, shivering from the cold, my head spinning from the mix of vodka and weed.

But despite all that, the second I hear a twig snap behind me I'm on my feet, feeling more sober than ever.

Images of finding her here that night play out in my mind like a fucking movie as I search the darkness for someone, for anything.

I come to the decision that it was just an animal when I see something.

"Wait," I call before taking off in the direction of the shadow.

The dark figure moves toward the exit, but there's no fucking way I'm letting her escape this time.

My feet pick up pace, and the second I'm in touching

distance, I twist my fingers in the back of her damp hoodie and drag her back into my body.

All the air in her lungs comes out in a rush when she collides with my chest.

I don't need to look beneath her hood to know it's her. My body knows.

"What are you doing here, Hellion?"

Refusing to answer, she tries fighting free, but this time, I'm prepared for her and I wrap both my arms around her, pinning her own to her body.

She doesn't give up easily though, even trying to stomp on my foot in the hope it'll be enough to make me release her.

Every time a part of her body collides with mine, causing even the slightest bit of pain, my cock hardens against her arse.

"I can go all night if you want," I growl in her ear, my arms tightening, crushing her curves against my hardness.

"I didn't come here for you," she finally hisses.

"No? So why are you here?"

She stills, no doubt fighting with her need to defy me. Until she lets out a long breath and finally spills the words.

"Theo said some things. Said you lost someone. I just thought..."

Anger rips through me at the thought of her learning my truths, my ugliness, but I fear it's too late to stop her now.

Fucking Theo. I fucking warned him not to say anything. To just pick her up and deliver her home like the white fucking knight he tries to be. But no, he had to run his fucking mouth.

"You thought you'd shove your nose into my life and hope to find some answers."

Taking a risk, I release one of my arms from around her body and drag her hood down, exposing her light blonde hair.

Threading my fingers into the soft lengths, I drag her head back so she has no choice but to look at me.

I flick my eyes over every inch of her face before focusing in on her eyes that are dark with anger.

My jaw tics as I stare at her, my cock hard as fuck against her arse.

She fucking knows it too, if the slight smirk playing on her lips is anything to go by.

Seconds drag by as we stare at each other, hate crackling between us. It's so fucking thick it's hard to drag in the air I need, especially when it's laced with her scent.

The drizzle picks up once more until fat raindrops land on both of us, soaking our hair through until it begins to run down our faces.

It should ruin her makeup, make her look a mess, but fuck, it only makes her hotter seeing her mascara smudging under her eyes as if she's crying. Crying for me. The only thing that would make it better would be seeing her lips swollen from my kiss.

No. Fuck no.

"You want the truth, Hellion?"

A shocked gasp rips from her lips as I force her forward with my hand in her hair. She stumbles, but I don't let her fall. Not yet.

Together, we splash through the puddles that have emerged in the grass as we approach Dad's gravestone.

Twisting my fingers, she hisses as I pull, giving her no choice but to drop to her knees in the mud.

"You're an asshole," she seethes, but it doesn't escape my attention that she doesn't fight me.

She could. We both know she could, yet she allows me to do this.

Is she really so curious about me to let this shit ride, or am I going to find myself knocked on my arse any second?

My cock twitches at the thought of her turning her rage on me, and I realise that any pain she's planning on dishing out will be worth it.

"There," I growl, forcing her head forward so she has no choice but to look at the carving on the stone.

Nothing but the sound of the rain soaking everything around us and our heaving breaths can be heard as she stares at it. Reading the words, the dates. The beginning of my life turning to utter fucking shit before my innocent eyes.

"Y-you were only a baby," she whispers, so quietly I would miss it if I weren't so invested in what she might say to all of this.

"I had no chance of remembering him," I force out through the emotion clogging my throat.

It doesn't matter that I never met him. I've always felt close to him. Always. I'm a part of him. The Family was a part of him.

"What happened to him?"

My body jolts at her question, and there's no way in hell she misses it. She's too perceptive.

"He was murdered."

Her gasp of shock cuts through the silence.

"But that's not all."

Hauling her backward, I twist her toward the headstone I was leaning against both tonight and the night she first found me here.

Her gasp of shock combined with her hand lifting to cover her mouth clues me into the fact that she immediately understands.

"Seb," she almost sobs.

The sound of her empathy threatens to make a lump of emotion crawl up my throat, but I swallow it down. Like fuck am I going to allow her to see how much all of this affects me.

Dropping to my knees behind her, I ignore the wetness that instantly soaks into my jeans as I pull her head back, putting my lips to her ear.

"Is this answering some of your questions?" I growl, making her shudder in my hold.

"Yes and no," she confesses.

"So what else did you want to know?" I ask, knowing exactly what's going to fall from her lips.

"What this all has to do with me?"

A dark, wicked chuckle falls from my lips.

I have her on her back in a heartbeat. Her chest heaves as I pin both of her wrists in the mud above her head and trap her thighs with my legs.

She squirms, but we both know she's going nowhere.

"It's cold. Is this really necessary?" she asks, her voice sounding almost bored while her body tells a whole other story.

"Do you still have my knife, Hellion?" I ask, my eyes darting over her features. Even in the dark night I can tell her pupils are blown, but I know it's not with fear. No matter how badly I might want her to be scared of me, I know she's not. Her lips are parted with her increased breaths and her chest is heaving.

She shakes her head, causing anger to surge through my veins.

If she's fucking lost that knife...

"No great loss," I lie. "I've got a backup."

Taking both of her wrists in one of my hands, I reach behind me and pull my spare knife from my pocket.

"Oh God," she whimpers as she watches the raindrops fall onto the cool metal in my hand.

"You made a mistake coming here tonight, Hellion. Hell, you made a mistake coming here at all."

"Why?" she cries. "Tell me why."

She thrashes beneath me, proving that if she wanted to get away she probably could. But I have a suspicion that escaping right now is the last thing on her mind.

Leaning over her, I rest the flat of my knife against her cheek.

"There's so much you don't know, Hellion," I murmur, dragging the tip of my nose down her cheek as I mimic the movement on the other side with my knife.

CHAPTER ELEVEN

Stella

*O*h *fuck.*

It's raining so hard it stings my skin. The water beneath me soaks every inch of me and my body trembles, but with his hips pinning me into the mud, it's not from the cold.

His eyes are dark as they hold mine.

That move was so tender that it threw me for a loop, but that's what this is.

It's a game.

I might have no clue where the finish line is, but I already know who's going to win.

With each flash of his wicked eyes, I already feel myself willingly handing myself over to him.

It's a dangerous place to be, but right now, I'm not sure I want to be anywhere else.

I need more. I crave more of his secrets, anything that

will help open up everything I'm desperate to learn about this place and why he turned on me the second he learned who I was.

"I'm all ears, Sebastian."

He visibly winces when I say his whole name, and it only adds more questions about who he really is.

He chuckles once more, his brief show of vulnerability gone as his face returns to its usual cold mask.

"You really think I'm going to make it that easy for you? All you need to know right now is that you're mine, Doukas." His knife continues over my chin and to my throat, where he pushes that little bit harder into my skin. Not enough to cut, but enough to ensure I'm aware of just how much a predicament I could be in right now.

"Mine to do with as I please. I deserve it, after all." His eyes drop from mine, lingering on my lips for a beat before dropping to where the point of his knife is. "I could just end it all here," he muses, talking to himself.

I have to bite down on the inside of my lips to stop any one of the millions of questions I have. I want him to say everything he has to say of his own accord. I already know that he'll shut down the second I demand anything of him.

His knife moves again, dragging over my collarbone with enough pressure that it stings.

His eyes flare, and I know instantly that he's drawn blood.

As he dips his head, I have to lock down the moan of pleasure that wants to rip from my throat when his lips close over the small wound and his tongue laps at the sensitive skin.

My hips grind into the soft ground beneath me as he tastes my blood, my pussy embarrassingly wet for him.

I should be repulsed. I should be demanding he get the hell off me and as far away from me as physically possible.

Any normal girl would.

I'm sure Teagan would.

But I'm not any normal girl, and if I didn't already know that, then this right now would be a huge fucking clue.

His lips leave my collarbone, brushing up my neck until his hot breath tickles around my ear, making a violent shiver rip through me.

"Mine," he whispers. "And I love nothing more than ruining everything I own."

My brain is still so lost to the fog of lust his deep warning voice causes inside me that I don't realise he's moved until a bite of pain adds to my desire as he catches the skin beneath my sports bra.

"Seb," I gasp as my eyes take in what he's doing.

The blade of his knife is beneath the fabric of my bra, poised ready to slice it from my body.

"Tell me no, Hellion. I dare you."

I tilt my chin up in defiance, and he smirks. "Fuck you, Seb."

"Nah, the only one getting fucked here tonight is you."

I blink the rainwater from my eyes, and in that split second, he moves, the fabric around me parting and leaving me exposed to him.

"Aw, hell, Hellion. I do like my toys to be pretty before I fuck them up. And I think breaking you is going to be the sweetest fucking torture."

My back arches when his burning hot hand lands on my bare breast. I tug at his tight grip on my wrists, trying to get free, to hit him or drag him closer I'm not sure, but it doesn't really matter because his hold on me is too strong.

"Seb," I cry when he pinches my nipple so hard I swear I feel it in my clit. "Oh shit." He twists, and it fucking burns, but fuck... "Fuck..." My hips roll, my thighs rubbing together with my need for more.

"I was right. So fucking beautiful falling apart beneath me, Hellion."

"Make the most of it. You won't see it again."

"You're full of shit, Doukas." And just to prove his point, he dips his head, circling my nipple with the tip of his tongue, lapping at both me and the rainwater that's still pounding down on both of us.

"Please." The plea falls from my lips before I manage to swallow it down.

His eyes flare with desire. Right as a loud crack of thunder pierces the air around us, he sucks my peak into his burning mouth and bites.

"Yes," I scream, everything south of my waist pulling tight with my impending release from this alone.

"You wanna come, Hellion?" he asks, shifting a little, cluing me in to the fact that I'm not the only one riding the wicked high from this little tryst.

"What do you think, asshole?" I hiss when it's clear he's done teasing me.

"I think..." He sits up as high as he can while still pinning my hands into the mud. They're beginning to sink, being swallowed by the cold, dirty ground above my head.

I want to care. I really do. But I can't find it in me when he's touching me, spewing his hatred at me. It does crazy shit to my insides. I might not want to acknowledge what those flutters are because I'm pretty sure only a very skilled shrink would be able to decipher them, but hell if I don't want them to continue.

"I think that only one of us is going to get what we want tonight." His free hand moves to his waist and I watch as he snaps his belt open and awkwardly shoves the sopping wet fabric of his pants down enough to release his cock.

My mouth waters as he wraps his fingers around himself, sitting up slightly so he's hovering over my chest.

I watch him shamelessly stroke himself for long minutes, my thighs rubbing together in a pathetic attempt to dull the incessant throb of my pussy. But it won't help. Nothing but his touch, his mouth, his cock will give me anywhere near what I need. It's just a shame that I already fear it's not going to happen.

Dragging my eyes from his cock, I look up until I find his almost dark eyes that are boring down into mine with a cold and unreadable expression deep within them.

The muscles in his neck are pulled tight and his jaw is set as he gives himself over to the pleasure.

My fingers flex. I'm slowly losing feeling in them with the cold and his harsh grip, but more than that, I just want to touch him, to feel his hard length beneath them and watch him fall at my own hand.

No words are said out loud, but I read more than one of his silent warnings when his orgasm begins to approach and his mask starts to slip just a little.

Pure unfiltered hate stares down at me. It's such a weird sight mixing with the movement right above my tits. He might hate me, but it's obvious that he wants me just as much as I do him.

I shouldn't. I should want Toby. Hell, even Theo. Both of them have at least shown me a little decency since I turned up at Knight's Ridge on Monday, unlike the guy currently jerking off to the high of his hate for me.

It's fucked up. It's wrong.

So why the fuck does it feel so right?

His body locks up and my lips part as I get a front row seat to the pleasure that covers his face seconds before ropes of his hot cum land on my cold, rain-covered chest.

The moment he's done, he tucks himself away and leans over me, pulling something else from his pocket.

"Smile, you filthy whore. I bet Daddy would love to see the truth about his precious little princess."

"Fucking cunt," I bark, thrashing against his hold as he takes photo after photo of me covered in his spunk, soaking wet and caked in mud. Safe to say, I've looked better.

"Start digging into my life again, Hellion," he warns, "and it won't just be the two of us who know what went down here tonight. All of Knight's Ridge, your father, your friends back in Rosewood..."

My brows pull together at his mention of my past.

"And *I'm* the one digging?"

He leans closer, his intoxicating scent filling my nose and reigniting my desire.

"Back off, Hellion. You're not going to like what you find if you keep going."

My lips part to argue, but he pulls back, the fierce look on his face making me forget my words.

"You should go home. You're a fucking mess."

The second he releases me, my first instinct is to reach for him, but I manage to stop before I embarrass myself.

Without another word but one look in the direction of

his sister's headstone, he takes off across the graveyard, another clap of thunder echoing around me as he disappears.

"Holy fuck," I breathe, pushing from the ground and pulling my soaked hoodie around myself.

Lifting my knees, I drop my head into my hands and immediately realise my mistake.

"Fuck. Fuck. FUCK," I scream, making the situation worse by trying to wipe the mud from my face. "I FUCKING HATE YOU," I bellow after him, hoping he's close enough that he can hear me.

My heart pounds and my stomach churns as I think about what he just did to me. The way he touched me, used me, degraded me.

I should be disgusted. He treated me like nothing more than the whore he accuses me of being.

But I liked it. Hell, I wanted more. I still do.

My cunt is still slick with need, desperate to feel something, anything.

And I know for a fact that if he turned around right now and came back, I'd let him do it all over again.

What exactly does that say about me?

Pushing to my feet, I look down at myself and wince.

He wasn't wrong when he told me I look like a filthy whore.

I pull up my hood in the hope it'll help me hide before tugging my hoodie tighter around my body and taking off in the direction he just disappeared in.

At the very last minute, I turn back and glance between the two graves.

How unlucky is it for your father and sister to die on the very same day fifteen years apart? That kind of loss is enough to fuck anyone up. But this is more than that. It's more than just the pain of losing someone you love.

I squint at the date of Seb's father's death. Seb was just a baby. Just like I was when I lost my mom.

Maybe the two of us do have something in common.

A bitter laugh falls from my lips at the thought. It's not like we're ever going to bond over such shit. It's clear the only kind of connection there will ever be between us is this burning lust-filled hate thing we have going on.

Maybe if I just fuck him again it'll get it out of both of our systems.

My thighs squeeze together once more. The throb between them has lessened, but it's still very much there. And it only increases once more as I think back to watching him come all over my tits like some kind of primal claiming of me.

Well, he can fuck right off. I have no intention of becoming anyone's property. Especially not an arrogant and conceited motherfucker like him.

With my head held high and those lies I just told myself still spinning around my brain, I march out of that graveyard, my sneakers squelching and my body trembling, finally giving into the cold.

By the time I walk around the back of the house in the hope of sneaking inside, my teeth are chattering violently, and my fingers and toes are numb from the ice-cold wind.

Slipping off my sneakers, I dump them straight in the trash as I head for the warmth of the house.

"Stella, is that you?" Dad calls the second I pull the back door open.

Of course he's here right now.

I roll my eyes at the coincidence. When I saw the

driveway was empty I breathed a sigh of relief. It seems I relaxed too soon.

"Yeah. I've been for a run in the rain," I lie. "Let me shower and I'll come back."

"Okay, sweetheart."

A smile plays on my lips that he doesn't even bat an eyelid.

When we spent a few months in Nevada, I used to bolt outside the second I saw one drop of rain, and I'd stay out there soaking wet until the last drop fell.

It was my happy place. Dad used to watch me from the kitchen window if he was home when it happened and laugh at me like I was a complete head case. He used to joke that my British roots ran through my veins with how much I loved the rain.

Back then, I never really understood what he meant. But tonight, despite the fact that I'm currently freezing my ass off and covered in mud, is what I used to dream of when we had endless days of scorching heat. Seb, the mud and his knife are just an added benefit.

I pause halfway up the stairs as a thought hits me.

Had he just ruined the rain for me?

Asshole.

I shed my wet clothes as I make my way through my bathroom to deal with later, and after turning the dial, I step under the shower. I get blasted with ice cold water for a few seconds, but I barely feel it. The second it begins to warm, it feels so fucking good.

I stand there, letting the torrent of water wash away the mistakes of the night along with the mud and the evidence of his twisted power trip that's lingering on my skin.

Thankfully, when I get back down to Dad with wet hair

and wrapped in the warmest sweater I could find, he doesn't see anything of concern. He just sets about checking in with me before dropping the not-so-shocking bomb that he's going to be away for the weekend. The fact that he's been here a few times this week is more than I was expecting.

"Maybe you could invite some friends around or something," he suggests as he sips on a tumbler of whisky.

I narrow my eyes at him.

"Friends?" I ask.

"Yeah. We're staying here, Stella. It's safe to get close to people." He pins me with a look.

"We'll see." I take a couple of steps out of the living room, more than ready to make my escape if this little chat was just all about making me promises I have no reason to believe he'll keep.

"I know what you think, Stel. But this is our home."

I don't know if it's the cold or Seb's influence, but I do something I hardly ever do with my dad.

"Well, how about you make me feel like it and share some secrets? You kept me locked up in this house for weeks when we first moved, and now you're more than happy for me to be running around in the rain? What changed? Hell, screw that... what's your actual job, Dad?"

"Estella," he warns, instantly making me feel like a six-year-old again.

"I feel like I don't even know who I am," I say, immediately hearing Seb's words in my ear from earlier tonight.

"Don't be so ridiculous."

His words are like a red rag to a bull. My anger bubbles over faster than I can contain.

"Ridiculous? You think this is me being ridiculous?

134

How can't you see how frustrating this is? I've let it all go before because I trust you, but this is crazy. Tell me something, Dad. Tell me something real." I throw my hands out, feeling utterly hopeless.

I hate that Seb's got to me. But I've had it with all the secrets and the bullshit.

We came here for a reason. A very good reason, and before, that was enough for me. But not now. Now I want some truth, something real.

Dad throws back the contents of his glass and stands. He's tall, his frame wide. For a man his age he's still really good looking and with a killer body, thanks to Calvin's regular workout sessions. Any woman would be lucky to have him. So why has he never had one? Why doesn't he even seem to want one? Or a man. Hell, I couldn't give a shit if he's actually gay.

Maybe that's the big secret.

No. I shake the thought from my head. This is bigger than his sexual preferences.

He doesn't stop until he's right in front of me.

Reaching out, he cups my cheek in his warm hand.

"You are the single most important thing in my life, Stella. Everything I do is to keep you safe and secure your future."

"Dad," I sigh, leaning into his touch. "I appreciate that, I really do. But I need more. Please. Moving here, it's been..." Harder. "Different than all the other times. I don't know who I am here."

"Didn't you like cheer tonight?" His hand slips from my face, leaving me feeling cold.

"This isn't about cheer. This isn't even about school. It's about me. It's about us. Our family, our lives."

He lets out a long breath, a tormented look I don't see very often passing across his face.

"When we first got here..." he starts, lifting his hand to his hair and pulling it back from his brow as if he's nervous. That can't be right. Galen Doukas never gets nervous. Ever. "There are some people from my past who don't want me here. And in turn, I was worried about you."

"Me? No one will care about me. I have nothing to do with your past."

"Sweetheart..." He sighs once more. "I'm connected to some dangerous people. Ruthless men who don't think twice about doing whatever is necessary to right some wrongs."

My brow wrinkles as I stare up at him, my heart sinking in my chest.

"Right. I don't know why I bothered."

Spinning on my heels, I storm away from him, furious that he can't for once just give me a straight answer.

Doesn't he think I've figured that shit out? We've got a team of security, for fuck's sake. I didn't think he was Mother freaking Theresa.

I slam my door, feeling like a petulant child who hasn't got her way, and throw myself on my bed.

Toby's lingering scent from the other night hits me, and I get the urge to call him. Something tells me he'd understand.

I second guess myself for ten seconds before I dig my cell from the bottom of my purse and find his number.

Sitting back against my headboard, I hold it to my ear as the call rings out.

My stomach flutters when the call connects, but

there's a commotion on the other end before the line goes dead.

"Okay then," I mutter to myself as I lower my cell.

I stare at the screen, waiting for him to call back, but it remains eerily quiet.

Emotion crawls up my throat and tears burn the backs of my eyes.

Bending my legs, I wrap my arms around them and rest my head on my knees.

I've been alone most of my life in one way or another, but I've never felt this lonely before.

It's my own fault. I allowed myself to need people in Rosewood, and now I crave that connection, that friendship I managed without for all those years.

I think of Emmie, of Calli. Hell, even Theo pops into my head as I refuse to allow a certain dark-haired boy with wicked intent in his eyes to slide back into my thoughts. Could any of them turn out to be what I need?

Pulling my sheets over me, I lie there with thoughts running at a million miles an hour around my head.

I'm exhausted, but sleep seems to elude me, my body happy to allow my brain to continue taunting me long into the night.

I have no idea what time it is when a soft knock sounds out on my door, but I don't react. I'm not in the right place to have another conversation with my dad when I know all he's going to do is lie to my face.

After a few seconds, he invites himself inside. The light from the hallway fills my room, but I still don't move. I keep my back to him and focus on keeping my breathing steady.

"I wish I could tell you everything, baby," he whispers, making my traitorous body jolt at the emotion in his voice. "But I'm terrified of what you'll think when you discover the truth."

I lie there, my head warring with itself. Part of me wants to flip over and demand more, but the other part hears the pain, the fear in his voice, and that finally wins out.

"I'm sorry, sweetheart."

It's not until he's left and my door has clicked closed again that I release the breath I didn't know I was holding and the tears I was fighting finally come.

And when I do finally pass out, it's because I've cried myself to sleep.

CHAPTER TWELVE

Sebastian

"What the fuck happened to you?" Theo asks the second I stumble into his living room looking like a fucking hobo.

"Got caught in the storm."

"Oh, I didn't realise it was raining mud." He quirks a brow.

"Don't be a fucking smart-arse. It doesn't suit you."

"Don't be a hater, bro. We both know my arse is way smarter than yours."

I flip him off as I march with wet, muddy shoes across his precious solid wood floors to the kitchen.

"Do you fucking mind?" he barks behind me.

"Not one single fuck."

Ripping open the top cupboard, I pull out a bottle of Jack that we keep for emergencies.

I fucking hate the stuff, but when you've had a night like I have it's a necessity.

"Wow, you must have had a really good evening," he quips as I tip the bottle to my lips and chug shot after shot. My throat burns like hell, but the second the warmth hits my belly and I get the first sign that it's going to do its job, I keep going.

"Whoa, Seb. Coach will have your bollocks in the morning if you turn up hanging out of your arse. Your focus has been shot all week."

"Is it any surprise?" I bark, finally pulling the bottle from my lips and wiping my mouth with the back of my hand as I fight the need to puke the lot back up.

Abandoning his laptop on the coffee table, he slides to the edge of the sofa.

"You've been with her, haven't you?"

Placing the bottle on the counter, I drop my forearms to it and hang my head.

"Fucking hell, Seb. She's gonna fuck you up."

Lifting my head, I find his eyes.

"More than I already am?"

He shakes his head, clearly not wanting to dive into my screwed-up brain.

Walking over, he swipes the bottle from the side and takes a shot of his own. He winces after he's swallowed and places it back down.

"You fuck her again?" he asks, his gaze dropping to my mud-covered hands.

"Nah. Didn't give her the pleasure."

A knowing smirk pulls at his lips.

"You're playing with fire. I hope you know that."

"Wouldn't be fun otherwise."

Jumping up on the counter, he takes another shot. "She's not like the others."

"You're fucking telling me. Bitch still has my knife."

"Yeah, about that. How come you won't even let me touch it, and she's had it for what? Twelve hours?"

"She's a better lay than you," I deadpan.

"Funny, because I'm not sure I remember ever being your little bitch."

"I also don't want to kill you with it. I'll let her keep it for a bit if it lets her think she's got the upper hand. But I will be getting it back, and it will have her blood on it."

If he's shocked by my words then he doesn't show it.

"Fair enough. Just don't do it here. I ain't dealing with the mess."

"I'll see what I can do. I'm going for a shower."

"And here I was thinking you wanted to keep the evidence of tonight on you."

The image of my spunk covering her chest pops into my head.

"The only one with evidence of anything that happened tonight is our little princess."

My phone damn near burns a hole through my pocket. My need to pull it out and stare at that image I threatened her with is almost too much to deny.

"What's that look for?" Theo asks. We've grown up like brothers since we were in diapers. He can read me almost better than I can myself.

"Nothing I'm fucking sharing with you."

"We'll see about that. I happen to think our princess would look fucking good between the two of us, don't you?"

A wave of overwhelming possessiveness hits me out of

nowhere. The thought of watching Theo touch what's mine makes me want to pull my knife back out.

My teeth grind as we stare at each other, him waiting for a verbal response—not that I think he needs one for a second.

"Touch her and I'll kill you."

"You'll be telling me you're falling in love with her and gonna put a ring on it next."

A growl rumbles up my throat at his words, but all he does is throw back his head and bark out a laugh.

"I'll be in my room if you need me. Sleep that off so I don't have to deal with Coach," he says, pointing to the now half empty bottle before grabbing his laptop and a bottle of Coke and disappearing down the hall.

I salute his retreating back before ignoring his request and taking the bottle with me as I head for my bedroom.

I swear to God that this coach house was designed with the two of us in mind all those years ago. It's a large brick building adjacent to Theo's family home. Not only are there four garages beneath us for our beloved babies, but every bedroom fits a king-sized bed with an en suite. The living area is big enough for some killer parties, and best of all, we're far enough from the main house that neither Theo's mum, dad nor younger siblings have a clue what we're doing inside.

Heaven.

The only time it's better is when I've got some company in my huge bed.

I glance over at my black sheets, my imagination running wild as an image of Stella writhing in it pops into my head. Her tits bare, her nipples hard and begging for my mouth just like they were tonight.

Reaching down, I rub my length through my pants.

Fuck punishing her. I should have fucked her tonight. My own hand only got me so far.

I fall into bed naked after a long shower that might have done the job of washing the mud from my body but did little to clear my head.

I thought shit was bad before, but with her here, now my head is spinning faster than I can control.

The thoughts of revenge have been at the forefront of my mind since the day I learned the truth. I always thought it was something of a pipedream, a fantasy. But now it's right here. Everything I've thought about, everything craved for so long is—was—right beneath my hands.

I have the power to cause the exact same pain that was forced on my family.

I could have done it by now. I could have done it that first night.

I had the gun right there.

I could have done it tonight while I had that knife to her throat. I could have done it and left her there for her father to find in hours or even a day's time. Her lifeless body in the middle of a muddy graveyard. He wouldn't have seen it coming, because he thinks his innocent little princess is safe with us. The boss may have given the order for us to protect her, but he has no clue about the ideas that have been running around my head for years when it comes to the most precious person in his life.

I lie there, staring at the ceiling, running the events of the day around my head. Every muscle in my body is locked tight as I continue to wonder if I should have just sunk inside her, if that would have helped settle something inside me. As it is, I'm lying here hard as fucking nails, replaying having her pinned beneath me over and over.

I have no idea what time I eventually pass out, but when I wake up the next morning, my head is pounding from the Jack on an empty stomach and my fitful sleep that was full of twisted, dirty dreams of Stella in that graveyard.

Reaching over to the bedside table, I feel around until I touch my phone.

Waking it up, I wince as I stare at the bright screen, but the second the image clears I bolt upright, my heart jumping into my throat.

"Holy shit," I breathe, my eyes locked on Stella's face.

In the hard light of day, the image I took of her hits entirely differently.

Fuck, she's beautiful.

Her hands and forearms are almost fully submerged in water. Her face is splattered with mud, her makeup smeared down her face, her lips full, almost as if we'd just spent the last half an hour kissing. Biting down on my bottom lip, my mouth waters as I remember what it was like doing just that.

Falling back onto my bed, I keep the image in front of me as I wrap my fingers around my length.

The sound of her moan as I teased her with my knife and sucked her nipple into my mouth fills my ears as I jack myself off, wishing like hell I was about to come over her perfect tits once more.

With my eyes locked on the second-best thing, I groan as my release hits me in embarrassingly short minutes.

"Seb, get your arse out of bed. We've got practice," Theo calls, pounding his fist on my door and scaring the shit out of me.

"Fuck off," I bark, pressing my head back into the pillow.

"No can do. You've got ten minutes or I'll go get the kids."

I groan. It wouldn't be the first time Theo let his little brother and sister in here to jump on me until I had no choice but to get out of bed if I ever wanted to have kids of my own one day. I can't imagine he told them to come in here and step on my junk at every opportunity, but that's pretty much how it went.

"You wouldn't want them seeing me right now."

"Stop jerking off, Seb. It'll fall off eventually."

His footsteps sound out as he leaves me to it. "Takes one to know one, wanker," I shout loudly enough to ensure he hears it.

I clean up before pulling on a pair of sweats and a Knight's Ridge t-shirt, grab my bags from the side, and swing the door open.

"Let's go then," I demand as I pad through the house. "You owe me a coffee on the way."

"How'd you figure that?" he mutters, reaching for his own bags and moving toward the door.

"You cock-blocked me."

"It doesn't count if it's with your own hand, dickhead."

"Sure it does. Your voice made me lose my high."

"Stop talking."

"I was right at that moment. You know it, the point of no return, and then your voice just... killed it," I say, fighting a smirk.

"My voice has never bothered you in the middle of action before," he quips.

"If you're referring to any time when there's been a

girl between us, that's entirely different. Her nakedness mitigates your presence."

"Unbelievable. I'll buy you a coffee if it'll make you shut up." He damn near rips the door of his Maserati off before throwing his bags into the back and dropping into the seat.

"Deal. I didn't really want to give you the details of my solo session anyway."

He glances over at me, his eyes narrowed in frustration.

"Oh, come on, like you didn't knock one out this morning. I saw the way you were looking at the emo chick yesterday morning. Bet you'd love to have her black lipstick on your—"

Theo floors the car, throwing me back in my seat and cutting off my words.

"Touchy subject?" I ask, humour laced through my voice.

"You're being a dick this morning. You really should have fucked her. It might have chilled you out a little."

I flip him off as he comes to a stop at the end of the driveway before gunning it onto the street and toward our closest Costa.

We're the last two into the locker room ready for our morning practice and every set of eyes turns our way. Most have the usual look of hesitancy on their faces, but there are always the couple who think they're man enough to stand up to us and square their shoulders in challenge. The only three who barely pay us any attention as we stroll in are Alex, Nico and Toby.

"What time do you call this?" Alex deadpans, pulling his boots on.

"That fuck was too busy jerking off over the princess,"

Theo announces, much to Alex and Nico's amusement. Toby's face, however, drops as his eyes find mine.

"You saw her last night?"

"You should have seen the state of him. Stumbled in soaking wet and covered in mud," Theo says, either oblivious to Toby's reaction or feeding it. It's hard to tell with him sometimes.

"Do we have to?"

"He's sulking because she didn't let him go all the way."

"Theo," I bark.

"He always is like a bear with a sore head when he don't get enough pussy," Alex joins in.

"It's too fucking early for this shit. Like any of you fuckers got lucky last night."

Smirks cover both Alex's and Nico's faces.

"Oh just fuck off, the lot of you."

Dragging my boots from my bag, I storm back out again, leaving them behind to gossip about me. I don't have the patience for this bullshit this morning.

I blow down the short walkway that leads out to our training field with the bench at the end in my sights when I run headfirst into a solid body.

"Whoa," Coach says, pressing his hands to my shoulders and pushing me back. He studies my face for a second. I have no idea what he sees. My hangover. My anger. The fact that I'm right at the end of my fucking patience. Whatever it is, it makes his brow crease in concern.

"You good, son?"

My lips part to lie, to tell him just like I do everyone else that everything is just fine. But for some reason, the words don't fall from my lips like they usually do.

"Come on."

He gives me a gentle shove in the direction of his office, and I have no choice but to head in that direction.

I fall on the chair in front of his desk before he takes his spot at the other side.

"I know it's a tough time for you right now, Seb."

I scoff, because tough doesn't even begin to describe what this time of the year is like.

Fucking excruciating is more like it.

I sit forward, resting my elbows on my knees, and look up at him, waiting for what else he's going to say to attempt to make my life any better.

"How's your mum doing?"

I continue staring.

There are only a handful of people who know the brutal truth of just how bad shit is with my mum, and Coach isn't one of them. He knows that she struggles since the loss our family suffered, but he has no clue that she's one shoot up away from leaving me an orphan.

"Same as. I think we're long past a miracle cure at this point, Coach."

He nods, looking totally out of his depth.

Back in the day, he had quite a prolific football career, but I'm not sure high school coach was ever really his calling in life. He wants to help, I can see it in his eyes. He wants to support us, help us achieve whatever it is our heart's desire, whether that be professional football or anything else. But talking about the heavy stuff with damaged teenagers isn't really his forte.

"I just need a couple of weeks," I lie. "Things will settle down, go back to normal." Whatever the fuck that is. "I'll get focused again."

"I'm not concerned about your focus on the field right

now, Seb. I'm worried about you. About the path you're headed down."

"I know what I'm doing."

He quirks a brow, silently asking, "Do you?"

Everyone knows who we are, what our surnames represent and the kinds of things that are—and will be—expected of us in the future. None more so than Theo. And I see concern in the eyes of most of our teachers.

I guess being a soldier in the Family isn't exactly what they consider a successful future. They want us to head to Oxbridge and make our fortunes as lawyers, doctors, MDs of huge corporations—just like the parents who pay the insane tuition this place demands to allow their kids to attend.

But that isn't our reality. We might make it to university—it's always been in mine and Theo's plans, depending on what the boss wants—but our futures were sealed the day we were born with Cirillo blood running through our veins.

"You've got nine months left here, Seb. Make the most of it. You're going to be an adult for a long time."

Don't I fucking know it. But what Coach doesn't understand is that I've been a fucking adult for years. Every single time I prized a bottle out of Mum's hands, carried her to bed, bathed her, brushed her matted hair, I grew up that little bit more until I was nothing more than a boy drowning in the reality of being a man in our world.

Blood, death, and corruption.

That's where we're all heading, and there's fuck all any of us can do about it.

I've been working for long enough to know exactly what's expected of me. I've got my hands dirty on more occasions than I want to think about just trying to keep Mum alive. It's a part of who I am.

It's a part of everyone around me.

Even my little hellion.

She just doesn't know it yet.

And it's going to be so fucking beautiful when she finally learns the truth. When she discovers what I'm really capable of and just how many ways I've dreamed of getting my revenge.

My fists curl, hunger for blood and retaliation making my hate burn red hot.

"So what do you say?" Coach's voice comes back to me, but I have no fucking clue what he just said. The images in my head are of our princess at my mercy, her skin stained with her blood courtesy of my knife—the one she's stolen. And they're all consuming.

"Y-yeah, you got it, Coach," I say, hoping like fuck it's what he wants to hear before pushing out of the chair, grabbing my boots and marching from his office.

By the time I'm booted up and jogging out onto the field, the rest of the guys are running drills.

I fall into step beside Toby, who glances over at me, a warning in his light blue eyes that I shrug off.

He's worried about the princess. Well, fuck him and fuck her.

She doesn't need anyone looking after her, and he needs to keep his fucking nose out of my business.

CHAPTER THIRTEEN

Stella

A shiver of awareness races down my spine as I stand at my locker a few minutes before the bell for the end of lunch on Friday afternoon.

Yesterday was suspiciously quiet from both Seb and his little gang, and Teagan.

I spent the whole day looking over my shoulder, waiting for the rug to be pulled from beneath me, but by the time I got to gym practice after school I soon discovered that Teagan and her bitches weren't just avoiding me, but they'd all skipped out on the entire day.

Practice was amazing without their piercing stares cutting into my skin. For the first time since starting here, I was actually able to just lose myself in something I loved and forget about all the bullshit with Dad and the idiots I seem to have found myself surrounded by. I want to say that I was able to put *him* and our second altercation in the graveyard out of my mind too, but that would be a big fat lie, because the memories of having him on top of me, pressing me into the soft and muddy ground beneath me won't leave.

Seeing as I had a car once again, I didn't even find anyone waiting to escort me home. My afternoon was almost enjoyable—hence I was waiting for someone to come running in to ruin it.

Despite knowing that he's watching me, I refuse to turn around. He shouldn't have this kind of power over me, and there's no fucking way I'm allowing him to see that his mere presence affects me in any way. His ego is already a few sizes too big. Teagan and her band of little bitches have blown it up nicely.

Everyone here, in fact, seems to either be terrified of Seb and his boys or worship the ground they walk on.

They're the school's kings—or knights, I guess—but they're no different to the arrogant pricks of every other high school I've attended. They've just got bank accounts that are the same size as their egos to buy whatever their little black hearts desire.

Toby's face flickers through my mind.

Why is he even friends with those jerks? I might have only spent a few hours with him, but he doesn't seem like them. Well, not like Seb.

I grab the book I need for this afternoon and slam my locker closed. Typically, the direction I need to go is where he's standing, but seeing as I'm refusing to go anywhere near him, I take a step the opposite way, more than happy to take the long route to my final class of the day.

I only take two steps when someone else appears before me.

"Oh my God, what happened?" I ask, staring up at Toby's black eye and split lip.

A smug smirk curls at the uninjured side of his mouth as he leans his shoulders against the bank of lockers beside us.

"You should see the other guy."

I roll my eyes at his attempt to brush it aside.

"I didn't have you down as a fighter." I know that Theo and Alex are still sporting wounds from whatever they got themselves into the other night, but I get those vibes from them. They're privileged, wealthy pricks. It only makes sense that they also feel the need to prove their worth with their fists too.

"There's a lot you don't know about me."

"Oh, mysterious."

His eyes hold mine, a soft smile playing on his lips before he glances behind me for the briefest moment.

"Oh my God, it was him," I breathe, realization hitting me out of nowhere.

"Just leave it, yeah?"

My fists curl and my lips purse.

Clearly Toby has a lot to learn about me too, because there is no fucking way I'm leaving it at that.

I spin on my heels, ready to march over to him, but just as I'm about to take a step it becomes abundantly clear that I don't need to move an inch.

"Hellion, how's it going?" he asks, his voice as smooth as melted chocolate and an accomplished smirk playing on his annoyingly handsome face.

"You," I spit, poking him right in the chest. "What is your fucking problem?"

"Me?" he asks, faux innocence covering his face before he leans into my ear so that only I can hear his response. His hot breath tickles my neck and I have to fight like hell to stop myself reacting to it. "I think we both know I've got more than a few problems. But right now, my issue is your company."

He pulls back, but not enough to get out of my space.

"I don't share my toys, Hellion," he warns.

"Well, it's a good thing I'm not yours to play with, isn't it?"

"Funny, I don't remember you saying that the other night."

My eyes narrow in warning, but Toby beats me to responding.

"Leave it, Seb."

"Butt the fuck out, Tobes. This doesn't concern you."

"Like fuck it doesn't. I won't stand here and watch you rip strips off her for your own amusement."

Seb's cold eyes finally release mine in favor of his friend's.

"Back off," he growls.

"Fuck this," I bark, having no desire to be in the middle of this macho pissing contest. Spinning away from both of them, I take a step when a hand grabs my upper arm.

The purse in my hand drops to the floor and I act on instinct, something which Seb is clearly not expecting when he finds himself pressed against the opposite wall three seconds later with my knee in his lower back and his arm twisted so far back that it's probably about to pop out of its socket.

I suck in a deep breath, my heart thundering at a mile a minute as my surroundings come back to me.

Silence ripples down the hallway a beat before the attention of every student loitering in here before class makes my skin tingle with awareness.

"You made your point, Hellion. You can fucking let me go now," Seb seethes, his voice low with his barely restrained anger.

I can't imagine anyone gets the better of any of these boys, let alone the new girl.

I try not to smile as he flinches against my hold, but I can't help it and my lips twitch up.

"Fuck me," a familiar voice announces from somewhere behind me. "That was the best thing I've seen all year. Princess," he breathes, pride oozing from his voice, "turn those moves on me, girl. I'll happily grapple with you all day long."

A growl rumbles up Seb's throat.

"Hellion," he warns, but I still don't let up.

Instead, I lean closer. I have to reach up on my toes, but I ensure my lips touch his ear.

"You've chosen the wrong enemy, Sebastian. Now ask me nicely," I demand with a smirk, which earns me a howl from whoever is behind me lapping this up like he's watching a fucking movie.

Seb's nostrils flare as he blows out a tense breath.

"I hope you know that I could have you on your back in two seconds flat if I wanted to," he warns. "I could fuck you over right here in front of the entire sixth form."

His words fall very far from the mark. He might be used to others being scared of him, but he won't get it from me.

His jaw tics as my only reaction is to laugh.

"Even if you did have the balls, you know I'd cut it off with your own knife before you got anywhere close."

Tension and hate crackle between us as I press my knee in harder.

The bell rings around us and the rustling of people starting to move about fills my ears, but the attention on the two of us never leaves.

"What are you lot doing?" a deep voice barks down the hallway. "Get to class."

I pull back just in time to see Mr. Davenport looking less than impressed at seeing almost all of his students loitering when they should be heading to class.

Seb is righting his shirt and tie as our Head of Sixth comes to a stop before us all.

"Everything okay, Miss Doukas?"

"Nothing I can't handle, sir." I smile sweetly at him, and he nods, giving the boys behind me pointed stares.

"Class, please. All of you."

"Sir," they all mutter simultaneously. He either believes them, or, just like almost everyone else around here, he's terrified of them and disappears around the corner.

Spinning around, I place my hands on my hips and narrow my eyes at my remaining audience.

My lips part to rip them all a new one when I notice something.

"Fuck me, are you multiplying?" My eyes focus on the new boy. It's obvious who he is, or at least who he's related to, and I groan, five has quickly become six.

"Princess," Alex says with a wide smile. "Meet my evil twin, Daemon."

I look between the two of them, noting all their similarities. Actually, they're so fucking identical that I doubt I'd be able to tell them apart if they weren't standing next to each other.

"Oh great. Another one to contend with."

A smile twitches at Daemon's lips. "Don't worry, Princess. I'm not around much." His voice is deep, deeper than Alex's, and as his eyes roll down the length of my body I can't fight the slight fear that creeps through me. And that really is something because I've been taught to never fear anyone. But this guy, there's something... actually, no. There's nothing. His face is a mask. I thought Seb wore his well, but it's really nothing compared to this guy.

"Right, well as fun as it's been watching Seb get his ass kicked by the princess, we should really get to class," Theo says, instructing his minions to move.

It didn't take much watching them these past few days to realize that he's the leader here. The second he barks a command, they all usually jump like good little puppies. It's almost amusing.

Theo, Alex, Nico and the new one all take off, leaving me standing between Toby and Seb once more.

"Well, as he said, this was fun and all—"

"This isn't over, Hellion."

"Of course," I mutter, reaching out to take my purse from Toby, seeing as he's a gentleman and rescued it for me after I abandoned it to kick his buddy's ass. "What would be the fun in leaving it here?" I deadpan, my eyes rolling so hard they hurt.

I shoot a look over my shoulder at him before dismissing him with a wave of my hand and taking off down the hall.

There are footsteps hot on my heel, but I know it's Toby. I don't feel the hate of Seb's stare burning into my back.

The second we're around the corner and out of sight,

his warm fingers brush my hand. Clearly, he learned a lesson from Seb, because he doesn't actually grab me.

"Wait."

I stop and turn to look up at him.

"Your surname," he says, his brow crinkled. "Is it Greek?"

"Uh... Y-yeah, although I'm not sure there's actually a Greek bone in my body," I joke. "Why?"

His eyes hold mine for a few more seconds. "N-no reason. What class have you got? I'll walk you."

"Nope," I state. "We're already late. I can take it from here. I can look after myself, after all." I wink at him, and thankfully he drags himself back to the here and now and cracks a smile. "That was hot as hell, just so you know."

"Glad you enjoyed it. Later." With a smile, I take off down the hall toward my last class of the week.

So I survived week one at Knight's Ridge... barely. It can only get better from here on out. It's not like I've made an enemy of one of the kings of the school, who, in his own words, wants me dead.

Whatever. I've handled worse.

"It's the weekend," Calli sings as we make our way back into the locker room after cheer practice.

Weirdly, Teagan and her bitches are still blissfully absent, something I could not be happier about. The entire squad just seems more relaxed without them.

"Yes," I sigh. "I'm more than ready for a weekend of nothing."

"Nothing?" Calli asks me, pulling open her locker and dragging her bag out.

"Yeah. This week has been..." I don't get a chance to come up with a word, because she takes over.

"Exciting. You took down Seb in front of the entire sixth form. Girl, we've not seen that excitement in like... ever. It was fucking epic."

A smile tugs at my lips.

Yeah, it was pretty spectacular if I do say so myself.

"He didn't even see it coming, from what I heard. You totally owned him."

"He needs teaching a lesson or two."

"Well, I think you definitely did that. No one is going to be messing with you anytime soon."

"I can only hope, right?" I mutter as I drop onto the bench and lift my bottle to my lips.

"So, you're coming to the party tonight," Calli announces.

"Err... I really don't think I am."

"Oh, come on. You need to celebrate."

"Celebrate what?" I ask, looking up at her as she pulls on a hoodie.

"Being Knight's Ridge newest bad-arse bitch."

"Is that a label I want?" I joke.

"It could be worse. You could be invisible like me."

"You're not—" Calli quirks a brow at me. "I've only been here a week. What do I know?"

"It's my fucking brother's fault. He scared off every single guy in a twenty mile radius before I even grew boobs."

I snort a laugh. "Who's your brother?"

She stares at me as if I just asked my own name.

"You're kidding, right?"

"It's been an intense week. I haven't exactly been learning everyone's family trees."

"Then you definitely need to come to this party tonight. Figure out who everyone is. I'll give you a masterclass."

"I think I've already figured out who I need to stay away from."

"That may be true. But is it working?"

Silence fills the space between us for a couple of seconds and thoughts of drinks and dancing pop into my head. Maybe it's not such a bad idea.

"Toby will be there," she adds, in the hope it might convince me.

"Which means the other idiots will be too."

"Fuck them. They don't own you. And you deserve to have some fun."

"What about you? Don't you have other friends to hang out with?"

Calli pales slightly, and the look on her face hits me like a baseball bat because I recognize it all too well. Hell, I'm living it.

She's lonely. Something tells me that whoever her brother is hasn't only scared the guys off, but the girls too.

"Do you know what? I'd love to party." Her face lights up like a freaking Christmas tree as the most genuine smile I've seen pulls across her face. "I need to go home, though. I've got to drop my car off and grab some stuff."

"I'll follow you," Calli says excitedly. "You can grab whatever you need and then we can go and get ready at mine. Our parents are away for the weekend, so you can stay. I mean, if you want."

"Sounds great."

After gathering our things, Calli practically bounces out of the locker room, and for the first time since moving here, I really feel like I could have found something outside all the drama.

CHAPTER FOURTEEN

Sebastian

"**B**ro, that was fucking brutal. Who knew she had it in her?" Alex laughs—and not for the first time since they found me pinned against the wall by the pocket rocket earlier.

"Are we not over this yet?" I ask after taking a pull on my beer.

"Mate, we're never going to be over this," Theo adds, dropping onto the opposite sofa and passing me another bottle. "It was that fucking good."

"Whatever," I mutter. "I made it easy on her. I could have got out of it in a heartbeat if I wanted to."

"Sure thing," Toby adds, his black eye from trying to get in the middle of this thing between Stella and me a constant reminder that it's none of his fucking business and that he needs to keep his fucking hands to himself.

I wasn't lying when I told both Theo and Stella that I don't fucking share.

I might have in the past. Theo and I, hell, even Alex and I, have had our fair share of fun with any willing girl. But that's not Stella. And not just because she's anything but willing.

"Where'd she even learn all those moves anyway?" Nico asks.

Theo's eyes meet mine, Alex's a beat later.

"She obviously does MMA as well as gymnastics and cheer," Toby says, although from the way he's looking between the three of us, I'd say that he's becoming more and more suspicious about what we're hiding.

"Explains her body, I guess," Nico adds. "She's fucking banging."

My head snaps to the side to glare at him.

"Stake your claim all you want, bro. She's clearly not interested in what you've got to offer. As far as I see it, all's fair in love and war." He winks at me before smiling at Toby.

"Nah, she's fucking mine."

Nico chuckles as he stands.

"And it's my fucking birthday," he quips before disappearing down the hallway with Toby hot on his tail.

"What the fuck was that?" Alex asks, taking a hit on his blunt.

"They suspect something." Theo says the exact thing I'm thinking. "We need to tell them."

"We need to tell them fuck all."

"Seb," he sighs, running his fingers through his hair. "I didn't mean everything. Just... who she is. The fact that she has no idea."

"Maybe it's time she learned," Alex suggests.

"So she can run? Fuck that."

They both stare at me in disbelief.

"Firstly," Theo says, holding a finger up. "I thought you wanted her gone. And second, does she look like the kind of girl who runs from anything?"

"I do want her fucking gone. But I want to be the one to make it happen."

"You need to chill out," Alex says, passing his joint over.

"Daemon coming tonight?" I ask him, taking a hit and holding it.

"He's working."

"No surprise there. Does he ever kick back and let go of the evil act bullshit?"

"Do you really need me to answer that?" Alex asks, demanding his joint back.

"Fair enough." The trill of the doorbell cuts through the house before footsteps head in that direction. "What time's the pussy getting here?" I ask, trying to ignore the fact that the only girl I want anywhere near me won't be here tonight.

She'll more than likely be at home. Alone. I rub my hands down the soft denim covering my thighs, trying to push aside thoughts of walking away from this party to have a private one of my own.

"That's not going to help." Theo mutters as if he can read my mind.

"Whatever." Swiping what's left of Alex's joint, I grab a full bottle of beer from the table and head for the back door.

"Seb," Theo warns. "Stay the hell away from her."

Flipping him off over my shoulder, I turn the corner and blow through the door.

Nico's house is on the same land as Theo's, although most people would never know it with the thick woods between them.

I head for the woodland at the end of the garden and drop down with my back against the old oak tree as I lift Alex's blunt to my lips.

Dragging my phone from my pocket, I open up that photo of Stella once more.

"Fuck," I snap, throwing it to the ground before quickly swiping it back up again. "Fuck."

Abandoning my beer, I find myself standing beside my car before I've even realised I've made a decision. And despite the fact that I know it's a bad idea, I climb in and fly out of the driveway.

The drive to Stella's takes less than five minutes. It seems that Galen wasn't too concerned about them returning, because he's moved them back right into the middle of Cirillo territory.

Her car is the only one parked at the front of her house when I walk up after leaving my own a little down the street.

Glancing through the windows at the front of the house, I find it empty. A smile curls at my lips as I slip around the back of the house and locate a door. I expect it to be locked, but to my surprise, when I push the handle down, it goes easily and the door clicks open.

Silently, I slip through the house and find the stairs. The sound of someone moving about in one of the rooms behind me has my heart in my throat as I make my way up, but it's nowhere near enough to stop me.

Poking my head into every room on the first floor, I don't stop until I find a room that can only be Galen's.

My need to step inside and wreak havoc is almost too

much to ignore, but as tempting as it is, fucking up his bedroom is hardly going to hit him where it hurts.

He might have left all those years ago, but it's clear from this house, the fact that Stella is attending Knight's Ridge, that he's still got plenty of money.

It makes me wonder if there's more to this whole story than we've all been led to believe.

I slam those thoughts down as fast as they emerge because none of it matters. All that does is that I right a wrong. That he learns that he can't just walk back into this Family like nothing ever happened. Like he never betrayed us.

Failing on the first floor, I head up to the second.

The moment I open the first door, I know it belongs to her. Her scent hits me and my cock instantly jerks in my jeans.

I scan the room as I slip inside for any clue that she might be here, but there's none. A door on the other side of the room catches my eye, and a smile tugs at my lips. If she's in the shower then I've hit the jackpot. Not only will I have the element of surprise on my side, but she'll have shed her armour.

Walking across the room, I take in everything she has on display, which to be fair isn't a lot. There's one photograph of her and two other girls that I assume is from America, but other than that, there's nothing personal. Just the standard makeup and discarded clothes draped over a chair in the corner.

I pause when I get to her dresser, shooting a look over my shoulder to make sure she's not watching me when I pull the drawer open and find exactly what I was expecting.

With a silent laugh, I pull out a red lace thong and swing it from my fingers.

Perfect to add to my growing collection.

I glance down at the rest of the drawer and consider taking the lot just to piss her off, but I refrain from filling my pockets full of her underwear and just stick to one pair.

Needing to act before I'm caught, I head for what I hope is the bathroom door, and after blowing out a long breath, I throw it open and step inside, ready to pounce on her.

Only, the room is empty.

"Fuck," I bark, spinning around, half expecting her to attack me from behind, but there's no one.

Not wanting to leave without letting her know that I've been here, I find an abandoned lipstick on her dresser and leave her a message on her bathroom mirror. It's old school, but I kinda like it.

I'm still smiling to myself as I head back down the stairs, but it's soon wiped away when I come face to face with an older lady with a rolling pin in her hand.

"Oh... uh... I was looking for Stella," I say, holding her eyes as if I'm exactly where I'm meant to be.

"She's gone out with a friend. Is there something I can help you with?"

"Uh, no. Her car was here so I just assumed... I'll call her instead. I'm so sorry if I scared you."

I take off toward the door that allowed me inside, her narrowed eyes following me the entire way.

"Have a good evening," I say, shooting her my best smile before disappearing from sight.

When I get back to my car, I find my phone where I

left it in the centre console lit up like Oxford Street at Christmas.

Theo's name flashes across the top and I groan. He's discovered I've disappeared.

"Fucking hell," I mutter when I find that was only one of fifteen calls since I left my car.

It takes him all of thirty seconds to try again.

"What?" I bark when the call connects.

"Where the fuck are you?"

"Driving."

"Seb, what have you done?"

"What makes you think I've done anything?"

"Because you're pissed, and I'm more than aware of some of the fucked-up choices you've made in the past."

"I'm not going to do anything stupid." Like break into the Doukas house and steal a pair of Stella's knickers like a creepy stalker.

"You need to get back here."

"Why? Is Alex off his head again?" I ask, although I know he's not. I stole his joint and I feel fine. Whatever was in that one on Monday afternoon clearly wasn't in today's.

"Just get your arse back here."

"Yeah, fine. Whatever."

I almost ignore him, get on Facebook and see if I can find where Stella's emo friend lives, but in the end, I decide I've probably stalked her enough for one night and follow orders like a good little soldier.

Nico's driveway is packed when I pull back up, and it makes me wonder how long I've actually been gone. The party had barely started when I left, but it seems to be in full flow right now.

I abandon my car, blocking a lot of others in, but I don't give it a second thought as I head inside.

The sun is starting to set, the temperature cooling quickly as we head toward autumn, but that doesn't bother the kids of Knight's Ridge who are happy to hang out drinking in Nico's front garden.

Eyes follow my movement toward the front doors. Guys watch me with jealousy in their eyes while the girls watch with desire.

I could have any one of them. More than one if I wanted, I'm sure. But why doesn't the thought of spending time with any of them interest me one bit?

With a sigh, I push the front door open and head inside.

The music pounds from the living room where Nico had some guys set up massive speakers earlier. Kids cover every inch of space, drinking, dancing, and making out.

I push a few of them aside as I make my way through the house, trying to find Theo or Alex as I move from room to room.

I spot them at the other side of the living room and set about forcing a path through the crowd who've turned the main space of the room into a dance floor. I'm halfway through when a flash of white blonde hair catches my eye.

Oh no she's fucking not.

Dragging a guy out of the way with the back of his shirt, I stand rooted to the spot as I watch Stella dancing with a drink in her hand, Calli in front of her and none other than fucking Toby behind her.

"Get out of my motherfucking way," I bark violently, shoving my way through the crowd to an unsuspecting Stella.

CHAPTER FIFTEEN

Stella

"Okay, your house is insane," I announce, following Calli through the entrance hall after we made our pit stop at my house to pack a bag.

"It's just a little over the top."

"Who's your father, Bill freaking Gates?" I joke.

The long driveway was beyond anything I ever thought I'd find in London. I thought it was meant to be cramped with people literally living on top of each other. But this place looks like it's right in the middle of the country.

"It's our family estate. We've had it for generations. It's... a lot."

"You don't say. I thought I'd lived in some big houses, but this," I say looking around the state-of-the-art kitchen, "is something else."

"You get used to it eventually."

She pulls open the huge refrigerator and grabs a couple of sodas.

"I thought we could order pizza before everyone arrives."

"Sounds good to me. Where's your brother?"

"Out causing trouble, probably."

I look around, searching for clues. "Are you going to tell me who he is yet?"

"Come on," she says with a laugh.

With my bags thrown over my shoulder, I follow her up the stairs but come to an abrupt halt when my eyes land on their first family photo.

"Your brother is Nico?"

"Unfortunately."

I nod as I stare at the family of four smiling for the camera. It's an old photo. Calli is probably eight, if that. She looks like such a sweet little girl with her golden hair hanging around her shoulders in ringlets.

Nico looks... less sweet. Even back then there seems to be a glint in his eye. Something that screams trouble. Their mom looks lovely, kind, like a mom from the TV, and their dad looks powerful, really powerful in his sharp suit and with a determined look on his face even while he's managing to smile. He reminds me of my dad, in a way. No matter what we're doing, there's always something so serious about him.

"Wait... is this Theo?" I ask, my eyes jumping to another image and finding a set of green eyes I recognize staring back at me.

"Yeah, we're all cousins. They're his little brothers and sister," she says, pointing to kids who are just babies and toddlers.

I continue working my way around the collage of family photos that line the huge wall.

"Shit," I breathe, locking eyes on an image with six boys all dressed head to toe in black.

They look... wow.

Theo's in the middle, standing slightly in front of the others, but it's not him who holds my attention. It's the boy with the dark, stormy eyes who stares at me like he hates me even in a photograph.

"They're really something, huh?" Calli mutters, coming to stand beside me. "That was the day they all—" She cuts herself off.

"The day they all what?"

Calli hesitates for a few seconds. "Come on, let's go to my room. We can talk there."

She glances around as if she's concerned someone might be listening.

"Where are they?" I ask. If the party is happening here in a few hours, I can't imagine they're far away.

"Probably in the basement. It's their den." Bitterness fills her voice as she takes off up the rest of the stairs.

"Their den?" I mutter. "Don't tell me, no girls allowed?"

"Something like that. They're idiots. Just because they've got a little power, they think they're God's freaking gift to the ma—"

She once again slams her lips shut.

What the hell is going on here?

Without another word, she walks toward a closed door and swings it open.

Letting myself in behind her, I drop my bags by the door and watch as she stands at a set of french doors that lead out to what looks like a massive balcony.

"Calli, what's going on?" I ask, closing her door behind me and stepping farther into the room.

"How much do you know about this part of London?" she asks without looking back at me.

"Uh... that everyone seems to have more money than sense," I mutter sarcastically, because honestly, I have no idea.

She laughs. "Well, there is that."

"But I'm assuming that's not what you meant."

She turns to me, her face serious as she looks at me.

"Have you heard of the Cirillo Family?"

"Uh... the Family?" I ask, amusement filling my voice. "Like a mafia family? No, I don't think I've seen that one. Is it on Netflix?" I ask, although from the look on her face, my comment has fallen a little far off the mark.

"It's not a TV programme, Stella. It's my life."

"Y-your life?"

She throws her hands out to her sides. "Callista Cirillo, long-suffering, smothered-in-cotton-wool, protected-from-the-reality-of-this-life mafia princess looking right at you."

"Fuck off. You're joking, right?" But as unbelievable as it all is, looking at the misery on her face, I know she's being serious.

"I wish." She falls down on her bed and stares up at the ceiling.

Sitting down beside her, I run her words through my head.

As crazy as they sound, they make some kind of sense.

After a few seconds, she turns to me.

"Stella?"

"Yeah?"

"Your surname. It's Greek, right?"

My brows pull together as I recall Toby asking me the exact same thing earlier.

"Uh... I think so, yeah." My heritage has never really been much of a concern to me when I've been too busy trying to figure out the present. "But what's that got to do with anything? Mafia are Italian, right?"

"The famous ones you've read about, yeah. The Cirillo Family? We're Greek."

My chin drops as a few of my missing puzzle pieces suddenly slot into place.

My friends in Rosewood joked about my father being part of the mafia, but it was just a joke.

Dad works in security. He runs his own company. And he... *fuck.*

"I'm sorry," Calli says with a wince.

"M-my dad is part of—"

"I don't know for sure. The fact that your name is Greek and you turned up at Knight's Ridge—here—might be total coincidence." But even as she says it, I think we both know it might be a coincidence too far.

"I guess that answers a lot of my questions. I've been trying to find out what my dad does for a living for years."

"I might be wrong," she tries again.

She rolls onto her side and looks at me, sympathy and regret written all over her face.

"It's okay," I say softly. "I'm glad you told me. Hell knows, everyone else has been keeping it a secret for long enough."

"You're not mad?"

"At you? Of course not. You're the only one who's been man enough to tell me how it really is. I do think I'm going to need something stronger than that, though," I say, nodding toward where she abandoned the cans of soda when we walked in.

"That I can do."

Calli makes quick work of placing an order for more pizza than we'll ever be able to eat in one night before slipping out of the room with the promise of alcohol on her lips.

Dragging my cell from my purse, I open up a browser and type my surname into Google.

Doukas: means 'duke' or 'lord'.

"I'll take that," I mutter to myself before typing *Cirillo Family* into the search. "Holy shit."

"You okay?" Calli asks me a few minutes later when she finds me staring at my cell with my mouth agape.

"Have you read all of this?" I ask, turning my cell around to show her what I'm looking at.

"A few years ago. I have no idea how much of it is true, and it's not like anyone willingly tells me anything around here. It's like the fucking Dark Ages. Men rule and women keep their mouths shut and look pretty."

"That's bullshit," I spit.

"Tell me about it." She rolls her eyes. "But I stole this from the boys." She holds up a bottle of vodka, an accomplished smile covering her face.

"Gimme," I say, making grabby hands at it.

She laughs and happily passes it over.

Twisting the cap, my hands almost tremble for a taste as I lift the bottle to my lips.

I'm not sure I've ever needed a drink more in my life.

My father is—I am—potentially part of a legit fucking mafia family. What the actual hell?

The first shot burns, but I don't let it stop me as I swallow mouthful after mouthful until the alcohol begins to warm my belly.

"Okay, take it easy," Calli says, reaching for the bottle and easing it away from my lips.

"I just... what the fuck, is this my life?"

"Fucked if I know. I live this shit and I have no idea what's going on around me most days. You need to find out if you're actually part of this before you get carried away."

"Calli," I sigh, "I think it would be naïve of us to assume this is a coincidence."

"But—"

"I get what you're doing, but with my dad's secrets, the money, the house, Knight's Ridge... Seb's reaction to me... The way Theo and Alex are. Toby and Nico, even." I scrub a hand down my face as my thoughts fly around my head at an incomprehensible speed. "They know things," I state, pushing to stand and beginning to pace back and forth. "They know things that I need to know. They—"

"Stella, you can't start digging. Not into their business."

I stop, looking at Calli standing at the end of her bed, her brow creased in concern. She's so sweet. Too sweet, especially for the likes of me. For the first time, I really appreciate what being sheltered really looks like. I might have a billion and one questions, there might be endless secrets surrounding my life, but Dad has ensured I was anything but smothered as I grew up.

"Don't you ever just want to rebel? Do all the things you're told not to?" I ask her, genuinely curious as to how she puts up with being kept in the dark like this.

"Honestly? Like, every day," she laughs, reaching for the bottle I'm still clutching like a lifeline. "But I'd never do it. I might not know a lot about this life, but I do know it's dangerous, and the last thing I want is to get myself in the middle of that."

"I get that, I do. But shit." I drop onto the bed beside her and take the bottle back, lifting it to my lips once more, desperate for the buzz it can give me.

A bell rings through the house as we sit there in silence, lost in our own thoughts.

"Pizza's here," Calli says, jumping up excitedly. "I think you're going to need it." Her eyes find the bottle and I quickly discover that I've drank more than I thought I had.

"You could be right. Tonight should be fun." I rub my hands together in excitement.

"Oh God. I made a mistake dragging you here, didn't I?" The smile she gives me is full of delight and mischief, and I love it.

"Go get the food. We've got a whole night of debauchery ahead of us."

She walks to the door but pauses with her fingers on the handle. "I think you're going to be a bad influence, Stella Doukas, and," she continues before I manage to get a word in, "I think it's exactly what I need."

Excitement bubbles in my belly as she slips from the room.

Oh yeah, Calli is my girl. I can feel it.

———

An hour later and we've eaten our body weight in pizza, finished the first bottle of vodka, and are dancing around

Calli's room in just our underwear as we attempt to get ready for this party.

It's exactly what I needed.

We never agreed to it, but the second we finished eating, talk of our lives and reality ceased and we just focused on enjoying ourselves, getting to know each other without all that bullshit. We've talked cheer, gymnastics, sixth forms and hopes for the future, and of course, boys. And that has led us to exactly where we are right now.

"You fucked him in a graveyard? Girl, that is freaky," Calli giggles, her cheeks pink with embarrassment.

"Oh yeah, it was freaky," I laugh, wiggling my eyebrows.

"Is it weird that I'm hella jealous?"

"You want Seb?" I ask, ignoring my own tingle of jealousy that wants to erupt.

"What? No. Ew. I wouldn't touch any of them idiots with someone else's. I just mean the freedom, even just having the opportunity to do something like that."

"Okay, we need to go out. We need to get away from this place, from your brother and babysitters, and show you what life is really like."

"I'm not old enough," she reminds me.

"Oh, Calli. You're so sweet. Leave it to me." I wink. "We'll find you a bad boy to get freaky with."

"Oh God," she says nervously, lifting a new bottle to her lips.

"You've been with boys, right?" I ask, although I immediately regret it because the way her face drops tells me everything I need to know.

She shakes her head.

"They literally scare everyone away from me. It's suffocating."

"Brace yourself, Cal. We're gonna find a way for you to spread your wings. Fuck your brother. Fuck his idiot friends. They can't control you. You're your own person, and you deserve to get out there and experience life. Experience boys." I wiggle my brows and she groans.

"I'm going to regret this."

I pin her with a look. "You can only regret the things you didn't do, Calli Cirillo. Now," I say, turning to my bag and pulling out the two dresses I brought with me and holding them up. "Which one?"

Her eyes dart between the two before they lock on one. "Black. Definitely black."

I glare at her. "I'm not dressing for him," I snap, more than aware that it seems to be their favorite color.

"I'm not suggesting you are, but equally, it'll knock him on his fucking arse, especially if your pert one is rubbing up against someone else's junk."

"You're wicked for someone who's been locked in your castle, Princ— *Motherfuckers*," I hiss, the reason behind their dumbass nickname slamming into me.

"What's wrong?"

"Those jerks have no idea who they're dealing with," I mutter, mostly to myself.

"Oh shit. What are you going to do?"

"I have no idea. But it's time they learned—Seb learned—that they're messing with the wrong girl. Everyone else might bend to their wishes, but I will not."

"Girl, I think I love you."

"You ain't seen nothing yet."

"I would legit pay to see you take them all to the floor. I have no doubt you can."

I can't help but laugh at the visual that pops into my

head of them all groaning in pain on the floor and me standing victorious in the middle of the mess.

"I'll give it a damn good shot. Now, what are you wearing?" I drag her wardrobe open and run my hand through the endless array of designer clothes staring back at me. "Does your grandmother shop for you or something?" I ask.

"My grandmother is dead," she shoots back, making me feel about an inch tall.

"Shit. Sorry, I—"

"It's fine. Honestly, she was a bitch. But no, my mother does, and she's all about making my dad happy, so..."

"Okay," I say, closing the door once more. "You can wear this one." I throw her the red dress she didn't choose for me.

"Oh, no no no no," she laughs, backing away from the dress with her arms wrapped around her waist as if it's about to attack her.

"Come on. You were just saying that you wanted a ride on the wild side. Break some rules, Cal. Be wicked with me."

"Nico, he'll—"

"Probably shit his pants, and it'll be fucking hilarious."

"He'll be furious."

"So let him. He's an asshole. You're in sixth form. You're not a kid anymore. Stop letting him treat you like one."

"But the others..."

"Can suck his tiny dick. We're doing this."

I launch the dress at her and place my hands on my hips as I wait for her to grow a pair and pull it on.

The second she does, I'm glad I stood my ground, because... wow.

"If I were into girls, I totally would do you right now."

"Stella," she gasps. "You can't say stuff like that."

"What? You look banging. Guys will literally fall over themselves to get a look at those tits."

"They're going to kill me," she mutters.

"I'd like to see them try."

I step up behind her, place my hands on her shoulders and direct her toward the full-length mirror.

"Look, you're hot." I gather up her hair into a messy updo, leaving a few strands falling around her face. "Dark eyes, blood red lips. They won't even recognize you."

"Promise you won't leave me," she begs, her eyes holding mine over her shoulder in the mirror.

"Promise, babe. And I won't let them touch you either."

"Okay. Do it."

A wide smile pulls at my lips at the determination I see on her face.

"Hell yes, girl."

CHAPTER SIXTEEN

Stella

"What the hell was that?" Calli slurs from behind me as I tuck my knife into my garter.

Lowering my foot from the edge of her bed, I straighten my dress.

"Protection."

"P-protection?" she stutters, her eyes bright with the amount of vodka she's already had. She's hardly had any compared to me, showing me just how smothered she really has been. She told me earlier that she usually just stays locked in her room whenever Nico throws a party after he threatened to make her leave the house once. So she just... did.

I find the whole situation bizarre, because the first thing I'd do in that situation would be the exact opposite of what I was told. But then, I'm not normal. And I'm certainly not Calli.

"You sound like one of them already," she mutters, walking around me to find her shoes.

"My dad brought me up so that I can look after myself. Calvin, our head of security, has been training me in all kinds of MMA for years. It's just my way of life."

Her shoulders drop as she looks up at me, her previously excited eyes suddenly filled with sadness.

"Why couldn't they treat me like that? Why couldn't they trust me to be a part of this instead of treating me like I'm a complete nuisance? I know Dad wanted another boy, another son to continue our legacy or whatever. But he got me. Just because I've got a foofoo, it doesn't mean I'm not capable."

I suck in a breath and take a step toward her. "Firstly, fuck them. All of them. You want to learn all this stuff, you want to take care of yourself? Then do it. Don't wait for their permission. This is your life, Calli. Take it by the balls. And secondly, never call it a foofoo in front of a guy. He'll never want to fuck it."

She snorts a laugh as she lifts her hand to wipe a stray tear from her eyes.

"We're going to make you a badass, Calli Cirillo. Princesses don't just wear frilly dresses and pretty diamonds. They also carry guns, wear shitkicker boots and stomp on anyone who gets in their way."

She smiles at me and my heart clenches a little. I have no idea how Calli and I are connected in all this, but I'm pretty sure we've already forged a pretty unbreakable bond.

"One more shot, and then we're going." I pass her the

bottle after she's slipped her feet into her shoes and she does as I suggest while I do the same.

Pulling up my strapless dress a little, giving the girls a wiggle, I take a shot and slam the bottle down.

"Look out world, Calli Cirillo has arrived." I don't give her a chance to freak out. Instead, I take her hand in mine and drag her from the safety of her room.

The booming music from below us gets louder the second we step out into the hallway.

Calli's hand trembles in mine, and when I look over at her, I find an apprehensive look on her face.

"Embrace that feeling, Cal. Don't let it stop you." She nods, and together we take our first step down the stairs.

Walking down to the party raging below is bizarre now I know everything I do. The staircase is so extravagant that I can't help feeling like the princess the guys call me, making my grand entrance.

Having every set of eyes immediately turn our way as we appear doesn't make that feeling lessen any.

"This could have been a really bad idea," Calli whisper-shouts beside me so I can hear her over the music.

"Never. Hold your head high. Every guy looking at you right now wants you. Remember that."

"I can assure you, there are a few who don't."

I follow her line of sight and find four very pissed-off looking guys staring up the stairs and right at Calli.

Nico's eyes are hard, his jaw tics in irritation, and there's a vein in his temple that I swear is about to explode.

I smother a laugh, but I don't think I do a very good job because not a second later do those hard and angry eyes find mine.

He takes a step forward, Theo, Alex and Toby moving as one with him.

Idiots.

Dragging Calli with me, I step up to her big brother and don't stop until I'm right in his personal space. The height of my heels means I don't have to crane my neck to hold his eyes, which are fucking deadly as they bore into mine. But I refuse to cower down to these idiots.

Reaching forward with my free hand, I grab him between the legs and squeeze, just enough to warn him.

His eyes widen, but his mask doesn't slip an inch.

"You fucking ruin this for her and I'll rip them clean off. You got me, Cirillo?" I hiss loud enough for only him to hear me.

"Do you have any fucking clue who you're dealing with?"

I take a step back, releasing him—much to his relief, if his long exhale is anything to go by.

Looking him up and down, I find his eyes once more.

"Do you?" A smirk curls at one side of my mouth.

I hold his deadly stare for another three seconds before I shoot each of them a 'fucking try me' glare.

Not one of them says a word. They just watch me with a mix of confusion, pride and utter disbelief.

"Come on, girl. We need drinks and then some hot guys to dance with. There's got to be plenty around here somewhere."

When I turn back to Calli, I find the exact same look on her face as was on the guys', although her pride wins out when she smiles at me like I'm literally the best person in the world.

She steps right up beside me, and together we turn our backs on them and make our way to the kitchen.

"Oh my God, that was fucking insane. Did you see Nico's face?" she screeches excitedly as we leave them behind.

"Told you he'd damn near shit his pants."

"Yeah, I just wasn't expecting it to be because you were going to squeeze the life out of his junk."

"That wasn't planned. I just didn't get the impression that my words would have been enough. And I think it's probably a little early in the night to pull my knife out."

"You're something else," she says, walking straight over to where there are bottles and Solo cups lining the counter and making us both a drink. A really fucking strong drink I realize the second I take a sip.

"Down the hatch. Let's dance," Calli instructs, having clearly found some inner confidence now we've dealt with her overbearing big brother.

She leads me through the mass of people toward what I assume is the living room. All the furniture has been cleared out and there's a crowd grinding it up in time with the music in the middle.

I smile as we get closer, my hips moving to the beat long before we join the edge of the bodies.

"Who are all these people?" I shout at Calli.

"Some are from school. No idea about the rest."

We dance together like we've got no cares in the world. The heat from the people around me means my skin is soon flushed as we move, bumping against each other and laughing as if half the room isn't watching us.

I know they are. I can feel them.

Calli might not know who these people are, but I'd put money on almost everyone knowing exactly who she is.

Maybe they even know me, who the hell knows. But I

don't let it faze me as I let go of everything and finally enjoy myself.

I have no idea how many songs pass us by or how late it is. I've even stopped noticing the watchful eye someone always seems to have on us by the time two guys appear out of nowhere and step up behind both of us.

"You two look lonely," one of them drawls in my ear. His deep voice and British accent hit exactly where I need them to, and I immediately lean back into him, continuing to dance.

Calli shoots me a concerned look as her guy makes a move and I give her a brief nod.

We're safe here. We've got a houseful of bodyguards, it seems.

The only two who aren't safe are the ones who are risking everything by touching us.

"I've been watching you all night," he continues, his fingers digging into my hips a little, dragging my ass back against him.

"Is that right?"

"The way you move is intoxicating."

Glancing back, I'm pleasantly surprised by what I find. Much like his friend, who's whispering something in Calli's ear, he's cute. Really cute.

"Well then, let's see what you've got." I dip, grinding my ass against him as he watches me with hungry eyes.

Oh hell yeah. I can definitely get on board with this.

Once I'm back at full height, I turn to face him, confident that Calli is okay, and throw my arms over his shoulders.

"Have we met before?" I ask, knowing full well that we haven't, but I need to get a feel on whether he knows who I am.

"Sadly not, babe. But I'm hoping that's all changed now."

His hands land on my waist, sliding down as we move together until he cups my ass, dragging my body to his.

"It sure looks that way."

Staring up into his eyes, I wait to see if he's got the balls to make an actual move.

If my reality is what I now suspect and he knows who I am, he wouldn't dare do it. Would he?

The heated stare of my protectors burns holes in my back as I run my tongue along my bottom lip. I'm more than ready to lose myself in someone. And not just because I want to prove a point.

His head lowers and my heart picks up speed as I wait for our lips to collide, but right before it happens, I'm dragged backwards and into another pair of arms.

"I don't think so," an angry voice growls in my ear as I stare longingly at the guy I was dancing with. "Fuck off now."

The guy holds my captor's eyes for a beat before he decides it would be a really bad idea to make a thing out of this and melts into the crowd.

Anger surges through me, turning my blood to lava as I rip myself out of the strong arms and spin toward him.

"Was that—T-Toby?" I stutter. I knew it was one of them. But I didn't think for a second that that cold and angry voice belonged to him.

Holy shit.

I glance at Calli, who's still dancing with the guy's friend.

Why haven't they stopped her?

"Surprise," he says, his mask dropping and his usual

easy, and slightly drunk, smile appearing on his handsome face. "Dance with me?"

"Uh..." I look back to where the guy vanished and then back at Toby. "S-sure."

Throwing my arms over his shoulders, I close my eyes and pick up where I left off, but it soon becomes obvious that my high from before has been totally obliterated when Nico comes marching over with two drinks in his hands.

His eyes are still full of contempt as they hold mine.

"Here," he spits, thrusting one of the cups at me.

"Wow, how thoughtful of you."

He scoffs before turning his back on me to face his sister and her guy.

I have no idea what Nico says to him, but three seconds later the guy damn near runs out of the room.

"Was that necessary?" I bark.

Nico doesn't even bother to reply. He just snarls at me over his shoulder before turning his attention back to Calli.

"Don't poke the beast, babe," Toby says in my ear.

"He's being a jerk. Calli deserves to enjoy herself too."

"You think any guy wants to see his little sister dressed like that and getting molested by a dickhead you don't trust?"

I ignore the last bit, because for all I know, Toby and the guys are aware of exactly who he was and just how trustworthy—or not—he is. "He wasn't molesting her, they were dancing. Innocently."

"Sure they were. Just like you were with that guy's hands on your arse."

"Careful there, Toby. You sound awfully jealous."

"Don't read into things too much, babe. You might not like what you find."

"Whatever." I wave off his cryptic comment. "You asked me to dance. Now make good on that or I'll find someone who's more willing."

Spinning around, I give him my back and start moving, cutting off anything else he might want to say.

Nico's gone, thankfully. Although now Calli is dancing alone.

Holding my hand out, I gesture for her to come closer, and after abandoning her empty cup she takes it and the three of us dance together.

It's not quite what it was before, but it's better than nothing.

It's a hell of a lot better than what happens next, anyway.

CHAPTER SEVENTEEN

Sebastian

I might have learned something from this afternoon, because when I get to Stella, Calli and Toby, I don't reach for her. Hell, I don't even touch her.

She's got her eyes closed, her head resting back on Toby's shoulder as she moves with him.

My teeth grind as I watch them, my frustration reaching dangerous levels.

Calli sees me coming and wisely steps aside to allow me in front of Stella.

Toby's eyes find mine, narrowing in warning, but I couldn't give a fuck what he thinks.

Stella Doukas is mine, and it's time he learned that.

I press the length of my body against her and her eyes ping open, locking on mine.

Reaching out, I wrap my fingers around her throat and lean in.

"You're not welcome here."

Instead of being scared like most, a smile curls at her lips.

"Fuck you. I was invited. Maybe you're the one who's not wanted here."

"Seb, just leave it," Toby barks.

"Butt. The. Fuck. Out, Ariti." His nostrils flare in irritation and his lips press into a thin line as if he's preparing to fight me on it.

He can try all he fucking likes. He's already wearing the evidence of how that went the last time he tried to get involved. "Let's go." I drag Stella away from him, my grip on her throat tightening.

Surprisingly, she doesn't fight me. I have no idea if that's because she's drunk or if she's just as much as a masochist I am and wants to see where this is going too.

I walk her backward through the crowd, which thankfully parts for me now they're aware that something is going on. She stumbles in her heels but I don't let up or allow her to turn around.

I don't owe her any niceties.

"Seb, let her go," Calli screams behind us. "Seb." Her small hand lands on my shoulder and I shrug her off.

"Toby, put the kid on a lead."

"Fuck you, Sebastian."

"This doesn't concern you, baby C."

"It does when you're manhandling my friend," she continues, still following us as I move Stella through the kitchen.

"You don't want to be friends with this piece of shit, Cal." I glance over at her. "I mean, look at the whore she's turned you into."

Crack.

I should have known that looking away from the feisty bitch was the wrong move.

My cheek burns from the slap and I suck in a sharp breath as I try to talk myself down from snapping her neck right here and now.

Shaking my head slowly, I hold her eyes.

"You're going to regret that."

"Make me," she hisses, taking my words as nothing more than a challenge.

We're almost at the basement door when it opens and Theo appears with a dark-haired girl attached to him.

He takes one look at me before his eyes shoot to the person behind me.

"Go to your room, Calli," he demands.

"Do you know what?" Calli, snaps while Stella smirks in accomplishment. "I'm sick to death of you lot ordering me around. If I wanna go down there, then I'm going to fucking go down there."

Theo laughs to himself and shakes his head.

"Fine. But don't say I didn't warn you." Calli races around us, ready to bolt down the stairs the second Theo moves out of the way. "You might think we're controlling arseholes, Calli. But trust me when I tell you that's only the half of it."

"Whatever. Jerk."

The second he moves, she's gone.

Finally, I spin Stella around, pressing my front to her back as we descend the stairs after Calli, but I don't release her.

The music changes as we move, the air around us becoming thick with cigarette smoke and weed. The main party might be happening upstairs, but down here in our den is where the real fun happens.

And Calli is about to get the shock of her life. I hope Stella knows what she's doing.

When we get to the bottom of the stairs and turn into the room that spans the entire length of the house, Stella sucks in a breath.

Nico lives down here. It's a huge self-contained apartment and has almost everything our dark little hearts desire.

There's a couple of guys snorting coke off the coffee table. Girls dancing who are wearing significantly less than the woman in my grasp, and right at the other end of the room, Nico is sitting on the edge of his bed, thankfully with his back to us, getting a special birthday blowy off one of the girls.

"Oh my God," Calli cries beside us. "This is what you do down here."

"Yeah, baby C. You still wanna hang out with the big boys?"

She turns to me, her eyes holding mine for a beat before she looks at Stella, who shrugs in my hold.

"Do you know what? I do. Maybe I'll even give my whore of a brother a little show of his own."

She marches farther into the room as someone shouts, "Cirillo, baby sister in the house."

If it weren't for the rat in my hold, I'd laugh my arse off at the way he jumps up, ripping his cock out of the more than willing mouth, and frantically tucks himself away.

His face is damn near purple as he approaches Calli and starts barking orders at her.

Stella jolts in my hold as if she wants to go and help her.

"Let's see how much you've rubbed off on our innocent little princess, shall we?"

Calli shouts back, giving as good as she gets.

I'm weirdly proud of her, seeing as she's usually as quiet as a church mouse when it comes to dealing with us all.

"Holy shit," I breathe in shock as we all watch Calli turn to the nearest guy and slam her lips to his.

He hesitates for a second—rightly so—before Nico pushes his sister aside and ploughs his fist into the guy's face.

"Whoops, that was probably a mistake."

"You're all a bunch of hypocritical cunts," Stella snarls.

"I've been called worse, Hellion," I growl in her ear, fighting my smile when she shudders against me.

Noticing my grip loosen, she slips from my hold and turns on me, her sparkling blue eyes holding mine.

She looks fucking beautiful with her heavy makeup and her hair pulled back from her face.

Unable to stop myself, my eyes drop from hers in favour of her body.

Her curves are encased in a sinful black dress. The only place it would look better is on my bedroom floor.

My cock swells just looking at her.

It sits high on her thighs, so high in fact that I get a glimpse at the lace that's wrapped around her legs.

Fuck me, is she wearing stockings?

Lifting my hand, I run my fingers through my hair as I take in the rest of her legs before making my way back up.

"Are you finished?" she asks when I finally find her eyes again before moving a joint toward her lips. Where the fuck did she get that from?

Seeing my confusion, she shoots a look to her left where Alex is standing with a grin on his face, also openly checking her out.

He winks and blows her a kiss before turning back to Daemon, who's decided to show his face for once.

Dragging my eyes back to Stella once more, I watch as her full red lips purse around the butt of the blunt and she sucks in a hit.

She nods, clearly knowing good weed when she finds it, before blowing out a slow stream of smoke from her lips.

The move is so fucking erotic I almost come in my pants right there.

"Well, this has been fun and all, but it looks like it's time to really party. Excuse me."

I stand there stunned as she stalks away from me, her arse swaying seductively as she makes a beeline for Alex—or more specifically, Daemon.

I have no idea why I'm surprised. It seems our new princess likes dancing with the devil.

"Hey, baby." A familiar voice fills my ears before hands slip around my sides and a body presses against my back.

Twisting to the side, I find Teagan smiling at me as if she's actually fucking missed me.

"Teag," I say as a greeting. If it weren't for the fact that Stella notices her attached to me then I'd physically remove her. "I didn't think you'd be here."

"Couldn't miss one of Nico's parties, you know how it is."

"Isn't your grandmother dying?" I ask, knowing it's where she's been the past couple of days.

"Yeah," she sighs, slipping around to stand in front of

me. She lifts her hand to her throat as she pouts as if she's actually devastated.

Teag is many things, but a good actress isn't one of them.

"It's been such a hard few days. I really need to blow off some steam, you know? Go a little wild, lose my inhibitions." She steps closer, skimming her hand down my stomach and quickly heading for my cock, which has zero interest in being touched by her.

"Not here, Teag," I say, wrapping my fingers around her wrist.

Her pout gets bigger.

"Aw come on, Seb. It's not like you to be shy. We both know how much you love an audience."

"Not tonight." It's a lie. I'd love a fucking audience. It's just not her who I want on her knees before me.

I wrap my hand around her arm, ready to push her away, but three bodies catch my eye across the room, and instead of putting some distance between us, I find myself dragging Teag closer as my eyes bore into Stella, who's pinned between Alex and Daemon as the three of them dance together.

She wants to play? I can fucking play.

CHAPTER EIGHTEEN

Stella

"I know what you're doing," Alex growls in my ear as he presses the length of his body against mine, ensuring there's not a hair between the three of us.

"I highly doubt it," I mutter, tracking every single one of Seb and Teagan's movements.

My fingers grip Daemon's waist tighter as his hips roll with mine.

I didn't come over here with the intention of dancing with the two of them, but it seems that Alex wants to have some fun of his own, and despite his twin's cold exterior, it didn't take much convincing for him to join us.

I stare into Daemon's emotionless eyes and try to get a handle on who he really is. I certainly didn't have him down as the dancing type, but he's definitely got some moves.

Ripping his eyes from mine, he glances over at where

Seb has dragged Teagan out into the middle of the room and is allowing her to rub herself all over him like the shameless whore she is.

"Ugh, is she even wearing panties?" I mutter to myself, although it's not quiet enough it seems, because Daemon turns back to me, and for the first time since meeting him earlier, I see something other than the need to kill someone in his eyes. The black orbs sparkle with mischief.

"No, I'm pretty sure she's not."

"Hussy," I hiss, much to his amusement.

"You really want to play this game, Princess?"

I rear back a little. "You really wanna start with that nickname?"

His brow rises.

"You wanna play, I'm all in, *Princess*."

"This is what you wanted, right?" Alex adds, clearly listening to every word. "You wanna push him. We're right here for it."

I glance over my shoulder, a smile twitching at my lips.

"I think the three of us could be great friends," I announce, sliding my hand up Daemon's sculpted chest and wrapping it around the nape of his neck.

"How far do you want to push him, Princess?" Alex asks.

"I want to fucking ruin him."

Daemon chuckles. It's a dark and dangerous sound that I'm sure would send a chill of fear through most people. "Your funeral, Princess," he says before slamming his lips down on mine.

Almost instantly, his tongue plunges into my mouth, searching out my own.

I still for a beat, not expecting him to go for it quite so forcefully, but the second Alex joins in, his hands running up my stomach and cupping my breasts, a moan of pleasure rips from my throat.

My head screams at me to look and see Seb's reaction, but my body has other ideas as it joins right in with what the twins are doing.

They work together in perfect sync. They've done this before. More than once.

The thought sends a rush of heat between my legs.

I've been with two guys before, but never twins. The idea is seriously hot.

"Fuck," I moan when Daemon rips his lips from mine, kissing along my jaw and down my neck the opposite side to Alex.

Both of them are hard against me as our hands explore and our hips grind.

"How many times have you two done this before?" I ask, trying to keep my head and not just dive straight into the pleasure they could no doubt offer me.

Daemon's dark chuckle is all the answer I need.

"Incoming."

Alex's words barely register before a hand slides into my hair and I'm physically dragged from between the two of them.

"What the fuck are you doing, you Neanderthal?" I growl, knowing exactly who it is.

"Enjoy the ride," I hear Alex shout behind us as Seb continues moving us.

"You want to act like a whore, then let's do it properly."

My knees collide with the tiled floor, pain shooting up my thighs as his fingers twist tighter in my hair, making my eyes water. He forces my head back so I have no choice but to look at him as he rips open his fly and drags his zipper down.

Oh God.

Heat floods my core at the thought of what's to come, my clit pulsating in time with the heavy beat of music filling the space down here. The murmur of voices reminds me that we're not alone, but at no point are they enough to stop me, to demand that he release me or to do something to make him.

Both of my hands are free and I've got a knife in my garter belt. I could get out of this in a heartbeat... if I wanted to.

Seb shoves his pants down, freeing his straining cock, and wraps his fingers around the width.

My mouth waters and my pussy clenches with desire as he moves my face closer to him.

"What makes you think I won't bite it—"

Ignoring the words I'm spitting at him, he makes the most of my parted lips and pushes his cock past them, his fingers tightening in my hair, forcing me to take all of his length.

I stare up at him, pure hate oozing from my eyes. And while his might be dark with anger that rivals mine, I also see the challenge within them.

He wants me to back down, to be a little pussy and freak out that we're in a room full of people.

Has he not learned anything about me this week?

Sucking him deeper, I hum in satisfaction when his eyes roll back and his hips jerk at the sensation.

Who has all the power now, motherfucker?

If my mouth weren't wrapped around his length, I'd smile in accomplishment. But as it is, all I do is allow him to pull me back slightly before he thrusts back inside, fucking my mouth as if he hates me. Which, of course, he does.

His thrusts are brutal, his grip on me painful as he forces the head of his cock down my throat.

Sucking in deep breaths through my nose, I relax my throat and take him, every fucking inch.

He stares down at me with hooded lids, his eyes filled with desire and... pride?

I push that thought away. He couldn't give a shit about me. He just wanted to make a point about me being a whore.

Fine. I have zero issue with admitting that I like sex. That I like the trickle of unease that flows through my veins. Anyone could walk around the counter and find me down here. Hell, the anticipation that any of his friends could come over and join us. I wouldn't put it past them to turn this into a group party. They've got those kinds of vibes going on with their closeness. The twins like to get freaky together, so it stands to reason that the others do too.

He thrusts his hips one more time, his cock going deeper than before, making me fight the need to gag before he stills and his fingers twist, damn near ripping my hair clean out.

His cock jerks, his entire body locking up a beat before hot cum shoots down my throat.

I keep my eyes on him as he throws his head back and roars out his release, ensuring that anyone who didn't know what was going on over here now has a very good idea.

The second he's finished, he tucks himself away and drags me to my feet. His eyes bore into mine for two seconds before hands wrap around my waist and I find myself flying through the air.

"What the fuck are you doing?" I scream, my head spinning. I've had way too much vodka to be hanging upside down.

He storms out of the kitchen as I stare at his round ass that's right in my face.

Reaching out, I cup one firm globe in my palm and squeeze as hard as I can.

"Put me the fuck down, ass—ow," I scream when his palm connects with my ass.

I wiggle on his shoulder, kicking my legs out, trying to force him to put me down, but all he does is hold on tighter.

We walk through into a different room and a door slams behind us, cutting us off from the pounding music and all the people.

My heart jumps into my throat, knowing that we're alone, and my head spins with thoughts of what could happen next.

A desperate ache tugs at my muscles and I rub my thighs together to stem it, although it does very little to help.

"Don't pretend you don't love it, Hellion. I know you're wet as fuck from sucking my cock. I can smell it."

My feet meet the floor a second before my back slams against the wall and his hand finds its home around my throat, squeezing with the most delicious pressure.

My lip curls in contempt as I stare at him. I can pretend all I like that I don't want him anywhere near me right now, but we both know it's a fucking lie.

"So what are you going to do about it?"

His fingers flex as if he's physically trying to restrain himself from squeezing the life out of me.

I'd like to see him try.

His other hand reaches out, and in a flash my strapless dress and bra are around my waist and his lips are making a beeline for my nipple.

My head slams back against the wall as he sucks me into his hot mouth.

"Yes," I cry, my fingers threading through his hair to hold him in place—not that he needs my encouragement.

He laps at me like a starved man, and I happily allow it.

"Argh," I cry, my fingers twisting in his hair until it must hurt when he sinks his teeth into the soft skin of my breast. "More. Fuck."

"Fucking whore," he mutters, dragging his tongue up my chest until he reaches my neck.

Desperate for him, I rip his hair back, forcing him to look at me.

"Kiss me."

"After you've already given your lips to someone else? I don't fucking think so."

I lean forward in an attempt to claim them anyway, but his grip on my throat tightens and I end up hovering just millimetres from my target.

"I don't share my toys," he hisses.

"And what makes you think I do?" I snarl, running my eyes up and down his body.

"I don't remember touching or kissing anyone else tonight, Hellion."

The image of Teagan's hands all over his body pop into my head making my stomach knot.

"Maybe I should have, though, because jealousy is a good look on you."

"Fuck you. You can walk out there and fuck any of those skanks if you want."

His eyes hold mine, searching for the lie he knows is there. I'd let it happen, though. I'd even fucking watch just to prove a point.

"Fuck," he barks, tucking his face into my neck once more and sucking on the patch of skin beneath my ear until I have no doubt I'll be wearing the mark for days.

Releasing my throat, his hands skim up my thighs, taking my dress with them before he lifts me from the floor, wrapping my legs around his waist.

"Fuck, Hellion. You dressed so pretty for me tonight," he growls in my ear, making all kinds of insane things happen just south of my waist.

"The only person I dress for is me."

"Hellion," he warns as his fingers find the switchblade that's tucked into my garter.

He pulls it free and holds the pink knife between us, flicking the blade out.

"Huh," he murmurs, twisting it around and taking it in. "For a second there I thought you had a piece of me strapped to your body all night."

"Why the hell would I want that?"

His eyes remain locked on the sharp point of the blade as he moves it forward and presses the flat against my bottom lip.

"Tell me, Hellion. Did you have intentions of stabbing someone tonight, or were you really hoping I'd use it on you?"

My eyes narrow. "I can assure you, I had zero intentions of seeing you tonight."

"Yet here we are."

"Yeah, tonight's been full of all kinds of surprises."

He sucks in a sharp breath, confirming what I already knew. He knows a lot more than he's telling me.

"It sure has." The knife lowers over my chin and begins a journey down my neck, the point scratching my skin but not enough to draw blood.

My heart races and my chest heaves as he continues, but I try to keep as still as possible—one wrong move and that knife is slicing right through my skin.

His touch is almost delicate as he circles my breast, his eyes watching the movement of the knife as if he's utterly mesmerized by the red mark it leaves behind— until he presses a little harder and the blade easily slices my skin right beside my nipple.

"Whoops," he says insincerely before leaning forward and licking at the small pool of blood that rushes to the surface.

When he pulls back, he's got a tiny bit of red on his lip. It makes him look even more dangerous than he usually does, and it doesn't have the effect on me that it should because a fresh wave of heat surges to my core.

The sound of the deep bass from outside of this room dissipates. The only thing I can hear is our heaving breaths as we stare at each other, daring each other, hating each other.

Flicking my knife closed, he pockets it before turning his attention back to me, wrapping his fingers around the sides of my panties and tugging until they fall away from my body.

Balling them up, they disappear in the same place as my knife.

"You can't just—Fuck," I cry, forgetting what I was saying when his fingers find my soaked pussy.

"Oh, Hellion. Look how much you hate me," he murmurs, attacking my neck once more.

He spears two fingers deep inside me, making me moan as he bends them just so.

"Oh God. Yes. Fuck."

This is what I needed that night when he left me without a second look.

My fingers grip onto his shoulders, my nails digging through the fabric of his shirt as he continues to rub at me.

"Seb, fuck," I cry, my back arching as he bites my neck hard enough to pierce the skin. "Fuck. Fuck. NO," I bark when he suddenly pulls out of me right before I fall. "I fucking hate you," I scream, but I soon change my mind when he lifts me a little and shoves his pants down over his ass, releasing his cock.

"You still on birth control?" he growls.

I nod, almost too lost to my desire to even hear the words.

He lines himself up and then drops me, impaling me onto his body as my eyes roll back in my head.

Not giving me a chance to adjust to his size, he almost immediately pulls out before thrusting back in so hard I see stars.

"Fuck me. Yes. Yes," I cry.

His fingers dig into the flesh of my ass as he holds me up with just one arm and his pistoning hips. His other hand grabs my breast, pinching and twisting my nipple and sending a bolt of extra pleasure straight toward my pussy.

His hot breaths tickle over my ear and down my neck as he continues his punishing rhythm.

"Who do you fucking belong to, Hellion?" he demands, his rough cheek brushing against mine, scratching my soft skin.

"Fuck you."

"Wrong answer."

"Argh," I scream when he pinches my nipple hard. Almost too hard.

"I am going to fucking ruin you, Princess." His words aren't a warning, they're a promise, and fuck if they don't make my orgasm come racing forward. "Come, Hellion. I want your cum all over my cock."

"Se—Oh God," I cry, refusing to let his name fall from my lips in case he takes that as me admitting his ownership of me.

My release slams into me right as Seb's cock jerks deep inside me and a deep growl rips from his lips.

I scream out my release, my nails digging into his shoulders as I ride out wave after wave of pleasure.

My orgasm is so intense it drains the life out of me and I cling to him, my body limp and lifeless.

That fucked out bliss only lasts for a few short seconds, though, because he pulls out of me and lowers my feet to the floor.

In a moment of panic, I reach out and grab his face, not ready to let him go just yet.

He allows me to drag him back to me until our lips are almost brushing.

"Kiss me. I dare you."

"No thanks." He's barely finished talking when he drops to his knees before me.

My first thought is "fuck yeah, that's hot," but then he pulls my knife back out and I swallow nervously.

"W-what are you—shit." Wrapping his fingers around

my ankles, he forces my legs wider, giving him the perfect view of my cunt and my thighs which are glistening in the evidence from our releases. "Seb?" I ask, hating that there's a slight quiver to my voice.

"I don't kiss whores, but no one out there will fuck anything that belongs to me."

"Holy fu—" My words falter as he lifts the knife to my upper thigh and begins carving an S into my skin. "You're fucking insane," I squeal, although it doesn't escape me that I never once try to get away as he pulls back to study his handiwork before adding a P.

"There," he says, rubbing the pad of his thumb over the sore skin to collect up the blood.

His lips part and I watch like the whore he accused me of being as he sucks on his digit.

Biting down on my bottom lip, my mouth waters to be the one attached to his mouth once more.

There is something seriously fucking wrong with me.

"You're so pretty when you bleed for me, Hellion," he whispers, staring at the wound as blood pools again.

This time, he forgoes his thumb and instead leans forward, lapping at the blood like I'm his favorite taste in the world.

A moan rumbles up my throat as his tongue licks at me, the sharp sting from the cut only making me wanton and needy for him again.

"Oh shit," I hiss when his finger runs through my wetness, swirling in the cum he left inside me.

"Open your legs for anyone else, and they'll know your mine, Hellion. Mine," he repeats, bending his finger and sending a wave of pleasure racing through me.

Pulling his head back, he rips his finger from me and runs it over his initials, mixing my blood and his cum.

It's like some fucked-up satanic ritual, and my eyes are glued to the patch of my skin he's touching.

Suddenly ripped from his trance, he pushes to stand.

"Open," he demands, holding his finger up, and my traitorous body follows orders like a good little princess.

His eyes flash with heat as I suck on his digit, swirling my tongue around just like I'd have done to his cock should he have given me the chance.

Pulling it out, he drags my bottom lip with it.

His eyes drop down my body, taking in my dress that's pooled around my waist and my garter belt and stockings on show.

Pulling his cell from his pocket, he holds it up. His eyes find mine. There's a challenge in them as he waits for me to tell him to stop.

But what's the point? He's already got one from the other night with my tits covered in his cum. What's another to add to his ammunition to 'ruin' me?

Tilting my chin, I force a smirk onto my lips.

"Whore," he breathes, but the word lacks the venom I'm sure he was hoping it would have.

"Better than an entitled cunt," I throw back.

With one more look at his handiwork on my thigh, he does up his pants, spins on his heel and marches from the room.

"Fucking asshole," I scream after him, and just before the door slams closed behind him, I swear I see his shoulders shake with his laugh.

Cunt.

I sag back against the wall, tilting my head up to the ceiling. I'm not sure what I'm hoping for. God certainly isn't going to help me after all the shit I've pulled.

Glancing around the room for the first time since I

was carried in here, I find a large black and white bathroom that would look quite at home in my house.

Making my way over to the toilet, I start pulling my bra and dress back up into place. The fabric brushes over my tender nipples and I wince.

There's nothing gentle about being with Seb, that's for sure.

His rough touches and wicked words feed something inside me, something I've been desperate for such a long time.

I knew something was missing. I guess that's why I had no issues going through guy after guy trying to find it.

But that...

Whatever just happened in here, just like our two times in the graveyard... It was exactly what I wanted. The hate, the passion, the pain. All of it.

And fuck if I wouldn't do it all over again if he were to barge back in here right now.

Pushing my messed-up hair from my face, I rest back and run those few minutes through my head over and over, my heart continuing to race as if it's happening right now.

Aware that the door's unlocked and anyone could come barging in, I finish what I'm doing and clean up, careful not to open up the cuts on my thigh more than they already are.

I stare at his handiwork, my feelings over the fact that he branded me like a fucking cow warring within me.

It was hot, no doubt about that, but fuck. Now I'm literally walking around with his name on me like I do actually belong to him.

One thing's for sure, though. He's fucking deranged.

I reach down to pull my panties up before realizing

my mistake. The jerk has fucking stolen them—and my knife.

I guess that's only fair, seeing as I have his.

Rolling my eyes at his caveman tendencies, I walk over to the sink to wash my hands, my thigh stinging as I move, reminding me of what he's done to me with every step I take.

I find my purse abandoned on the floor and pull out my lip gloss, attempting to fix myself so I look less like I just got fucked over by a baby member of the fucking mafia.

I soon give it up as a bad job. My lips might not be swollen from his kisses like I wanted, but my neck is littered with hickies and I've got red, angry scratch marks down my chest from my own knife.

Sucking in a breath, I prepare to walk back out there. Everyone will know exactly what went on in here only moments ago. Okay, probably not *everything*. I'd like to think the little brand on my thigh is between the two of us.

Just before I move from the sink, the door swings open and none other than fucking Teagan comes stumbling inside.

"Ew," she says, turning her nose up the second she finds me standing in her way. "I didn't realize this bathroom was full of trash."

"Whatever," I mutter, swiping my purse from the counter and throwing it over my shoulder. I don't have the energy for another sparring match with this bitch. I've got someone else I want to piss off more. "Excuse me." I storm past her, ensuring my shoulder collides with hers.

She yelps like a little bitch before I swing the door

closed behind me, leaving her in the room that smells like the sex I just had with the guy she's so desperate for.

I don't see him immediately, but I sure as fuck feel his hate-filled stare from across the room.

Marching up to the counter where he stood not so long ago and forced himself into my mouth, I reach out for one of the bottles of vodka sitting there.

Interested stares from the rest of the room burn into my back as I line up a row of shot glasses and slosh vodka into each one.

"Okay," a familiar soft voice says to my left, "I'm not sure that's such a good idea."

"No offence, Calli, but you can't possibly understand why it's completely necessary."

Picking up the first glass, I throw it back, wincing as the alcohol hits my throat.

"Um..." Calli hesitates, not knowing what to do.

"Here." I offer her one of my shots. She takes it, but she makes no move to drink it. "Gotta be honest, I'm surprised Nico hasn't carried you out of here yet."

She shrugs, tilting her head toward the corner of the room. "He got distracted."

Glancing over, I find him dry humping a girl. A completely different one from the one who was blowing him when we first arrived. I guess it is his birthday, after all.

"Nice."

"He's a pig."

"I hate to burst your bubble, Cal. Every guy down here is exactly the same."

"I wouldn't know," she mutters sadly. "Most won't even talk to me, let alone come anywhere near."

"Well, after Nico punched that guy, I can hardly say I'm surprised."

"He even scared that guy off from upstairs." She sighs, looking emotional and exhausted.

"Maybe you should call it a night," I suggest.

"Maybe. You wanna head up?"

Movement over her shoulder catches my eye, and I find Seb talking to Theo and Teagan's little bitches.

"Maybe in a bit. I've got something I need to do first."

Following my stare, she groans.

"You're not going to beat them, you know that, right?"

"Says whom? They haven't come up against someone like me before."

She studies me for a moment as if she can read my intentions on my face.

"Those idiots take bromance to a new level. You won't break them. Trust me, more than a few have tried."

"Again. Not me."

Turning to my drinks, I knock each one back, the liquid warming my belly the second it hits.

"You go. I'll be up in a bit. Promise."

I drop a kiss on her cheek then walk away, slapping her ass as I go.

Almost every set of eyes in the room follows me as I stalk across the vast space with my head held high and a determined look on my face.

Passing Alex, I swipe the joint from his fingers and suck in a hit, seeing as my high from earlier was easily killed by the asshole whose eyes are shooting so much hate at me I'm surprised I haven't gone up in flames yet.

Theo leans toward Seb and whispers something in his ear, but my eyes are locked on Seb's angry ones, so I don't have a chance of lip reading whatever it was. Not that I really give a shit.

Shoving both Lylah and Sloane out of the way, I step right up to Theo.

"Watch where you're going, bitch," one of them whines, but I pay them zero attention.

With my hand in the centre of his chest, Theo allows me to push him back against the wall as I continue holding Seb's eyes.

The warning in his is loud and clear, and it only spurs me on—that along with the alcohol and the blunt.

"Princess, I really don't think—"

CHAPTER NINETEEN

Sebastian

All the air rushes out of my lungs as Stella presses the length of her body against Theo's and slams her lips down on his.

He's my boy, so I'm not surprised that his first reaction isn't to immediately kiss her back.

His hands go to her shoulders, ready to push her away as his eyes find mine, but he never gets the chance to do anything because she grabs his wrists and drags his hands to her arse.

He hesitates longer than he should, but I get it. She's fucking hot and just thrown herself at him.

Resting back against the pool table behind me, I fold my arms over my chest and watch them.

She's doing it to piss me off, to punish me for not kissing her in the bathroom. But what she doesn't realise is that she's missed the mark by a fucking mile.

I trust my boys with my life. And while I might have warned them not to go anywhere fucking near her, I also trust them with her.

I've ensured they won't go after her, but that doesn't mean they'll always behave, especially with my permission.

His eyes continue to hold mine as she kisses him, urging him to return her attention.

All it takes is one single nod of my head and he caves. His eyes slam closed and one of his hands moves from her arse, skimming up her curves until he threads his fingers into her hair and takes control of the kiss, tilting her exactly as he wants.

My stomach twists as I watch them... but equally my cock swells and my need to go over and join in almost becomes too much to bear.

I'm about to push off the table when I spot two people approaching from different directions.

Calli is the first to get to me.

"What the fuck are you doing?" she squeals. Her eyes are wide, her face flushed in a way I've never seen before. That probably has something to do with the fact that we've never let her party with us. Nico seems to have forgotten that she's here as he wraps some slut's leg around his waist, blatantly thrusting into her on the other side of the room.

I'd put money on the fact that Calli hasn't seen what he's up to, otherwise I've no doubt he'd be on the wrong end of her wrath right now instead of me.

She waves her hand in the direction of Stella and Theo, her eyes impossibly wide as she stares at me.

"Why are you letting that happen?"

"Seb," Toby warns, his lips pressed into a thin line when he joins us.

"Why do we do anything we do, baby C? We're just having fun. Ain't that right, Tobes?" I sit up on the pool table and rest back on my palms, my eyes firmly on Stella and Theo, halting the game the couple of drunk guys were attempting to play behind me. Unfazed, they both wander off.

"No, we're fucking not. You need to stop this bullshit before she ends up getting hurt."

"Aw, Tobes. It's so cute that you care. But she's nothing more than a fucking whore. I'm just letting her get her kicks."

His fist flies toward me, but I see it coming a mile off and catch it before it connects with my face.

"You're wrong, she's nothing like that."

"No? So she didn't just blow me in the kitchen, fuck me in the bathroom and then come straight out here and start all over again with Theo?" I hop back down, more than ready for another drink.

Stepping up to Toby, I tap my palm on his chest. "You're fucking deluded if you think she's an innocent little princess sent from above, man." I lean into his ear. "She's one of us. Let her act like it."

I don't need to look at him to know anger covers his face. It radiates off him in waves.

"If you can't hack it, maybe take baby C and go and play with her Barbies or something."

With a smirk, I walk off toward the kitchen and the half-empty bottle of vodka Stella left behind.

"Enough for me?" Teagan asks, sliding up to me and wrapping her hand around mine that's holding the bottle.

"No," I snap, ripping it away from her when she tries to take it.

"You know, if you're tense, I've got a great way to help you relax."

Ripping my eyes from Stella and Theo, I stare down at Teagan. I've always known she's a desperate wannabe who wants a taste of our lives, but she's not the kind of girl who can actually hack it. She cares too much about her hair, her nails, everything that's on the outside. Maybe she'd be the perfect trophy wife for one of the other guys. But she certainly isn't for me. I'm not interested in that kind of fakeness. The only reason I've let her stick around for so long is because I know I'll never fall for her, and that makes her safe.

Love makes you weak, and ultimately, it leaves you a broken-hearted shell of yourself.

All you need to do is look at my mum for evidence of that. I have no idea who the woman was before she died right alongside my father. Losing Demi only made it worse.

"Why are you still trying?" I ask her.

"What do you mean?" The fake innocence in her voice makes me cringe.

"You know full well I just fucked Stella in that bathroom. Don't act stupid, Teag. You might be a blonde, but you're not fucking dumb." Her brow crinkles as I say the words, and I start to doubt whether they're actually true or not. Is she really just this fucking dim?

"We've got something."

"Something so special I just fucked someone who wasn't you?"

Tears burn her eyes, but she tries blinking them away.

I should care, but I really fucking don't.

She doesn't want me. All she's interested in is her social standing.

"Come on, Seb. Don't be like that. It's a party, we all do crazy shit. You clearly don't want her or you wouldn't be standing here with me while she's got her tongue down Theo's throat."

"When did I say I wanted her? All I said was that I don't want you," I say, my voice cold and lacking any kind of emotion despite the jealousy that wants to bubble to the surface. "You should leave."

Turning my back on her, I walk away with my bottle and drop down onto one of Nico's massive sofas.

There's a couple dry humping beside me, blocking my view of where Stella and Theo are now dancing.

"Fuck off," I growl.

The guy takes one look at me and lifts the girl to her feet, both of them damn near running away. Anyone would think I pulled a gun on them or something.

Propping one foot up on the coffee table, I continue watching the show Stella is insisting on putting on for me.

She thinks she's winning.

I'll allow her to think that for a while. It'll only make the fall all that more delicious when it comes.

She spots someone over her shoulder, and when I follow her line of sight, I find Alex at the end of it.

She gestures him over, and without a second thought, he lights up a fresh joint and walks over to her, handing it over before lining up behind her and rolling his hips in time with hers.

The sofa moves beside me as someone joins me.

I'm about to rip them another one for even thinking about it when he stretches his long-arse legs out and copies my stance.

"Thought you were working tonight?"

"Got off early," is Daemon's quick reply. "So that's her, then?" I don't look over, but I know he nods toward Stella.

"Sure is. What have you heard?"

The six of us might have grown up together, but Daemon has never really been one of us. He always preferred to hang out alone, lose himself in his computer and follow his father around like a needy puppy.

He has lived and breathed the Family for as long as he's understood its importance and his place. He wants it. He wants it so much I swear it borders on an obsession, but I'm not exactly one to criticise people's choices. My own are questionable as best.

"Galen's been given a pass. Did you know he's been working all this time, just from over the pond?"

My grip on the bottle in my hand tightens.

"No, I didn't." Although I'd kinda figured as much, seeing as he's returned with no issue and his precious spawn is important enough for the boss to demand we babysit her.

"Does he shit fucking gold or something? You don't pull a stunt like that and get away with it."

"We don't know the whole story," Daemon muses.

"Not right now, but we will."

"Maybe. I know one thing, though."

"Oh yeah?" I ask, finally turning toward him and narrowing my eyes. Daemon isn't usually one to say much, or to openly have an opinion on anything. He's usually too busy following orders in the hope of jumping a few rungs on the Family ladder.

"She fits right in. Fucking good kisser, too." He slaps me on the thigh, muttering, "I'm out," and pushes to stand. If I didn't already regret not kissing her earlier and forcing her into her little one-woman show, then I really fucking do now.

I sit back into the sofa cushions and tip the bottle to my lips, readjusting my jeans as I watch my boys grind up against my little hellion.

The way she moves, even while pressed up against them, makes me hard as fucking steel.

CHAPTER TWENTY

Stella

Fuck my life.

My tongue is stuck to the roof of my mouth when I come around to the sound of a fucking marching band inside my brain.

I groan, attempting to shift my body, but it's sunk into the most comfortable bed I think I've ever slept on.

Loud snoring from somewhere else in the room fills my ears, forcing memories from the night before to come back to me.

None of them make me feel any better.

Oh God.

"Morning, Princess," a deep, rough voice says from beside me.

My stomach bottoms out. Who the hell am I in bed with, and how the hell did I get here?

The last thing I remember was messing about with

Theo and Alex. There was dancing, kissing, grinding, weed and vodka. God, there was so much vodka.

I suck in a deep breath before cracking an eye open.

Theo's face appears in front of me, and I groan when I lower my gaze and find him on top of the bed in nothing but a pair of boxers.

Please don't tell me I went there. Please.

"How are you feeling, beautiful?"

"Exactly as I deserve. Does Nico have any painkillers?"

"Check the bedside table." He flicks a look behind me, and I muster up as much energy as I can manage to turn around.

I almost sigh in relief when I find a glass of water and a packet of pills waiting for me. Someone was organised. Or saw what a fucking mess I was last night.

It's all *his* fault. If he'd have just kissed me...

Thoughts of him have me looking around the room. He's here, I know he is. My skin tingles with awareness.

I find Nico passed out on the floor with a half-naked girl on either side. Alex is curled up on the pool table, an empty bottle of vodka still in his hand.

I keep searching, my eyes squinting against the sun that's streaming through the wall of floor-to-ceiling windows I didn't see the night before.

I gasp the second I find him.

He's sitting on the couch in the exact same place I remember him watching me from last night. He's resting back, his legs spread, and instead of a bottle of vodka, he's got a bottle of water hanging from his fingers. But his eyes, just like last night, are trained right on me.

I swallow nervously as images of my behavior flick through my mind like a movie.

I shift on the bed and my thigh stings as I do so.

What the...

My knife. The bathroom. His initials.

Jesus, how many regrets can one person possibly have from just a few short hours?

I need to get out of here.

Ripping my eyes from him, I sit up and for the first time take note of what I'm wearing—or not, as the case may be.

The image of him stuffing my ruined panties into his pocket fills my mind, and I squeeze my thighs together, earning me a chuckle from the guy beside me.

"What?" I snap.

"Princess, you've got nothing left to hide."

Dropping my head into my hands, I press my thumbs into my temples.

What the hell happened last night?

Without looking at anyone—namely the angry guy on the couch—I throw back two of the pills and drain the glass of water.

Silence ripples through the room, aside from Nico and Alex's snoring. The tension is thick, completely unbearable as eyes burn into my back.

"Excuse me," I mutter, pushing from the bed. The words aren't directed at anyone specifically, and no one replies as I make my way across the room, my body aching, my head pounding with every step I take.

"Jesus," I whisper when I get closer to Nico and find both him and his two little friends stark naked on the floor. How much did they drink to not notice yet?

At least Alex still has his pants on as I pass him curled up on the pool table.

There aren't any other bodies loitered around like I'd

have expected, and it makes me wonder who was with it enough to actually clear the place out.

I wonder what happened upstairs. Are there still people up there passed out and regretting their alcohol-fuelled decisions from the night before?

What happened to Calli?

My heart sinks knowing that I abandoned her after promising I'd keep an eye on her. Everything flew straight out the window as soon as Seb dragged me down here into the basement of sin.

His stare still burns into my back as I slip into the bathroom and close the door behind me, cutting myself off from everything that happened out there last night. It's not until I turn around that I realize my mistake. I might have left some regrets on the other side of the door, but I have plenty from in here, too.

My thigh aches as I vividly remember Seb on his knees before me, cutting into my skin.

"Motherfucker."

Was he right, though? Did his initials on my thigh stop anyone else fucking me?

Shit. I wish I could remember how I ended up wearing only Theo's shirt and passing out beside him on Nico's bed.

Lowering myself to the toilet, I drop my head into my hands. I groan out my frustrations at myself.

Why did I agree to come here last night?

I picture Calli's sweet face and remember all the things she told me about being smothered by the guys on the other side of the door, along with her father and the rest of the Family.

Fuck. The Family.

I sit bolt upright, snippets of our conversation flashing through my mind.

I need to go home and do some research. I need to speak to Dad. I need to...

I sigh, my shoulders sagging once more. Will he even tell me the truth?

All my life I've trusted my father. Through all our moves, his absence in my life, I've always trusted that he was doing what was best for me.

But keeping something like this a secret?

It's rocked me, and my trust in the man I love more than anything is hanging right in the balance.

I gasp when I look at myself in the mirror. How Theo managed not to burst out laughing is beyond me. My hair is a matted mess sticking up in all directions. My makeup is everywhere, lipstick smeared across my lips, over my jaw and down my— "Fuck." Lifting my fingers, I run them over the hickies and bite marks that litter my throat.

Those were all from Seb... right?

Fuck my life.

With only water, I do the best job I can at washing away what remains of last night's makeup. I look better than I was expecting once I've mostly managed to clear it away. And after finger-brushing my teeth, I feel almost human again.

I find a comb on the shelf above the sink which helps me to tame my wild hair, and when I wrap my fingers around the handle to finally escape the sanctuary of the bathroom, I almost feel strong enough to deal with the jerks on the other side.

All I can hope is that two of them are still passed out and that, by some miracle, Seb will let me slip out to find Calli without any drama.

Yeah, it's wishful thinking, and I realize my mistake when I step into the main room and find all four of them sitting on the couches with coffees in hand.

Nico's girls are nowhere to be seen, and thankfully, he's got some pants on.

"Morning, Princess." Alex winks, his eyes dropping to my stocking-clad legs. Theo's shirt sits high on the thighs, so it's no secret what I'm wearing beneath. Although if his words from earlier are anything to go by, then I could be standing here naked and it wouldn't really matter.

I swallow, dragging my eyes from him to the other three idiots whose hungry stares are trained on me.

"W-where's my dress?" I stutter, hating that I sound unsure of myself.

Silence ripples through the room, sending a shiver of unease down my spine as Seb leans forward, resting his elbows on his knees.

"Come here, Hellion," he demands, his dark eyes holding mine and daring me to defy him.

A part of me wants to. A really fucking huge part wants me to spin on my heels and run as fast as I can from this den of sin. But I don't, because locked in his stare, I lose control of my body and find myself taking a step toward him.

A smirk twitches at his lips, satisfaction that I followed orders filling his eyes.

The others all track my every movement as I round the coffee table that's got two steaming mugs sitting in the middle and come to stand in front of him.

His face is totally unreadable as I stare at him. His mask is firmly in place. It makes the hairs on the back of my neck stand on end, because I can't read anything about his intentions—and that's dangerous.

"W-where's Toby?" I ask, although the second his name rolls off my tongue I realize it was probably the wrong thing to say, because Seb's jaw tics in frustration.

Without saying a word, he reaches for my hand and tugs, ensuring that I fall down on his lap.

His hands encircle my waist and he spins me, placing me exactly where he wants me between his spread thighs, my back to his front.

Leaning forward, his hot breath races over my ear, making me shiver. It's something he doesn't miss, if his low chuckle tells me anything.

"Did you have fun last night, Princess?" he asks, loud enough for the others to hear.

Unable to look at any of them, my eyes find the steaming coffees on the table before me. My fists clench with the need to reach for one.

Seb must sense my desperation, because just as I'm about to move, he reaches out and collars my throat with his hot hand.

Asshole.

"Answer me, Hellion," he growls, sending traitorous tingles south of my waist.

"Y-yes?" I don't mean for it to come out as a question, but I've got so many unknowns about what went down last night that I have no idea what the correct answer could be.

"Oh yeah? So you enjoyed whoring yourself around my boys, despite what I told you about who you belong to?"

I don't respond, and I sense he doesn't actually want me to.

"You did, didn't you?"

Despite his harsh words, the second his other hand

lands on my stomach and begins sliding up until he cups my breasts through both Theo's shirt and the bra I'm still thankfully wearing, my chest begins to heave and my breaths begin to increase.

I really am just a whore.

I've got one guy's hands on me and three others watching, and my body is burning up faster than I can handle.

"I think I need to teach you another lesson. Don't you, Hellion?"

He squeezes my breast harder, and I can't stop the moan of pleasure that rips from my lips.

Tucking his feet behind my calves, he drags my legs wide, and like the shameless slut I am, I let him.

Heat burns my cheeks, blooming down my neck and onto my chest knowing that Theo, Alex and Nico can literally see everything now. It's not just them seeing my cunt that fills me with humiliation, but Seb's brand. The red angry scar that now bears his initials, probably forever, if the depth of his cuts is anything to go by.

Not wanting to appear weak, I drag my eyelids open and glare at the three of them.

My breath catches when I find pure danger and lust staring right back at me.

Alex's eyes flick between my face and my pussy as his hand lifts to run through his messy bed hair.

Nico's attention is firmly on my cunt, his own arousal at this fucked-up situation more than obvious behind his sweats.

And Theo? He just looks fucking intrigued. Asshole.

Despite knowing that he's not here, I search the basement for Toby.

He wouldn't allow Seb to do this, to humiliate me in front of his friends.

But he's not here. And Seb is more than aware of that fact. Although something tells me that Toby might just be the real one he wants to give this message to.

"She's fucking dripping for it, man," Nico damn near growls as he palms his cock through his sweats.

Fucking dog. You'd have thought he got his fill last night with his two little friends.

Seb's fingers tighten on my throat and fuck, another wave of heat pools in my pussy.

"Say it, Hellion," he growls in my ear, and my spine goes straight at the roughness in his voice.

I know Nico's not the only one affected by this little show. I can feel Seb's cock hard and ready at my back.

It seems this little bit of exhibitionism really gets him going.

Tilting my chin once more, I keep my lips firmly shut, refusing to give him the words I know he wants.

He wants me to submit.

Well, he can go fuck himself.

"You really think you're in any position to defy me right now?"

"I don't give a fuck, Sebastian. Do what you want with me, you'll be the one who has to live with your actions. I, however, already know I'm a whore, so you may as well make use of it."

A growl of frustration rips up his throat the second I call myself a whore.

So what? It's okay for him to, but not me?

Fucking hypocrite.

Dropping the tone of my voice, ensuring it comes out

all raspy and needy, I look between the three guys before me.

"What do you say, boys? Wanna have some fun? I'm all here for the taking." I wink a second before my head is ripped back, my scalp burning at almost having my hair clean ripped out from his brutal movements.

"No one fucking touches you, Hellion. You're mine." His dark, bordering on deranged eyes hold mine and all the air rushes from my lungs.

Right now, there's no way I could refute anything that Calli told me last night. I might have seen Seb with both a gun and a knife in the past couple of weeks, but he has never looked more dangerous, more deadly than he does right now.

"Mine," he mouths.

Releasing my hair, I breathe a sigh of relief when he removes his hand and I don't find strands of it between his fingers.

That feeling only lasts so long, because his hand drops between my legs, his fingers dancing up my thighs and making my muscles bunch in desire.

"Are you going to put on a nice little show for my brothers, Hellion? I think they need to see who you belong to just as much as you need to understand it."

My chest heaves, my breaths coming out in short, sharp gasps. Biting my lips together, I try to refrain from demanding he stop teasing me and just do it.

Nico wasn't wrong. I'm so fucking ready to feel him inside me.

My pussy aches to be stretched open, to be punished by him for whatever went down last night that I don't remember.

A needy whimper escapes as he gets higher, dragging

his finger over my lips but not going near where I need him.

"Look how badly they want you, Princess. All of them are fucking dying for a taste of you."

Unable to do anything but follow orders in the hope it'll get me what I need, I find each of their eyes.

The green in Theo's is brighter than ever as they follow Seb's movements, his cock bulging against his pants. Alex and Nico's eyes are so blown with desire that they look like the dark depths of hell, much like Seb's do behind me. Nico, though... he's taking it to the next level, because his hand has slipped under his waistband and he slowly strokes himself as he watches me.

Sensing my attention, his eyes lift to mine and he winks.

Nothing like helping me out, asshole.

A scowl pulls at my lips, but all he does in response is smile.

"Oh God," I breathe when Seb finally grazes my clit before pushing lower and sinking two fingers inside me.

"Fuck, Hellion. You do like driving my boys wild, huh?"

He curls his fingers inside me, and I lose any thread of control I was holding onto.

My body sags back against his, giving myself over to what he's doing. My eyes fall closed as I focus on the sensations and my quickly building release.

"Watch them," he barks, his fingers stilling. "I want them to see exactly what they can't have."

An argument is right on the tip of my tongue, a demand to know if this is actually about punishing them for last night more than it is about me.

Although the second I open my eyes, I quickly realize

that they're all enjoying this as much as I am. Not that I'd ever fucking admit it.

Nico has given up attempting to hide what he's doing to himself. His sweats are now around his thighs, his thick cock openly in his palm as he fists it.

Alex has his pants undone and his hand is quickly sinking beneath the fabric. Theo is the only one who looks even slightly composed as he sits there with his hand moving slowly over the bulge in his pants.

The sight of them falling apart before me is so fucking erotic I almost find my voice and demand they just shed their clothes, let me see exactly what this is doing to them.

But doing so would probably put pay to the intense release I'm flying toward, so I settle on moaning out Seb's name instead, more than aware that it's what he wants and willing to play this little game of his.

I'm not sure if he was anticipating me enjoying it, but fuck, I'm not sure I want to be anywhere else right now.

"Who do you belong to, Hellion?" he tries again, knowing that I'm beginning to fall.

I fight to drag in the air I need as he keeps me riding that torturous edge of pleasure. If I say or do the wrong thing, he's going to rip it away from me, and that can't happen. Not this time. I'm too far gone, and it'll result in doing something stupid like running straight to Nico, who I'm sure would be more than willing to finish the job—assuming he was alive long enough to do so.

"Y-you," I breathe, part of me hoping he can't hear it over the increasing grunts and groans that are filling the room.

"Louder," he booms, startling me. "Tell my boys who you fucking belong to."

"You," I cry as a loud crash sounds out somewhere in

the room. "You, Seb. I belong to you," I shout as his fingers pick up pace once more.

I'm just about to fall when my eyes find a figure on the other side of the room.

Toby.

CHAPTER TWENTY-ONE

Sebastian

About fucking time.

My lips curl as Toby's murderous eyes find mine after he's taken a moment to assess the scene playing out in front of him.

I might want to make a point to the three assholes jerking themselves off in front of us at the sight of my hellion falling apart under my hands, but really there's only one person who needs to see this warning for what it is.

Ownership.

Toby might have been the only one not to get a taste of her last night, but he's also the one who looks at her differently, like she's not just a game. And that is a fucking problem, because he's going to fuck everything up for me if he keeps going. If he keeps trying to protect her and treat her properly.

She doesn't fucking deserve either of those things.

I know I should probably just be honest about my reasons behind all of this, but fuck that. He should trust that I know what I'm doing. He's my fucking brother in all the ways that count. He should fucking trust me.

His lips part to say something, to attempt to rip me a new one, but I move first, thrusting my fingers deep inside Stella's cunt and grinding the heel of my hand against her clit. And like the fucking devil she is, she falls right on cue. Much to Toby's horror.

"Seb." Her cry echoes through the almost unbearable silence of the basement as her body clamps my fingers and her juices gush down my hand.

Fucking perfect.

Toby's eyes widen more than I thought possible, his fists curling at his sides in anger as the recognisable sound of one of the guys finishing covers Stella's lingering whimpers of pleasure as she trembles in my arms.

Dragging my fingers from inside her, I lift my hand and push them into my mouth as I continue to hold Toby's eyes. Her taste explodes on my tongue, making my cock ache for her.

"What the fuck are you doing?" he snaps. I don't know why he looks so fucking horrified. It's not like this is our first group party. And I happen to remember that he's been all in in the past. He might try to look like he's all straight laced and shit, but it's a fucking lie. He's as freaky and wicked as the rest of us when you peel back a few layers.

"Join in or fuck off, bro. We're enjoying ourselves."

His jaw tics as he fights to make a decision.

"Let her go," he demands, taking a warning step toward us, although I'm not entirely sure what he's about to do unless he's planning to pull a gun from his pants, which is unlikely seeing as he's hardly ever packing.

"How about we ask her?"

Sliding my hand around her body, I squeeze her breast, pinching her nipple through the fabric.

She stifles a moan so I up the ante, pushing my hand down her stomach, circling her swollen clit.

"What do you say, Hellion? Should I let you go?"

Her response is a loud moan, so I dip my fingers back inside her again.

Toby's eyes bore into mine. They never drop lower to watch what I'm doing to her body. Respect for his self-control, because hell knows the other three have fuck all.

"Right answer," I growl in her ear. "Now get on your knees."

She stills as my words register in her post-orgasm haze.

"U-uh."

"Get on your fucking knees for me, Hellion."

The second she follows orders and drops between my spread thighs, Toby turns his back on the lot of us and storms from the basement, leaving only the echo of the slamming door behind him.

"Who pissed on his chips?" Nico quips.

Ignoring him, I focus on the woman between my legs.

Resting back and stretching out, I lift my hips in invitation and raise my brows.

Her gaze lifts from my obvious arousal, her eyes rolling up my shirt-covered chest until she finally meets my eyes.

I swallow down the groan that wants to rumble up my throat at the sight of her.

Fuck, she's beautiful.

Her face is clear of last night's makeup, and her eyes are blown with desire, the light blue now resembling the deepest ocean. Her lips are parted, allowing her sharp gasps to escape.

"What are you waiting for, Hellion?"

In a moment of weakness, she looks over her shoulder toward the door Toby disappeared through.

Reaching out, I take her cheek in my hand, forcing her back to me.

"Fuck him, Princess. He's a pussy. Now," I say, undoing my belt to help her out.

Her hands lift, and in seconds she's got my jeans around my hips and my aching cock in her palm.

"Remember this, boys. It's the closest you're ever gonna get to experiencing it."

Sliding one hand into her hair, I guide her forward as I rest the other on the back of the couch.

Jealousy burns through the air as she sucks me into her mouth and I fucking revel in it, because she is all fucking mine.

Unlike last night, I allow her to do her thing, and fuck am I glad I do. Fucking her throat was good, but the feeling of her licking up the length of my cock, worshipping me as if I'm her fucking king is every-fucking-thing.

My fingers tighten in her hair, but I never take control as my eyes watch her every movement.

I know what the guys are doing around us. I can see their movements out of the corner of my eye. But my only reaction to them getting off over this is to smirk, because they are never gonna fucking experience it.

"Mine," I growl when she pulls off my length, my fingers twisting until it hurts.

Her eyes flare with desire before I push her back down and lose myself in her hot little mouth.

I want to hold on forever, but it's all too soon when my balls start to draw up, the familiar tingling erupting at the base of my spine.

Feeling it too, she ups her pace, sucking me harder and sending me spiralling headfirst into an intense release I'm not going to forget for a while, if ever.

My cock jerks as I moan in pleasure, my cum coating her tongue.

Her eyes hold mine as she swallows, licking at my tip, taking every drop she can get.

Releasing me, she stays on her knees, her lips beautifully swollen from my cock.

My chest aches at the sight of her at my feet, and my muscles burn to reach out and lift her to my lap. But that's not what this is.

"You can leave now," I force myself to say, pulling my jeans up and walking away from her as if she's nothing.

Storming to the bathroom, I have every intention of not looking back, but my body betrays me. Just before the door slams behind me, I fucking turn around.

The sight of her on her knees with her head bowed in shame does something to me, but it's not something I have the capacity to acknowledge right now.

Resting back against the closed door, I listen for movement or voices on the other side as I will my heart to stop pounding in my chest and for my doubts to vanish.

She needed that.

They fucking needed that.

She's mine. And mine only.

The image of her at my mercy between my thighs

comes back to me and a smug, satisfied smile pulls at my lips.

Yeah. She fucking knows it now, too.

Pushing from the door, I take a slash before regretfully washing her scent from my fingers as I wonder how soon I can have her screaming my name all over again.

Her knickers burn a hole in my pocket.

Yeah, maybe I'll be making another little visit for another pair sometime soon.

I'm not surprised, although admittedly a little disappointed, when I emerge from the bathroom to find that she's gone.

I did tell her to, after all.

Three intrigued sets of eyes follow me as I walk to the kitchen for a fresh cup of coffee, seeing as my last one is sitting on the table, cold and abandoned.

"What?" I bark when I fall on the sofa once more.

"That," Nico starts, "was hot as fuck but completely unnecessary."

"Really?" I ask, my brows almost at my hairline. "I stood around last night watching each of your tongues in her mouth. Sorry for feeling the need to make a point."

"She's a feisty bitch," Alex says happily. "I like her."

"Yeah, that's the fucking problem," I mutter, sipping on my too hot coffee.

"Bro, we get it. We really fucking do, but—"

I shoot Theo a look that cuts his words off. Nico doesn't know what we know, and as far as I'm concerned, I want it to stay that way.

"It's fine. You three can have your little WI meeting if you want. I'm going for a shower. I've got girl all over me," Nico huffs.

Alex laughs at his comment but doesn't point out the obvious fucking reason for it, and the three of us watch as he disappears into the bathroom.

"I know what I'm doing," I tell them, my voice firm, confident.

They both stare at me, their eyes saying everything their mouths don't. I'm thankful, because the truth is, I have no fucking idea what I'm doing.

I thought I did, but Stella surprises me at every turn, and the plans I had only yesterday get shot to shit because right now, the only thing I can think about when it comes to my little hellion is how I'm going to get an up-close view of my initials on her skin sometime soon.

CHAPTER TWENTY-TWO

Stella

My legs and lungs burn by the time I fly through Calli's bedroom door and crash to the carpet in an exhausted, humiliated heap.

"Stella?" The concern in Calli's voice as her sheets rustle makes a sob want to rip up my throat. But I refuse to allow myself to go there.

I'm stronger than Seb and his idiot friends.

It's just my exhaustion, I tell myself.

I always have been a really shitty liar.

Warm hands wrap around my upper arm. I push my initial reaction to fight aside and allow her to help me stand.

I haven't looked in a mirror since running from the basement, but I don't need to to know I look like hell.

"What happened?" Calli asks, standing before me as I perch on the edge of her bed.

"Uh..." I hesitate, not wanting to tarnish her purity and innocence with the horrific truth.

"The last time I saw you, you had your tongue down Theo's throat," she states matter-of-factly with her hands on her hips.

Thankfully, there's no judgement there, just curiosity.

"I had too much to drink. And Alex's blunt was fucking strong," I mutter, dropping my head into my hands.

"Do you need pills? I've got—"

"I've had some, but thank you. I should go. Get out of your way and let you get on with your day."

"I'm not letting you walk out of here like this. Talk to me. I might not understand, but I want to help."

She drops down beside me and reaches for my hand.

"No offense, but you smell like boy. And from the state of your neck, I can guess why."

A bitter laugh falls from my lips.

"Can't say I'm surprised."

"What happened, Stella?"

I give her a very brief, very vague rundown of my time with Seb in the bathroom before coming out with the intention of teaching him a lesson.

I remember kissing Theo. I remember Alex joining us and there's a very, very hazy memory of his lips too.

But anything past that is just a blur of nothingness.

From the way Nico looked at me this morning, I know that he was involved somewhere.

The only thing that makes me feel a little bit better about everything I can't remember is that when Seb pushed his fingers inside me earlier, I wasn't sore like I'd been fucked seven ways from Sunday.

I hope that means my night maxed out at kissing, and that Theo was lying when he said they'd all seen everything already.

I internally cringe as I think about how I ended up out of my dress and who might have put me into Theo's shirt.

Looking up at Calli, I smile softly, more than appreciating her support right now.

"Can I use your shower?"

"Of course. Use anything you like. Do you have clothes?"

I nod—I packed for today.

"Maybe we should go out once you're ready, get breakfast or something? Get out of the house, away from them."

My first reaction is to refuse in my need to go running home and lock myself in my bedroom. But then I look into her kind eyes and realize she needs the time out as much as I do.

"Okay. I'll shower then we'll go for food. You can tell me all about your night." I wink at her, and she blushes.

"I can't believe I saw Nico getting—" She slams her lips shut, her cheeks only getting brighter.

"Head? Don't worry, he woke up with two naked girls on either side of him. It got worse."

"Oh my God. How am I related to that dog?"

Laughing, I leave her to her mortification in favor of her shower.

I sigh in relief when I find that it looks completely different to the one in the basement. It's certainly a girl's bathroom, and my back straightens a little. I'm safe in here.

Turning the shower on as hot as I can, I strip out of Theo's shirt, drag my bra, garter and ruined stockings from my legs and step under.

The water burns, my skin rejecting the temperature, but I force myself to stand there, to endure the heat that will help wash last night, them, *him,* from my body. It's just a shame that I can't get all of them out of my head quite so easily.

I make the most of Calli's fancy shampoo and conditioner that I've never heard of, and I don't step out until every single part of my body has been scrubbed within an inch of its life. Well, that's not entirely true. There was one patch that couldn't handle that kind of treatment, a part I refused to even look at. If I ignore the existence of those two little letters, then maybe they'll disappear as if they never happened.

Yeah, nice thought.

By the time I step out, dressed in fresh clothes and with my wet hair hanging around my shoulders, I feel a little like the usual me once more.

"Here, I snuck out for coffee."

"Oh my God." I race over and take the mug she offers me, hugging it to my chest as I breathe in the scent of the freshly ground beans. "It's good stuff, too."

"Of course. Only the best in the Cirillo house, you know." She puts on a prissy English accent. I have no idea who she's mimicking, her mom maybe, but it's funny.

"Drink that, dry your hair, then we're out of here. I'm taking you for a real breakfast. None of the pancake and bacon crap you're used to."

"Crap?" I ask, faux offended.

"There's only one way to deal with hangovers, and that's the British way."

An hour later, I find myself sitting across a table from Calli in a backstreet London café. It's not where I was expecting her to bring me, but after the night and morning I've had, hiding here couldn't be any more perfect.

I didn't even bother looking at the menu when we arrived, I just let Calli handle it. She seems to know what I need to fix everything that's gone wrong in my life over the past twelve hours, so she can have at it.

"Look what I've got," she says excitedly, slipping a screwed-up piece of paper across the table.

I stare down at the scribbled phone number and my brows pull together.

"Whose is that?" I ask, a proud smile tugging at my lips.

"The guy I was dancing with before we went to the basement. I had no idea until I took my dress off and found it in my pocket."

I'm not sure what I'm more surprised about—that he did it or that the dress she borrowed from me had fucking pockets.

"Are you going to call him?" I ask, excitement beginning to bubble in my belly at her finding a life outside of her prison.

"I messaged him when I found it." She giggles like a schoolgirl.

"And?" I urge, more than happy to drown in her boy drama, rather than relive my own.

"I apologised for my brother, and told him he was a little overbearing." I scoff at that description. "He said he understood that he's got a little sister too. He wants to meet me."

"Oh my God. Are you going to?"

A nervous grin appears, her eyes alight with excitement. "I said I would."

"Eeek," I squeal. "That's so exciting."

Her nervousness increases with my reaction.

"What is it?"

"I... uh... said you'd come. His friend wants to see you again, too."

"Calli," I sigh, dread already settling in my belly. "I can't. Can you imagine if—"

"They won't find out. We'll meet them somewhere on the other side of town."

Her eyes plead with me to say yes, to stand beside her as she sheds the chains that have held her back for so long.

And I guess she's got a point. If we make up a good enough lie, they should buy it... right?

They might be protective, but they can't follow her every single minute of the day. No one is here watching us right now at least.

A shudder runs through me at the thought of one of them being close after what happened this morning.

"Are you okay? All the color just drained from your face."

"Y-yeah. I'm just hungry, I guess." I look over my shoulder, hoping our breakfast might magically appear to change the subject, but there's no waitress heading our way.

"So what do you say? Want to meet them with me?"

"When?" I tentatively ask.

"Next weekend."

I breathe a sigh of relief that she hasn't planned

something for this afternoon. I hold her eyes for a beat, but the anticipation of doing something so normal as meeting a boy for the first time cracks my black little heart and I find myself agreeing, although somewhat reluctantly.

"Yesss," she hisses. "Ant says Enzo was really into you. He'll be stoked."

I force a grin on my face, although I don't feel it.

Spending time with the two guys Nico threatened to get away from us is a bad move. A really fucking bad move, but it's too late now. Plus, Calli needs this. Really needs this.

Thankfully, our breakfasts finally arrive and I get to experience for the first time just how good a full English breakfast is for a hangover.

"Oh my God, that was so good," I moan, sitting back in my chair and rubbing my hand over my swollen belly.

"Told you so," Calli says with a wink. "Are you feeling better now? Because I've got plans."

"Oh?"

"Come on, you'll see."

"Mysterious. I like it."

We pay the bill before heading back out to Calli's Mercedes. The sun is shining, so the second we climb in, she presses the button to lower the top and looks over at me with a smile.

"You really are the perfect princess, huh?" I ask, taking in her long golden hair, her light pink sweater and her car.

"Maybe, but something tells me that's all about to change."

"Figured out I'm a bad influence already?"

"Stella, I think you're everything I need."

She starts the car and we take off through the city streets. It's surprisingly quiet for a Saturday afternoon, and before long we're pulling up outside a fancy glass building.

There's no sign or anything outside, so whatever it is is hella exclusive.

"What's this place?"

"Wait and see."

I follow her lead as she climbs out.

"I've always wanted to do this," she says excitedly as we enter the sparse foyer. Everything is glass, and even the woman behind the desk looks fragile. Perfect, but fragile.

"Hi, I have appointments booked under Calli Cirillo."

The second Calli's surname rolls off her tongue, the woman's demeanor immediately changes.

"Oh of course, Miss Cirillo. Would you like an escort?"

"No, thank you," Calli looks at the woman's name badge. "Julie. I think we can navigate the lift."

I smother a laugh at the sarcasm in my friend's voice and mentally high five her.

I really am a bad influence. Something tells me she never would have spoken up like that before. Julie's widened eyes only confirm my suspicions.

With a nod, Julie lets us head deeper into the building.

"Did you see her face?" Calli asks excitedly once the elevator doors close behind us.

"I'm assuming you come here often."

"Pretty much. I'm usually with Mum, though."

The lift rises, the numbers increasing until we get to the twentieth floor.

With a ding, the doors open and I get my first clue as to where we are. The familiar scent is a dead giveaway. So are the candles and bubbling water features as we step out into the much more lavish foyer.

"Good morning, Miss Cirillo."

"It's Calli, and this is Stella," she says, turning to me.

"Nice to meet you, Stella." Her voice sounds sincere, but her eyes are as assessing as hell.

"Don't worry, Stella has full approval. You may ask my father for confirmation."

My brows shoot up at the mention of him. Does he know that Calli and I are friends? Does he actually know we're here?

Hell, can I meet him and get some damn answers about my life?

"I'm sure everything is fine, Calli. Why don't you both follow me? We'll get you set up and then I'll call you both through once we're ready."

"Sounds great, Ellie. Thank you."

We both follow her through a set of double doors and my eyes almost bug out of my head when the room behind emerges.

"Oh wow," I breathe, taking in the glistening blue pool, the waterfall and the bubbling jacuzzis. But best of all, it's empty, and aside from the water, it's blissfully silent.

Ripping my eyes from the piece of heaven in front of me, I look at Calli.

"You booked this entire place for us, didn't you?"

She shrugs as if it's nothing. "Come on, I want a dip."

"You know where everything is. I'll ensure drinks and snacks are ready and let the therapists know you've arrived."

Calli thanks the perfectly-styled woman who showed us in, and she disappears back through the door.

"Calli, this is insane."

"I never said everything about my life sucked," she deadpans. "Having one of the most dangerous men in the city as your father allows you certain privileges."

"Not to mention the money that comes with it."

"Mom owns this place. A whole chain of them, actually. Pretty sure it's just a way for Dad to launder his dirty money, but whatever. It works for me."

I want to be shocked by her words, but the truth is, while I might have been surprised at her revelation of this whole mafia situation, I'm not naïve enough not to know the kinds of things they might be up to in order to fund their extravagant lifestyle.

It certainly helps to explain the kinds of houses we've always lived in.

My stomach sinks as I consider all the things my dad could actually do for a living. Has my life not only been a lie but totally illegal too?

Calli's hand slips into mine, pulling me from my thoughts.

"Come on, pure relaxation awaits."

She drags me toward the locker rooms where we find two swimsuits waiting for us in exactly the right sizes.

"How'd you—"

"I have my ways." She winks, pulling her suit from the hanger and making quick work of stripping out of her clothes.

I hesitate for a beat, knowing exactly what this tiny suit is going to expose on my thigh that I didn't confess to earlier.

"What's wrong?"

"Um... There's something else I need to tell you about what happened last night."

"R-right?" she says, lifting a brow.

Undoing my pants, I pull them off before twisting my leg to show her.

"Oh my fucking God, Stella," she squeals. "Y-you let him brand you?"

"I don't remember letting him, as such."

"Well, it seems you didn't stop him."

My lips part to argue, but I soon find I have no words. She's right. I did absolutely nothing to even try to stop him.

Calli lets out a sigh. "You're in trouble with him, Stella. He's not going to stop until he gets what he wants."

"Yeah, whatever that is."

We both change in silence, Calli's concerned eyes finding mine more than once before we head back out where we find fresh orange juice and an insane array of fruit waiting for us.

"I'm guessing there's no fizz in these bucks?" I mutter, tipping the glass to my lips.

Calli shoots a look at me with her brow quirked. "You really want more alcohol after last night?"

I shrug. "Something's gotta help me forget."

"And this morning?"

I groan. "You don't need to remind me."

"Have you heard from Toby?"

"Nope. Nothing. Pretty sure he hates me."

"Nah, it'll be Seb he hates. He won't blame you for this."

My cheeks heat as I remember exactly what he witnessed.

Yeah, there's no way he doesn't hate me.

CHAPTER TWENTY-THREE

Sebastian

Theo jumps up from the couch the second he looks at the screen of his ringing phone and disappears out of the doors that lead to the garden.

"Something tells me we're about to get summoned," Alex mutters, scrubbing his hand down his face and over the beard he seems to be trying to grow.

"Get dressed, fuckers," I bark, pushing from the sofa and taking all the dirty mugs to the kitchen. Hell knows Nico won't do it.

"Suit up. We gotta go," Theo booms, confirming my suspicions about who was on the phone.

"For real?" Alex moans.

"For real. Nico, you're good. You can stay and rest your tiny, overused cock."

I chuckle as Nico fumbles for a comeback.

"You're just jealous, bro. No one so much as touched your cock last night," Nico mutters, a smirk playing on his lips.

"I dunno, Stell—"

"Finish that sentence and you won't make it to whatever this job is," I warn Theo, much to Alex's amusement.

"Bro, you are so fucking gone for the princess," Alex announces.

Before he knows what's happening, Alex's back slams against the wall as my forearm presses against his throat.

He barely reacts, just stares at me with knowing eyes.

"I am not fucking *gone* for her. I can barely stand looking at her."

"Sure. Sorry," he says, completely insincerely.

My teeth grind as I stare at him, my free hand clenching into a fist, ready to wipe the smirk off his lips that I know is coming.

"Children, we've got a fucking job to do," Theo barks, slapping me upside the head as he marches past the pair of us.

"I'm going to fucking hurt you," I warn Alex. He just rolls his eyes and mutters, "I'd like to see you try, fucker."

Leaving Nico behind where he's still lying on the sofa with his hand in his joggers, we head toward our cars.

An hour later and we're sitting outside, waiting for Alex to get his ass out of his house, dressed and ready to work.

"You gonna tell me what we're doing yet?" I ask Theo, who's still white-knuckling the steering wheel despite the fact that we're sitting still.

I know his issue. It's the same every time the boss calls and demands something of him. Theo wants to impress, wants to prove that he's got what it takes to fill his father's shoes one day. And most of all, he wants to prove to Nico that, despite being younger, he's still above him and deserves his place there.

He lets out a frustrated sigh that Alex still isn't ready.

"Marco didn't pay."

"Shit. I thought we'd delivered a pretty solid message on Monday night."

"Yeah, apparently not. Dad's pissed." He doesn't need to say more. I already understand why.

Marco's diner is right on the edge of our territory. All of the Cirillo businesses on that side of town are constantly at risk with the Mariano Family running things just over the street.

If Marco isn't paying, then it could mean...

I shake my head, not wanting to consider the possibility.

Things have been good between the Cirillos and the Marianos for years. Almost all our lives. None of us really remember a time when they were fighting for dominance over this side of the city, but the losses from back then can still be felt. We lost good soldiers. Family members. Friends.

The last thing we need is the Marianos getting fed up with the small patch they ended up with and beginning to push back once more.

We knew there was a chance after their boss stood down a couple of years ago, handing power to his eldest son.

"It'll be fine. He's probably just going through a rough patch or something."

"You willing to put your life on the line for that?" Theo asks, his voice tense, his patience on the verge of running out. "Thank fuck," he mutters when the front door to Alex and Daemon's house opens.

"Why the fuck isn't Daemon doing this shit?" I murmur my thoughts out loud.

"Fuck knows. Boss said he wanted us. He didn't say the words, but you know it's some initiation bullshit."

I groan, briefly remembering the other shit we've been forced into to prove our worth, our dedication to the Family.

"Great. Couldn't have done it on a day when we're not all hanging out of our arses, no?"

"Exactly why he's done it, man."

"Who the fuck is that?" I ask, ignoring Theo when a woman emerges from the house instead of Alex. Although the more I study her, the more she seems familiar.

"Fuck this, I'm going to get him." Theo's got his hand on the door and is about to push it open when Alex finally emerges, shooting the woman a death glare as he jogs past her.

He's dressed the same as us, head to toe in black, and looking lethal with the anger swirling in his eyes. Exactly what the boss expects of us.

"What the fuck, bro?" Theo barks, not bothering to wait for Alex to even shut the door before he starts backing up.

"My father's latest fucktoy."

"She's hot," I add, taking in the woman who's now standing at a beat-up old car.

"She's our fucking housekeeper."

"Your dad's fucking the help?" Theo asks, dragging his head from our impending task.

"Apparently so. She's from the fucking Lovell Estate."

"Not his usual type," I murmur.

"He's gonna need to think again if he's planning on making this one my latest stepmother."

"Can we focus on the fucking job?" Theo grunts, his irritation levels at an all-time high.

"Tell me what it is and maybe I could," Alex says, poking his head between the seats and glaring at Theo.

"Marco. He didn't pay," Theo repeats. "We need to find out why."

Alex cracks his knuckles. "Fine by me. Let's go grill this motherfucker."

The drive to the edge of our territory takes forever thanks to the late afternoon traffic, but the second we pull up out the front of Marco's diner, we drag our game faces on and get to work.

"We don't leave here without answers."

"You got it," I say, pushing the door open.

"Let's go."

We might not be made yet, but the second we step into Marco's in our black suits and scan the space, a ripple of fear races through the air.

One of the waiters looks at us and rushes out the back, all the blood drained from his face.

"Looks like he's here," Theo mutters. "Let's go find him."

Eyes follow our every movement as we slip uninvited behind the counter and push through to the kitchen.

Knives clatter at our sudden arrival, and the previous chatter immediately stops.

One girl looks over her shoulder, down a long corridor, and Theo takes off in that direction.

Pushing open each door we pass, he looks inside before we come to the final door.

Reaching under my jacket, I wrap my fingers around my gun, and he rushes through the door, no fucking care in the world.

"Fuck's sake," he mutters, heading for the stairs.

Of course the pussy has fled to his flat. Does he really think he can hide from us?

The second we storm into his living room, we find him standing in the centre. He's as white as a sheet, his body trembling with fear. The bruises we left him with from our little warning Monday night have barely faded, yet here we are again.

"We didn't think we'd have to come back here, Marco." Theo's voice is low, deadly. Alex and I flank his side, ready to go to war with him should we have to.

"I-I'm sorry. I-I—"

"Where's the boss's money, Marco?"

Theo takes a step forward and we follow until there's a creak behind us and a pained grunt from Alex.

Lifting my gun, I have the safety down and my finger on the trigger the second I recognise the three men standing over Alex as Marianos.

"Motherfucker," Theo growls when he looks back and finds one of the Marianos with his gun trained on me. "You're a fucking stupid motherfucker, Marco."

His terrified whimper fills the room, but I don't look over to see what he's doing. My eyes are fixed on the guy with his gun pointed in my direction.

"Marco's, and this entire street, belongs to the Marianos now," one of them states.

"You're starting a fucking war, you know that, right?"

"Following orders, man. You know how it is," the other Mariano says as Alex gets to his feet.

"Yeah, we fucking do."

Before I know what's happening, Alex launches himself at the armed guy, knocking his gun from his hand, although not before he fires.

I wait for the pain, but when it never comes, I jump into the fight, swiping my gun across the face of the guy who comes at me while the third goes for Theo.

All three of them are older than us, but that means fuck all. We've been trained for this kind of shit since we first learned to walk and make a fist.

Managing to get the upper hand, I get the guy to the floor, pummelling his face with my fists until he finally passes out. I stop the second his body goes limp, killing any of these motherfuckers will only be pouring fuel on this situation.

They're clearly making a move, trying to prove a point.

I'd rather we didn't send a fucking massive one of our own by putting these three into body bags before we've been instructed to.

My chest heaves and my face aches like a motherfucker where he managed to get a hit in as I climb to my feet, shaking my fists out.

"Seb," Theo booms, dragging my attention to where he's grappling with one guy while the other has Alex pinned beneath him, his hand wrapped around Alex's throat hard enough to make his face turn purple.

"Shit," I hiss, but before I manage to get over, a small red laser dot appears on the guy's temple.

I glance out the window and narrow my eyes but see nothing.

I can only hope he's found his target and it's not a fucking Mariano trying to take us the fuck out.

I don't get another second to consider the possibility of that sniper not being on our side before he takes his shot.

The warmth of the guy's blood sprays me, covering my face and body as he falls limp on top of Alex.

With one final hit to the guy Theo is fighting with, he drops to the floor like a sack of shit.

"Bro, you okay?" I ask, pushing the dead body from Alex and helping him up as he heaves in deep breaths.

"Yeah, man. I'm good. What the fuck just happened?"

The door behind us opens as we stand in the middle of the carnage and a smug as fuck Daemon comes strolling in with a fucking rifle in his hand, as if he hadn't just killed a man and saved his twin's life.

"That was the beginning of war," Daemon says as casually as if he's talking about the fucking weather.

"And we were put in the middle of it because..."

"A test."

"Great," Theo mutters, clearly pissed off that Daemon was in on it when he should be one of us.

A noise comes from the corner of the room, and we all turn to find Marco hunched in the corner. I'm not sure if it's him or the dead body lying on the floor, but it smells suspiciously like someone's pissed themselves. From the look on Marco's face, I'd be tempted to say it's him.

"Alex and I will take him in. I've already got men on the way to take those idiots. You two clean this fucking mess up and meet us back at the hotel."

Before either of us has a chance to argue, Daemon has Marco off the floor and is frog marching him out of the flat.

"Later then," Alex says, shooting a salute to Theo.

"Is he for fucking real?" Theo barks the second their footsteps have disappeared.

"Daemon's a fucking psychopath. The boss might let him in on this kinda shit, but he'll never take control."

Theo's teeth grind in frustration before he pulls his phone from his pocket and sets about calling in the clean-up team. He doesn't bother updating the boss—he knows full well that Daemon and Alex will do that for him.

"Go find a bathroom and clean your fucking face," he mutters, reaching down to pick up the couple of guns littered on the floor. "You're covered in Italian blood."

Thankfully, backup arrives before either of the Italians wake up, and it's just over an hour later when we finally make our way out of the diner. Only this time, we go via the back door.

If we wanted this place shut down, we could do it in a heartbeat, but Marco's diner is a good earner, thanks to the extra kitchen in the basement—hence why the fucking Marianos want it.

"This was not how I was expecting my day to go," I mutter as we make our way back to Theo's car.

"What, finger banging the princess in front of us all and then ending up in a fight with the Italians? Thought that would be what you spent the night dreaming of."

"Well, when you put it like that."

We fall silent as Theo pulls away from the pavement and joins the queue of traffic.

He's still white knuckling the wheel, or at least he would be if his skin wasn't completely busted up and covered in blood.

"You okay, man?" I ask, wondering where his head is at.

"Yeah, I'm good. A fucking heads up would have been nice, though. We were fucking bait."

"Yeah, we did the job though."

"Alex could have died."

"We all could have died, T."

"I guess," he mutters, pulling into the left-hand lane, ready to head back to our side of town.

We only make it a few streets when someone up ahead catches my eye.

"Pull over," I demand.

"What?" Theo startles, clearly lost in his own head.

"Pull the fucking car over."

"Why? What have you—" He follows my line of sight, his words faltering as he sees what—or whom—I see. "Seb," he growls, not happy about our pit stop.

"Fucking pull over."

"Fine," he sighs, cutting someone off and screeching to a halt on the side of the road right behind Calli's Mercedes.

CHAPTER TWENTY-FOUR

Stella

"That place is like heaven on Earth," I sigh as we make our way out of the building. "And your hair looks amazing."

"My mum is gonna kill me," she laughs, not giving two shits about it by the sound of it.

Gone are Calli's long, golden locks in favor of a shoulder-length, chocolate bob. It looks amazing, and the colour totally suits her.

"Meh, it's your hair."

"Exactly." She beams at me, confidence shining in her hazel eyes.

I try to fight a yawn as the bright afternoon sun hits me.

"Let's get you home. You look like you could sleep for a week."

"I feel it."

"You remember anything about last night yet?"

"Nope. Nothing. Either they're gonna have to tell me or it's forever going to be a dark hole of nothingness."

"It can't have been that bad," Calli says, trying to reassure me.

"You heard me explain what happened this morning, right?"

"Yeah, I'm still horrified. Toby?" she asks, concern pulling at her brows.

Shoving my hand into my purse, I rummage around until I find my cell and pull it out.

My heart sinks when I find nothing from him.

"Nope. I'll message him when I get home."

"Try calling him. Toby isn't like the others, he'd probably appreciate it."

Embarrassment floods me as I even consider what I'm meant to say to him after what he witnessed this morning.

"I'll see."

Calli takes off around the other side of the car and I open the door, ready to get inside. But right before I take my foot off the ground to climb in, I'm pulled backwards and slammed up against the side of her car.

I reach out, ready to react, to attempt to fight off whoever it is, but his hand collars my throat and familiarity washes through me.

"Seb, what are you—holy fuck," I gasp when I focus on his face, finding blood splattered over his skin.

He's tried to wash it off, that much is obvious, but he's done a really shitty job.

"What the hell have you done?" I breathe, my heart in my throat as my eyes scan over his face.

A smirk curls at his lips, and it only serves to make him look even more dangerous.

"You were a beautiful little whore this morning, Hellion." Lifting his other hand, he runs his fingertip over my lips. "I can still remember how this wicked mouth felt wrapped around my cock."

I suck in a breath, hating that his dirty words affect me.

"Seb, get your hands off her," Calli calls from the car. "Your big bad scary act isn't working."

His eyes hold mine for a beat before they drop to my heaving chest.

I fight to keep my breathing steady, but it's pointless. There's no way he can't feel my pulse thundering against his fingers.

"Are you sure about that?" he asks, his eyes crawling back up to meet mine.

"Seb, come on, bro. Boss is waiting."

"Yes, Sebastian. Time to run along like a good little soldier."

His jaw tics as he stares at me.

"Seb," Theo barks, his voice low and terrifying.

His lips twitch and he leans forward until our noses are almost brushing.

"I'll see you real soon, Hellion." It's said as a promise, but I hear the underlying threat in his voice.

"Great. I can hardly wait," I hiss, sucking in a deep breath when he removes his hand from me.

I stand there watching him as he marches back toward Theo's Maserati, each of his strides more powerful than the last. The black suit oozes wealth and importance. I want to say it's a turn off, but honestly, I'd be lying.

I don't move until he's back in the car and Theo wheelspins off down the street.

Falling into Calli's passenger seat, I tip my head back and close my eyes.

"Wow," Calli breathes. "I'm pretty sure you two haven't got whatever that is out of your systems yet. That was intense."

"Can you just take me home, please? I'm sorry, but I just need... I need to be alone."

"Of course."

The car rumbles to life beneath me and Calli pulls out.

I have no idea how long I stay there unmoving, but eventually I cave to one of the questions spinning around my head.

"Do they often turn up covered in blood?"

Calli hesitates for a second, and it's long enough for me to drag my head forward and look at her.

"It's not that common, no."

"But it happens?"

"Yeah."

"Whose was it?"

She shrugs. "I like to assume it's always someone who deserved it. It's too much of a head fuck otherwise."

"I can't believe they kill people."

"They might not."

I raise a brow at her. "You really like to focus on the positives, huh?"

"What else is there? I'd rather they just treat me like an equal and let me know what it is they do, but no, I'm just the stupid little girl who can't be trusted with the big bad mafia secrets."

"They don't think that, Cal," I assure her.

"Really?"

"No, they're just..." I let out a breath, because as

much as I'm trying to reassure her, I know she's not going to want to hear my next words. "Trying to protect you."

"Well, I don't fucking need it. I'm a big girl who can look after herself."

"I know that. But men are idiots."

"A-fucking-men, sista," she jokes, lifting her hand up for a high five.

"Have you shot a gun before?" I ask.

"No," she sulks. "They won't let me. We've even got a freaking shooting range at the back of our house."

"I'm going to teach you."

"You can shoot?"

"Yeah. I've been shooting for as long as I've been able to lift a gun."

She huffs out a frustrated breath. "Why can't my dad be more like yours?"

"He's lied to me my whole life, Cal. I'm not sure that him teaching me to shoot makes all that much difference."

"Maybe not. But at least you can defend yourself. They've left me to be a damsel in distress if anything happens."

"We'll fix it. I'll get Calvin to train you, and I'll teach you to shoot."

"Do you think he would?"

I smile, thinking of the big teddy bear of a man we have as our head of security. "For me, I think he'd do pretty much anything."

She nods, and when a song comes on the radio that she loves, she turns it up and we fall into a comfortable silence. As much as I appreciate it, being left with my thoughts is dangerous. Really freaking dangerous.

"My car," I squeal when Calli pulls into my driveway and I find my gorgeous matte black Porsche waiting for me and the red monstrosity nowhere to be seen.

Calli pulls her car to a stop beside it, and I turn to her.

"Thank you for everything."

She opens her mouth to say something, but I beat her to it.

"You've answered so many of my questions. Given me so much more than anyone else since I arrived here. And you've made me feel like I might actually have a home here."

She reaches over and squeezes my hand.

"Of course you do. Fuck those arseholes. I want you here. Now go and get some sleep, try to speak to Toby and maybe call me later, yeah?"

"I will. Thank you."

"Anytime."

I climb from her car and grab my bags from the trunk before waving her off and walking over to my Porsche.

I run my fingers over the sleek lines and smile to myself—until I get to the windshield and find a white envelope tucked under the wiper.

My stomach somersaults as I remember the first little 'gift' I found the other day.

Opening the flap, I pull out the card. This time there's no image. I take that as a good sign. I'm not sure I could stomach the knowledge that Seb's been spying on me again. I've kept my curtains closed since I found that first photograph, but something tells me that won't put him off.

Turning the card over, I find red writing scrawled across the back.

Someone's been a very naughty girl...

"What the fuck?" I mutter to myself. "Stop being suck a fucking creep," I shout, assuming that he's probably watching me right now and Theo's words about going to the boss were bullshit. "It's weird."

Not hearing or seeing anything to confirm my suspicion about him watching me, I lift my bag up higher on my shoulder and head for the house.

Silence greets me, and I sigh in relief. As much as I might want answers, I want them from my father, not our staff.

I grab myself a bottle of water and a bag of chips from the kitchen before forcing my exhausted legs to drag me up the stairs.

The spa might have been relaxing, but all I want to do now is curl up in bed and sleep for the rest of the weekend.

I'm so up in my own head when I get to my bedroom door, I don't even notice that it's ajar as I push it open—but I sure as fuck realize something is wrong when I step inside.

"Holy shit," I breathe, my eyes scanning all the new additions to my room. My heart is in my throat as my trembling hand reaches behind me blindly to close my door.

Photographs line my walls, all taped there and fluttering in the breeze coming from my open window.

Rushing over, I close it and drag the curtains closed. That motherfucker isn't getting any more of a reaction out of me over this.

I stand there in the middle of all of my mistakes. The answers to the questions I've been asking myself, plainly laid out in front of me.

As I stare at each one, memories flicker through my mind.

Kissing Daemon. Dancing with him and Alex.

Disappearing into the bathroom with Seb. Thank fuck there's none from what happened inside that room, but as my eyes keep moving to the next image, my stomach turns.

Theo with his tongue deep in my mouth, his hands firmly on my ass as we moved together.

Then I was with Nico and another girl, one I vaguely recognise from this morning, only in this image she was wrapped in a barely-there purple dress.

There are images of me with Toby, but he's the only one I'm not completely molesting.

No wonder he was pissed, seeing as I was all over his friends.

"Oh God," I sob when I get to some of the final images to find that it was him who carried me out of the bathroom, stripped me out of my dress and helped me into Theo's shirt—after he helpfully dragged it off his body for me.

I'm not sure if the photographer was meant to capture it, but he's at the perfect angle to be able to see everything in Toby's eyes. His softness, how much he cares, his frustration, his anger. The only thing I don't see that I should is his judgement and disappointment in me.

I'm a limp, drunken mess in his arms. He's watched me with all his friends and he's still the one trying to hold me up.

I sink to my knees in the middle of my bed and crumble.

I'm a mess, and my need to punish Seb for his cruel words and vicious touches is hurting the wrong person.

Toby—Calli and Emmie aside—is the only one who's tried to help me since I started at Knight's Ridge.

And look.

I risk a glance up and find his wrecked expression as he stares down at me flat out on the bed. Theo's shirt might be long enough to cover me, but it's ruched up and with the way I've fallen, Seb's brand burning bright on my inner thigh.

"Oh God."

I fall on my side onto my bed and let out a loud sob.

But my pity party only lasts for a couple of minutes, because I manage to find some strength from somewhere deep inside me, and with my cheeks soaked with my tears of regret, I begin stripping all the images from the walls and ripping them to shreds.

It's not until I get around to the last one, my chest heaving with emotion and exertion, when my eyes land on my mirror.

Whore.

"I'm going to fucking kill you," I seethe, stomping to my bathroom for a washcloth, only to be confronted by another message.

You never should have come here.

I clean it off the best I can, leaving red smears around the edge of the glass before going back to my bedroom to do the same with the other.

I'm emotionally and physically exhausted by the time I'm done and have stuffed all the scraps of paper into a bag, vowing to have a private bonfire later to watch everything about last night go up in flames.

It's just a shame I can't watch Seb go with them.

Stripping out of my clothes, I walk naked into my bathroom and turn the shower on. I might have only had one before leaving the spa, but I feel dirty all over again. My skin prickles with their touch and my lips tingle from their kisses. Not to mention my stomach clenches with regret.

There is something I do know about all of this, though. Given the chance, I'd probably do it all over again.

Despite hurting Toby, I wanted to get to Seb. I wanted to hurt him, to prove a point, and from the effort and time it must have taken to break in here and decorate my room with my misdemeanours from last night, it's clear that I've got myself well and truly under his skin.

My cell pings in my purse, and my need to know if it's him makes me pause with one foot in the shower.

The second I see his name illuminated on my screen, my stomach turns, and I have to fight the need to vomit.

He knows I've seen it all, and he clearly just wants to gloat about his little prank. Asshole.

I'm not entirely sure what I'm expecting when I open the message, but my eyes widen in shock when I find a photograph of a red pair of panties resting on what's obviously his chest. His shirtless chest.

As I'm staring at him with my brows pinched in confusion, another comes through. This time, it's of the bottom half of his face—not enough for anyone else to know it's him, but I do. Namely because he's holding the pair of panties he ripped off me last night to his nose.

I let out a curse when the sight of him doing

something so disgusting... so erotic, sends a wave of heat between my legs.

The third and final image doesn't include him, but it has the very first pair of panties he stole from me hanging over the barrel of his gun.

Then I get a message.

Asshole: I wonder what colour I'll collect next?

My brow furrows as I think about that red pair of panties. He's only ripped two from my body. He—

Realization dawns on me and I twist around, my eyes landing on my top drawer that's slightly ajar.

Pulling it open, I find one more note.

Mine.

I force myself to put my cell down in the bathroom and walk into the shower to cool off for a few minutes before I fire back something I'm going to regret.

I need to think about my next move, not just act out in anger and hatred. Both of those things make me hot-headed and way too irrational. Last night is evidence enough of that.

It's not until I step out of the shower and reach for a towel to wrap around me that inspiration strikes.

Okay, yeah, I will probably regret it later. But it seems like a really good idea right now. Even if I am summoning the devil himself.

CHAPTER TWENTY-FIVE

Sebastian

I sit back on my bed at Theo's, fresh from my shower with a towel around my waist and my hair dripping onto my chest as I lift a can to my lips for a drink and raise my phone.

I almost choke on my Coke when I see that she's actually replied. I wasn't expecting to hear anything in response to my pictures—well, not until Monday morning when she castrates me, anyway. I'm weirdly looking forward to it.

I take another sip as the image loads thanks to Theo's shitty WiFi, but the second it does I spit Coke all over my phone and hand.

"Holy fucking shit."

I move my phone closer, ignoring the liquid dripping from the bottom of it as I stare at the image.

In true Stella fashion, she once again shocks the hell out of me.

"Jesus, baby," I mutter, placing my can down and running my eyes over every inch of her.

She's sitting naked on the closed toilet in her bathroom, her legs spread, showing me everything I've been obsessing about since that first night in the graveyard. Her hand is covering my brand on her thigh, she's got her head to the side with a 'fuck you' tilt to her chin, and she's got her phone in her hand taking the photo.

On the mirror is a message in reply to the one I left for her.

In the same red lipstick I left on the basin.

I belong to no one.
Cunt.

She's even drawn a little heart, which makes me smile. She might think she's a total bad-arse, but she's also such a girl at heart. The mixture of the two threatens to bring me to my knees—not that I'll ever admit that to anyone but myself.

Dragging the towel from beneath me, I finally wipe the sticky mess off my hand and phone before setting about my reply.

She started this little game, and I'm more than happy to continue it.

Wrapping my fingers around my hard length, thanks to her dirty message, I snap a picture and tap out a reply.

Seb: Don't tempt me, Hellion. I know exactly where you are and how to get to you.

I add a little devil emoji, because why not, before scrolling back up to that image and getting myself comfortable as I wait for a reply.

It only takes her thirty seconds max.

Hellion: Feel free. I've got my gun and your knife ready. Imagine that, being killed by your own blade. How embarrassing.

Seb: I'm willing to risk it for another taste of what's mine.

I can almost hear her groan of frustration down the other end. Predicting that she's not going to reply again, I focus on the image of her body as I let my imagination run away with itself about what actually might happen if I were to let myself into her bedroom right now.

It's tempting, really fucking tempting. But after the day I've had, all I really wanna do is pass out. Especially after I come with her name almost a plea on my lips.

I wake to my phone vibrating somewhere in my bed.

Groaning, I move around, running my hand over the mattress until I locate it, and at the very last minute, I crack my eye open to see who it is.

I tried not to hope that it might be her calling for an early morning phone sex session after the images we exchanged last night, but still, my heart sinks a little, and so does my excitement, when I find my sister instead.

"Killjoy," I mutter as I swipe the screen and put my phone to my ear.

"Forgetting something, bro?"

"Uh..." I hesitate, trying to get my brain to focus on anything other than Stella and her sexy arse curves. "I-I don't—"

"It's Sunday lunchtime, Sebastian," she growls, disappointment dripping from her words. "You said you'd be here."

I sit up, pull my phone from my ear and stare at the screen to look at the time.

"Fuck. Fuck. I'm sorry. I'm coming now."

"If I burn all this shit then it's your fault."

"Zoe's there, right? I'm sure you can figure it out between you two. I'm only the baby, remember?" I say with a laugh, knowing how often they like to play that card on me.

"Yeah, yeah, just don't complain when the Yorkshire puddings aren't to your standards, master."

"You're funny. See you soon."

Dragging on some clothes, I run some wax through my hair and race from the house. Theo is nowhere to be seen, but the trail of both his and a female's clothes that seems to disappear into his bedroom clues me into the fact that he's actually here.

How fucking hard did I sleep last night?

I guess that's what happens when you spend the entire previous night watching to make sure a certain drunken princess didn't choke on her own puke. That and the fact that you wanted to make sure no one else fucking touched her.

I'm pulling up at my house in only minutes to find both Sophia and Zoe's cars parked out the front.

Excitement bubbles in my belly, my gorgeous niece is going to be inside waiting for me.

Pushing through the door, I make a beeline for the kitchen. I'll deal with whatever state Mum is in later—I've got another woman in my sights right now, and she's way less of a handful.

"Ah, look what the cat dragged in," Zoe mutters from her place at the stove.

"Where's my girl?" I ask, barely sparing her a glance as I scan the array of toys scattered around the kitchen. "Phoebe!" I say excitedly when I find her and take a step toward her.

"No," Sophia shouts from somewhere. "Wait for her to come to you."

"Uh, okay."

Phoebe's huge dark eyes hold mine as a gurgle of excitement bubbles up her throat. I remember Sophia telling me on the phone the other day that she was almost walking. Has she done it and they haven't told me?

"Come on then, Phoebe," I say encouragingly, dropping to my haunches and holding my hands out for her.

She gets herself onto her hands and feet as if she's about to do some weird kind of crawl over to me, but then she reaches for the cupboard door and pulls herself up.

"That's it, baby girl. Come to Uncle Seb. Come on."

She takes one step, her face hard with concentration, before she lets go of the cupboard and takes another.

"Oh my God, she can do it," I breathe, watching in amazement as she takes one wobbly step after another. My sister rushes out from the pantry and steps behind her just in case she stacks it on the marble floor, but she doesn't need the support. She absolutely fucking kills it.

Tucking my hands under her arms when she gets to me, I sweep her off her feet and spin her around, making her squeal and laugh.

The sight of her happiness and the sound of her joy settles something inside me that I didn't realise was quite so messed up.

"You're so clever, Phoebe. I'm so proud of you." Pulling her into my body, I hold her tight and breathe in her incredible baby scent.

"You seem to have cheered up," Sophia says, walking over and dropping a kiss to my cheek.

"You woke me up."

"It was quarter to twelve, Seb."

"Yesterday was... Yeah. I needed it."

Sophia's brow wrinkles. "Is everything okay? Jason said something happened." Concern for both me and her husband is obvious on her face.

"Yeah, everything's good. Nothing to worry about."

I smile at her before returning my attention to Phoebe, but I know she doesn't buy a word of it.

"So have Mummy and Aunt Zoe managed to decimate dinner yet?" I ask her.

"Shut up. We're more than capable," Zoe mutters.

"He's got a point," Sophia adds. She might now be a housewife and mother, but I would never use the word domesticated to describe my sister in any way. Thankfully, she's a kick-arse mother to Phoebe, so it totally makes up for her lack of culinary skills.

As kids, we pretty much lived on takeout until we all discovered that I could cook without almost burning the house down. It was a relief to have something other than pizza, burgers, and fried chicken.

"Shall we show them how it's done?" I ask my niece,

walking over to the fridge to pull out the eggs and milk for my Yorkshire puddings. They might have done the rest, but I'm not letting them anywhere near those.

"Where's Mum?" I finally ask as I beat my batter with Phoebe attached to my hip.

"Getting showered and dressed," Sophia announces, much to my surprise.

"Oh?"

"She was already awake when we got here."

"Huh." I don't want to say anything positive, something like it's a good sign, because past experience tells me that it's not. She'll have days, weeks, sometimes even months where we all start to believe that life could return to some kind of normal, but then it all crashes down around our feet.

Only three minutes later, the woman herself appears. I actually have to give her a double take because she looks almost alive.

"Hey, Mum," I say.

"My boy. How are the Yorkies coming?"

"Perfect as ever, I hope."

She takes a seat at the table after getting herself a glass of water, and we all stand a little awkwardly, waiting for the other shoe to drop.

Our bi-weekly Sunday lunches are always a surprise. We can have something akin to a normal family meal like we could be heading toward today, or it could be a complete disaster. I'm grateful that today could be along the normal lines, because I'm not sure I've got it in me for any more drama. I've just about had my fill these last few days.

As the seconds draw out, we find ourselves falling into an everyday conversation about our lives as I lower

Phoebe to the floor and sit with her, playing with her toys.

"So, are we going to talk about the mess some poor girl's made of your neck, or what?" Zoe asks, her voice full of teasing and mischief.

"Nope. I already said yesterday was interesting."

"Work-wise, yeah. That doesn't look much like work to me," Sophia joins in.

"You haven't met her," I mutter, mostly to myself, but they both hear it.

"Well, we can't wait to."

"Un-fucking-likely."

Sophia drops the spatula and glares at me.

"How many times? No F's in front of the baby."

I roll my eyes at her. "She's hardly gonna repeat me."

"One day she will. I'm already convinced it's going to be her first word."

"She's gonna be a bad-arse. Of course it will."

My words conjure up an image of another bad-arse princess that I really don't need in my head. My phone burns a hole in my pocket as I think about that image once more.

Damn, she really missed the mark with that message.

I—hopefully—subtly tug at my jeans, hoping that my reaction to talking about Stella isn't obvious to every other adult in the room.

"Did she try to kill you, too?" Mum says, being weirdly observant. "Looks like someone's had a knife to your throat as well as their teeth."

"Yeah, actually. She did. Excuse me," I say, jumping from the floor and leaving the kitchen as the sounds of their teasing voices follow me all the way to the bathroom.

I stand in front of the basin and groan when I take in

the state of my neck. No wonder they couldn't leave it alone.

When I got back yesterday, I showered to get the rest of that cunt's blood off me, but I didn't pay much attention to my appearance aside from that. And I was in too much of a rush this morning. Clearly a fucking mistake, because her bright red hickies and teeth marks mar my skin.

I run my fingertips over the angriest mark and my mouth waters to storm over there and give her a matching one—assuming she doesn't already look like she's been attacked by a starved bear, which is possible after the way I took her in Nico's bathroom.

I have no idea how long I spend in the bathroom attempting to get my head together, but when I get back, I get curious looks from all three of them.

"You good now, or do you need a little more private time?" Zoe deadpans.

Sophia smothers a laugh.

"What? I wasn't in there banging one out, if that's what you think."

"Oh my God," Mum whines. "My sweet baby boy."

"Sweet, my arse," Zoe mutters. "No sweet boy ends up like that after a night with a girl."

"Can we please stop? None of you need a play by play about this." Or how I carved up her skin to ensure no one else gets to her.

"Sure. The buzzer just went off on your Yorkshires. You might wanna check them out."

"Great. Let's just focus on the food."

"Oh, we can talk all day about what you've been eating."

I grab the tea towel, and Zoe screams like a little bitch when I whip her with it.

"Because you're so innocent, Zo. I happen to remember very vividly walking in on you with your li—" Her hand clamps down on my mouth, cutting off my words.

"Fine," she hisses. "We'll leave your sex life alone."

"Dear God, will you two please stop?" Sophia begs.

We have a nice afternoon together. Too nice.

Okay, so Mum insists on getting the brandy out after we've all eaten, and by the time we leave, she's already three sheets to the wind, but drunk is a hell of a lot better than some of the states I've found her in over the years, so I leave almost confident that we're not going to find her dead in her own puke in the morning.

When I get back to Theo's place, his cars are parked in the garage but he's not upstairs. Glancing out of the living room window, I discover why when I find him sitting around with his own family as they pretend to be normal.

We all know the truth. All of us are far from fucking normal.

As Damien and Evan Cirillo sit there eating their roast dinner, they're silently plotting the deaths of every member of the Mariano Family. Theo and Nico are probably scowling at each other over the table, their constant battle never more obvious than when they're forced together in family situations like that. Both of their mothers faff around, making sure everyone has everything they need with forced smiles on their faces, despite the fact their housekeeper has already done everything to ensure everyone is happy.

It's fake. All of it. And exactly what I do not want.

The weak Stepford wife, the pretentious family events.

Bullshit. All of it.

I'll take Zoe grilling me about my questionable choices any day over that.

Grabbing a beer from the fridge, I take myself to my bedroom and grab my school bag with all good intentions of getting everything done for the week. With an impending war, there's a very good chance that school is about to take a back seat.

Putting my AirPods in, I attempt to block out the world.

It works for a good few hours until my music cuts out and my phone rings.

"Oh great," I mutter, knowing I'm about to get a grilling.

"Tobes, how's it going?" I sing lightly.

His growl of irritation rumbles down the line.

"What the fuck are you playing at, Seb? You've crossed a fucking line."

Pushing my laptop aside, I rest back on my pillows.

"It's taken you this long to call me and say that? You're losing your touch."

"I-I..."

"Spit it out. Or grow a pair of balls and come and beat the shit out of me, if you think you're man enough."

"Can you grow up for just a fucking second? Stella has done fuck all to you, Seb. She doesn't deserve this kind of bullshit."

"You don't even know her," I hiss.

"And you do? Just because you touched her, it doesn't mean you know her."

"You don't even know who she is, Toby. All you see is her pretty face and a sweet pair of tits and you're smitten. Pull your head out of your arse for a few minutes and maybe search for some facts."

"What the fuck do you think I'm doing?" he booms. "Who is she, Seb? Why do you hate her so much that you'd humiliate her like that?"

A smile pulls at my lips as I cast my mind back to the event he's talking about.

"I might hate her, Tobes. But she fucking loved that. You should have felt how wet she was with all our eyes on her."

"You're a fucking cunt."

"Tell me something I don't know. Now if you didn't have anything more interesting to say, can I go? I've got better things to be doing than listening to you trying to rip me a new one when you don't know all the facts."

"Stay the fuck away from her, Seb. I mean it."

"Yeah, yeah. You know, now you say that, I might go and pay her a surprise visit. I'm sure she'll be thrilled to find me in her room in the middle of the night."

"Don't even think about it," he seethes.

"Too late, motherfucker."

I hang up, the idea already firmly planted and growing roots.

CHAPTER TWENTY-SIX

Stella

"Argh," I scream, throwing my cell across the room. It hits the curtains and drops with a thud to the floor.

Toby is ignoring me, and it's annoying the shit out of me.

I should let it go, but the look on his face in that one image won't leave my head.

He looked utterly devastated by my actions, by the state I'd got myself into. And I know that apologizing won't really do all that much in the long run. Clearly, he's never going to look at me the same again, but still, I need to try. I need to do something. I can't leave him believing that I'm the total waste-of-space whore Seb's trying to make me out to be.

I wanted to reach out to him yesterday, but that fucked-up exchange with Seb that I regretted instantly—

even if I did drag my vibrator out of my drawer and get myself off—pretty much killed me off, and I passed out still wrapped in my towel and with wet hair.

I wanted to say I woke up feeling better, but that knot was still in my stomach, and the events of the previous forty-eight hours were still spinning in my head.

Calvin found me in the basement a few hours later, beating the shit out of the punching bag that I was imagining was Seb's face.

He put me through my paces and taught me some new techniques—ones that I can't wait to try on Seb at the first possible opportunity I get.

I'm pretty confident that I could break his nose now with one punch, and I really want to put it into practice.

I bet he'd still look drop-dead gorgeous with a busted-up nose.

I shake the thought from my head and banish him from my mind as I try to focus on my homework, but it's hard when my cell continues to taunt me from the floor.

I've had a few messages from Dad this weekend just checking in. I have no idea where he is, and I don't expect to find out anytime soon unless Calli happens to overhear where her parents have been, because I'd put money on them being together.

The more I think about all the secrets and lies, the more my anger begins to poison me. The betrayal from the one man I've always trusted stings more than I ever could have thought.

The sun's sinking behind the trees at the bottom of our backyard when I finally give it up as a bad job and close my computer. I've done everything that's due for the beginning of the week. I'll just have to hope that tomorrow will be a better day and I'll be able to focus.

I grab my cell and check the screen, but there's still no response from Toby—just a message from Calli excitedly telling me that she's spent all day messaging Ant. Even through her typed words, I can tell she's buzzing about meeting him next weekend, and it's enough to convince me that I did the right thing by agreeing to go. I'll just have to set Enzo straight from the moment that we arrive that I'm there for Calli and not him, because I have zero intentions of bringing another guy into my life. I've got enough to deal with right now. I don't care how good looking he is, or what he might have to offer. I'm firmly off boys for the foreseeable future.

I've got two vibrators that do the job almost as well as any guy, and that'll do me until I get all this bullshit sorted in my head and can actually embark on finding a decent guy who isn't only interested in shaming me in front of his equally douchey friends.

After tossing and turning and forcing images of *him* and the feelings and pleasure he manages to drag from me out of my head, I finally fall asleep, twisted up in the sheets.

But my attempt to put a barrier up between the two of us seems to vanish the second I drift off.

The sound of my door opening startles me, but the second I discover who it is, my panic subsides as I roll onto my back, pulling the sheets away from my body, I invite him in, forgetting everything I've told myself about what I'd do to him the next time I see him.

Reaching behind him, he drags his shirt up his body, revealing his toned stomach and sculpted chest to me. The tattoos that cover both his arms ripple and pull as he drops his shirt to the floor and starts working on his pants, ripping the button open and shoving the fabric over his hips, showing me that he's bare and hard beneath.

Oh hell yes.

If I have to put up with his presence, I'll more than happily take it like this.

His knee presses into my mattress, the entire bed dipping under his weight and making me slide toward him a little as he reaches out and cups my breasts, pinching my already hard nipples beneath my thin tank.

"Seb," I moan wantonly as a bolt of pleasure shoots to my core.

Pulling one of my knees up, I widen my legs in the hope of enticing him exactly where I need him.

As much as I've tried to push it from my mind, the memory of how he works my body into a frenzy is never far from my mind.

"Fuck, you're so beautiful," he breathes, his voice softer than I think I've ever heard it before, and I melt.

His lips find my neck, kissing and sucking, driving me to the brink of insanity before he drags the neck of my tank aside and sucks my peak deep into his mouth, dragging his teeth over it until my hips start writhing on the bed with my need for him to touch me.

"Oh God. Please," I whimper.

"Not God, Hellion. Just the devil," he says, his voice sounding like pure sex as he drags his eyes up to mine.

The heat and burning lust that stares back at me is almost enough to tip me right over the edge.

"You gonna come for me, Hellion? I've not even touched you."

"Seb, please. I need—"

"Shh... I know what you need. Do you trust me?"

I try to focus for a second, but my brain has turned to

mush. My body and its insatiable need for him have completely obliterated it.

But despite my lack of brain function, when I finally manage to respond to his question, the truth falls out.

"No. Not even in the slightest."

"Wise, Hellion. Very, very wise."

He chuckles against my breast, and I moan a curse as he switches to the other side.

"Touch yourself, Princess. Show me how you do it."

Unable to do anything but follow his wicked orders, my hand slides down my stomach until my fingers hit the lace. Dipping them beneath the fabric, I find myself dripping wet.

I moan as I circle my clit, imagining it's his fingers working me and not my own.

"That's it, my dirty little whore. Show me how you make yourself come when you're thinking about me." His voice sounds farther away when he speaks this time, but I'm too lost to the sensations running rampant around my body that I don't think anything of it.

I push my fingers lower, dipping one inside me. I can't get as deep as he can, but still, it feels so fucking good that my hips buck off the bed and I add a second, stretching myself open. My other hand drifts up my body until I find my breast, pinching and tugging at my nipple as the pleasure in my lower belly grows almost to the point of no return.

Something soft brushes against my lips and I startle for a second before I hear his voice once more.

"I'm so hard for you right now, Hellion. You've no idea what you do to me."

Reality threatens to rip me from this body-consuming bliss and I fight to stay asleep, to stay in the moment, to remain on the brink of losing myself to a vision.

"Suck me, baby. You're so fucking good at it."

I part my lips, doing as I'm told, but the second I lick at the tip of him and the taste of his precum coats my tongue, everything comes crashing down around me and I'm dragged back to reality with my body screaming and my core clenching violently at my lost impending release.

"Seb?" I cry as my eyes fly open and I discover my wicked fantasies weren't something my subconscious dragged up in my slumber but reality. "Get the hell out," I scream, writhing about beneath him, but he's got me pinned to the bed, my wrists now cuffed with one of his giant hands.

"Oh yeah, because I'm just going to walk out after watching you lose yourself to your dreams of me. I thought you'd know me better than that by now."

"Oh my God, you're a fucking psychopath," I shout, thrashing about once more despite the fact that I know it's a pointless waste of energy.

CHAPTER TWENTY-SEVEN

Sebastian

Getting inside Stella's house was a hell of a lot smoother this time, thanks to the fact that I got a copy of her key cut after she passed out at Nico's on Friday night. It was easy, too fucking easy, to ensure I've always got a way to get to her.

The entire house was in silence as I made my way upstairs. I had no idea if their staff lived in, or if they were in the outbuildings that came with this property, but I was silent as I moved just in case.

I was hopeful that I'd find her asleep and be able to take her by surprise. Hell, there was a part of me that didn't even want her to know I'd visited at all. I had images in my head of me slipping inside, taking what I needed from her, and disappearing again, leaving behind only a small piece of evidence from my little visit.

But what I got, in reality, was way, way more than I ever could have expected.

She was fast asleep, her eyes closed, her face peaceful with her lips parted, but her body was out of the sheets and her skin covered in a sheen of sweat. She'd pulled her tank down, exposing her breasts as she pulled at her own nipple and palmed her breast. Her other hand had vanished beneath her knickers as she writhed in pleasure, chasing her release even in her slumber.

The sight was so fucking beautiful. And without a second thought, I pulled my phone out and flipped the camera to video to capture her fall.

And only two seconds later, it got even better.

"Seb," she moaned, and I nearly came in my damn pants on the spot.

"That's it, my dirty little whore. Show me how you make yourself come when you're thinking about me," I murmur, my eyes locked on her writhing body, my cock aching to be inside her, to feel how tightly her cunt is squeezing her fingers right now.

Taking advantage when she was sleeping was a dick move, I knew that, but also, I really didn't give a fuck.

She clearly thought she was with me, so why not make her fantasy a reality?

"Oh my God, you're a fucking psychopath," she screams, waking up with me on top of her, trying again to buck her hips to push me off.

"I've been called worse, Hellion. Now, where were we? Oh yeah, you were knuckles deep in your dripping pussy as you called out my name."

Her jaw tightens, her teeth grinding as she stares up at me.

"I was asleep, asshole, and I was clearly having a nightmare."

"Oh, it sounded and looked terrifying." Trailing a finger down her chest toward her still bare tits, I whisper, "Your skin is still flushed from the fear."

"I hate you."

I smile. "I know, isn't it fun?"

The growl that rips from her throat does all sorts of weird shit to my insides, not to mention making my cock weep with need.

She glares up at me, her chest heaving, her nipples begging for some attention.

"W-what are you doing?" she hisses when I push my free hand under her pillow and root around. If I know her like I think I do, then I won't find it empty.

I smile the second my fingers connect with something.

"Seb," she warns, knowing exactly what she hid under there.

"And you claim not to be scared. Is that why you sleep with a gun under your pillow, Hellion?"

"I'm not scared, I just want you to leave me the fuck alone," she barks. Her words might be dripping in venom, but we both know they're far from the truth.

"Oh yeah, you wanna tell your body that?"

Her teeth grind once more as I brush the barrel of her gun down the soft skin of her cheek.

Her entire body flinches as the cool metal makes contact and her eyes narrow.

"I didn't put it there as a fucking sex toy, Sebastian."

"Maybe not, but I already know that a little gunplay gets you all kinds of horny." Leaning forward, I brush my lips over the shell of her ear. "I haven't forgotten a single second of our time together, Princess."

"You really should," she seethes, "or I'll start to think you've got a bit of an obsession with me. I already think you're fucked up, and it's going to get worse."

An obsession? I think it's abundantly clear to both of us that I'm completely fucking addicted. Why else would I be collecting her underwear and breaking into her bedroom to watch her sleep in the middle of the night?

And as for fucked up... I've been that for a long time.

"It's cute that you think I care what you think of me, Hellion. I couldn't give a fuck. I know what I want, and I know what the endgame is going to be. I'm just enjoying the ride."

"Oh yeah, care to enlighten me?"

Pulling back, I trail the gun down her neck and over her collarbone as I move toward her breasts.

An image pops into my head of her curled on the ground, her body shaking, tears streaked down her face as her father finds her. Broken, ruined. Fucking destroyed.

Yeah, that's what I want. I want him to watch his world fall around his feet. I want to watch as he experiences just a taste of what he's put my family through.

"You're going to have to wait and find out, Hellion. What would be the fun in telling you, huh?" She growls once more, but it's accompanied by a shiver as I run the tip of her gun around her nipple. "What I can tell you? It's going to be a lot of fun... for me."

She stares at me for a beat, thoughts flickering through her eyes, escape plans that we both know are going to fail. I'm the one in charge right now.

"Fuck you," she spits.

"Do you know, that's a really good fucking idea, Princess."

She tilts her chin up in defiance, ripping her eyes from mine, staring across the room as if she doesn't care.

Lies, total fucking lies. I can read her body better than she thinks I can, and she wants me more than she'd ever admit to right now.

Reaching for my waistband, I drag my belt free.

"Seb," she warns. The slight quiver in her voice makes my wicked heart sing as I loop the leather around her wrists and then attach them to her metal headboard, tugging to ensure I've tied her tight enough.

"There. Now you're totally at my mercy. What should I do with you?"

"I'm going to fucking kill you." The rise and fall of her chest increases, her breaths coming out in short, sharp pants as her narrowed eyes hold mine.

"Oh yeah? Good luck with that without the use of your arms."

Her hips thrash, but I'm too heavy for her to get anywhere.

"Careful or you'll find your ankles bound, too. Then you really will be powerless. Is that what you want?"

"ARGH," she screams, loud enough to sound out through the house, and I panic. I have no idea if anyone is here, but if they are I really don't need them rushing in to rescue her.

Slamming my hand over her mouth, I cut off her cries.

"If you want someone to join the party, Hellion, you should have just said. I can call my brothers now. You know they'll be up for it."

"Fuck you," she shouts against my palm.

Keeping it in place, I slide down her body, picking her gun back up and gliding it down the toned skin of her stomach until I can run it along the edge of her knickers.

"These will be perfect to add to my collection," I muse before looking back up at her.

Placing her gun on the bedside table, I release her mouth to free up both my hands. She doesn't say anything, but I'm not stupid. I know that's not because I warned her against it.

I wrap my fingers around the straps of her vest and tug until the sound of ripping fabric fills the room and it falls away from her body.

"Better," I murmur, moving down to get to her panties.

The second they're off, I stuff them into my back pocket.

"I wonder how many I'll have before I finally break you, Hellion."

"Not going to happen. I'm not some weak damsel in distress. I won't cower to you. You'll have to kill me first."

"Oh, that can certainly be arranged. But then we'd miss out on all this fun."

Wrapping my hand around her thighs, I push her legs wide, settling between them.

She fights, but not enough to stop me, and the second I blow a stream of air down on her swollen cunt, she immediately stops, losing herself to what she wants the most.

Her body jolts when I do it again, only closer this time, and her hate-filled eyes bore into the top of my head.

Rolling my eyes up her body, I capture them with mine and smirk.

She wants to demand I leave again, I can see it in the hard set of her mouth, but the slight frown that mars her brows point to her inner turmoil.

"You smell like sin and really fucking bad decisions, Hellion."

"Then walk out as fast as you entered," she grits out, although the roughness of her voice tells me she wants the complete opposite.

"You'd only be torturing yourself and you know it."

"I don't need you. Remember that vibrator I mentioned? It's fully charged and ready to go."

A laugh falls from my lips and the line between her brows deepens. "It's funny that you think I'll allow that to happen."

"You don't control me, Seb. I can do what I want. It's my body. *My* pleasure."

"Not anymore. It's mine. All of it."

Spreading her wider, I drop my lips to her cunt before she can snap out a biting comeback.

I lick up the length of her before sucking her clit into my mouth and nipping at her until she can't hold her tongue any longer and squeals in pleasure.

"Fucking hate you, Sebastian."

I chuckle against her and she moans, her hips rolling against my face, trying to get exactly what she needs.

Dipping my tongue lower, I push it inside her, lapping at her juices and letting her taste explode in my mouth.

Yeah. Obsessed doesn't even come close to what this is.

Wrapping my hands around her hips, I hold her still as I continue working her, feeding my addiction as she moans and cries out above me.

I watch all of it, my cock impossibly hard with its need to sink deep inside her.

"Oh fuck, please," she begs when I pull back a fraction just before she's about to fall. "Seb."

I laugh, brushing my lips over the healing skin on her thigh that bears my name.

Fuck yeah.

I give her five seconds to come down from the impending high before I start again.

I'm not ready for her to fall. When she does, I'm going to be so deep inside her that she'll be able to feel it until this time next week.

"Oh my God," she sobs, tugging against her bindings as I lap at her once more. "S-Seb."

CHAPTER TWENTY-EIGHT

Stella

My body burns up, my skin flushed with sweat as he continues to drive me toward the brink of insanity.

It was a dream. Just a dream. I was sure of it.

Until it really fucking wasn't.

My head spins as I race toward my release once more, although I already know he's not going to let me fall. Sadistic cunt.

If I were dreaming, I'd have come by now, he'd have left, and I'd be in a peaceful slumber. But no, here he is, torturing me with his tongue and dark eyes which shoot up to me every few minutes to ensure I'm still watching him between my thighs. Spoiler alert: I can't fucking rip them away from him, no matter how close he gets me.

His belt cuts into my wrists, my fingers going numb

from the lack of blood flow up there, but with the pleasure building once more in my belly, I forget all about them.

Tears burn my eyes as frustration washes over me once more when he pulls back. I want to cry, scream and lash out but I try to keep it all contained, because that's exactly what he wants.

He craves my hate, my anger, my violence.

I get it, because I feel the same. His wicked moves, barbed comments, and brutal touches feed something dark inside of me too.

This thing between us, it's lethal. And if we're going to continue with whatever this is, then one of us is going to end up burned. Badly.

I kind of can't wait.

I cry out once more as he thrusts two fingers deep inside me, bending them when he finds my G-spot, rubbing it until I see stars.

"Yes, yes, yes," I chant, hoping like hell that he's going to let me fall this time. "Cuuuuunt," I squeal when he rips his fingers from me. "I fucking ha—Oh God." I cut myself off when I watch him sit up, swipe his hand across his mouth and move his cock to my entrance.

He teases me for a few seconds as our eyes hold, hate and desire oozing from his dark depths, and I'm sure the same look is staring right at him as well.

He pushes the tip inside and my muscles clamp down, desperately trying to suck him deeper, but he holds still.

"Who do you belong to, Hellion?" His thumb presses hard against my healing wound as he says the words, sending a bolt of pain through me.

I growl, still not wanting to say the words.

"Say it, or I'll walk out right now."

I glance at the door, and he pulls back.

My panic forces my lips to move before my brain has had a chance to make a decision.

"No, no. Don't. I'm yours. Yours, okay?"

The most deliciously dark grin curls at his lips, but I only get to enjoy it for a second because he pulls out of me and flips me over as if I weigh no more than a feather.

I land on my knees, my ass high up in the air.

Crack.

"Fuck," I scream, grateful as hell that the house is empty. If it weren't, I'm sure someone would be up here by now thinking I was getting murdered.

His palm soothes the explosion of pain on my ass cheek before his cock glides through my pussy, finding my entrance once again.

Instead of teasing me, this time he slams inside me, forcing me to take all of him in one quick thrust.

My entire body lurches forward with his power before his hands land on my waist, pulling me back against him as he circles his hips and makes a loud moan rip from my lips.

He pulls out and sets a punishing rhythm, fucking me like a man possessed. His fingers dig into me hard enough that I know I'll have bruises when I wake in the morning.

"Too right I'm fucking obsessed," he mutters as if he's talking to himself, but I hear every word loud and clear even through my lust-filled haze. "Can't get e-fucking-nough."

I don't say anything for fear it'll make him stop.

"Your pussy. Fuck, Hellion."

"Argh," I cry when he brushes his hand up my spine until his fingers sink into my hair. His other hand frees his belt, obviously sensing that I'm no longer a threat to him,

329

and I'm lifted from the pillow my face was smashed against as he fucks me into oblivion.

My back presses against his shirt-covered chest as his lips find my neck.

"Do you have any idea how good you look impaled on my cock? It's almost like you were sent here just for me. For my pleasure."

I'm too lost to the sparks firing off around my body and my impending explosion to reply. I just soak up his rough voice and help it feed my climb toward the mindless pleasure I really hope is coming.

"Fuck. Fuck," he grunts in my ear, his fingers brushing over my stomach seconds before they find my swollen clit.

He pinches me hard as his cock swells inside me.

"Come for me, Hellion. I want to feel you milking my cock as I fill you."

My head falls back against his shoulder as he pinches my clit once more and his cock jerks with his own release.

"Seeeeeb," I cry as I fall, my entire body locking up as pleasure finally slams into me. My eyes close, my chin drops, and I swear to God that just for a second, I pass out as he holds my limp body up.

His arm bands around my waist as our heaving chests fight to drag in the air we need. Nothing is said as we enjoy the endorphins and aftershocks from our explosive collision.

His breath tickles over my neck, and my need to turn and capture his lips in that kiss he's still withholding from me almost gets the better of me.

His cock softens, although not a lot, and all too soon he pulls out of my body.

The quiet, soft lover he was for barely a minute

vanishes the second he presses his palm between my shoulder blades and shoves me forward, face-first into my pillow, my ass still in the air.

A violent shudder rips through me when he trails his finger through my hyper-sensitive pussy.

Dipping his digit inside me, he drags it through his cum before ripping it back out.

Using my hair to twist my head to the side, he trails his wet finger over my bottom lip, coating it in our joint release before he barks, "Open."

Powerless but to do what he says after that mind-blowing release, my lips part, and he pushes his digit inside, allowing me to taste both of us as I lick it clean.

"So the princess can do as she's told," he mutters to himself before lowering the length of his body over mine, forcing my hips to the bed.

His entire freaking weight presses me into the mattress as the tip of his nose traces around my ear.

"I'll be seeing you real soon, Hellion. Try to stay out of trouble."

He drops a kiss to my cheek before his weight leaves me. I flip my head over so my freshly kissed cheek presses against the pillow and watch as he tucks himself back into his jeans and folds his belt into his hand.

Then, without so much as a glance back in my direction, he disappears out of my room and jogs down the stairs as if he didn't just rock my fucking world and then leave me cold.

"Fuck," I breathe, flipping onto my back as the evidence of his little visit drips from me. "Gross," I hiss, I'm going to have to get up and have another shower.

"Good morning, sweetie," Angie says when I shuffle into the kitchen the next morning.

My body aches, my ass cheek stings, and my eyes burn from lack of sleep. To put it bluntly, I feel and look like shit.

"Didn't you sleep very well?"

And apparently, it's just as obvious to others as it was to me when I looked in the mirror. Great.

"No," I grunt. I've got a lot on my mind.

She gives me a soft smile and turns toward the coffee machine, knowing exactly what I need.

"Angie?" I ask while she busies herself making breakfast.

"Yeah."

"D-do you know where my dad is?"

She looks back over her shoulder, a deep frown line between her brows.

"No, I don't. I'm sorry. He just said he'd be gone until last night. Did he not come home?"

No, he certainly wasn't here for that. And Seb damn well knew it too, didn't he? Asshole.

"Not that I know of."

"I'm sure he'll call."

I mutter an agreement, thinking of all the bullshit messages that are sitting on my cell.

I don't want a fucking message. I want the truth.

"Here you go. Hopefully this will perk you up a little. Is there anything I can do to help?"

There are a million questions on the tip of my tongue, but I swallow them all down. I know Angie cares about me. She's been the closest thing I've ever had to a mother, but ultimately, she's on my father's payroll, so I'd be naïve to think that her loyalties weren't to him, and if I start asking questions, she'll tip him off.

I need answers, but I'm going to have to wait. I guess I've already waited almost eighteen years.

"Thank you," I say sincerely when Angie places the coffee mug in front of me.

I don't feel any better for it when I pull up at Knight's Ridge just over an hour later. The only positive thing is that I'm back in my own car and that asshole didn't leave me a little note as a reminder of our time together last night.

I don't need any more than those he left on my body. I swear to God my skin looks like a dot to freaking dot of Seb's wicked kinks.

I sit in my car as long as possible, but after watching almost all the other students head inside ready for homeroom, I know I need to shift my ass.

There has been no sign of Seb and his band of twisted douchebags, and I've still had no contact from Toby.

My stomach twists once more as I stare at their empty parking spaces.

I was hoping to enter after them, but it seems that plan has failed.

With a heavy sigh, I drag my exhausted body from the car and make my way toward the building.

The rumble of a motorbike behind me forces me to turn back, and when I do, a smile tugs at my lips.

Of course Emmie would turn up at school on the back of a badass bike.

She climbs off and rips her helmet from her head before grabbing her bags from the top box. It gives the driver a chance to pull his own helmet off, and my chin damn near hits the floor.

Fuck me.

He says something to her before she turns and marches my way.

"Holy shit, is that your dad?" I ask, my eyes still locked on him.

He's way too old for me, sure, but he is hot. Like... H.O.T.

"Uh, ew. He's like... ancient."

"Emmie," I laugh. "You are neither blind nor stupid. You know exactly how hot your old man is."

"He's got a freaking six pack too," she mutters as she takes off toward the entrance, much to my amusement.

"Oh my God. Tell me more."

She shoots me a death glare over her shoulder.

I'm pretty sure she knows I'm joking.

"Sadly, you're a little too late. I'm pretty sure he's banging Miss Hill," she announces as I catch up with her.

"No fucking way."

She shrugs. "Something is going on. He's being secretive as fuck. Even managed to convince him to finally buy me my own bike."

"Yeah?"

"Just a shame the engine of it will be worth shit."

"Only for a year, then you can get a bigger one, right?"

"I damn well will be, too."

The second we step into the common room, all eyes turn on me.

Well, any hopes of what happened on Friday night being kept on the down-low were wishful thinking.

"What's happened?" Emmie almost groans.

At least one person has missed the gossip.

My eyes find Teagan in the crowd of students and a spiteful smile pulls at her lips.

Of course the rumor spreading was all down to her.

I guess I can't really blame her. I seem to have acquired exactly what she wants.

Seb's fingerprints on my hips and his brand on my thigh burn as our stare holds.

"Hey," Calli says, popping up out of nowhere. "We should probably get out of here."

"I'm not cowering down to that bitch," I spit.

"I'm not suggesting you do. I'd just rather not start my Monday prying you off her when she starts something."

"A bitch fight to start the day sounds like exactly what I need," I mutter as Calli's hand wraps around my arm and she pulls me back out of the room. "Spoilsport."

Emmie follows as we make our way down to the bathroom.

"Where are the guys? Their spots are empty."

"They'll be here."

Emmie slips into one of the stalls and I take a step closer to Calli.

"Any news on what happened Saturday?" I ask, thinking back to finding Seb covered in someone else's blood.

She shakes her head. "No, but Dad is tense as hell. He and Mum came back from their trip early and we had to spend almost all of yesterday at Theo's while our dads basically locked themselves in my uncle's office. I've got a bad feeling about it."

Concern passes over her face as the toilet flushes.

"Everything will be fine. This is what they do, right? Kill people and shit."

"Who knows," she mutters.

"Did you spend all last night sexting Ant?" I ask loudly as Emmie emerges.

"Who's sexting who?" she asks, falling right into my trap.

Calli groans, her cheeks heating as she ducks her head.

"Calli's met a boy."

"You really should have come to my brother's party on Friday night, Em," Calli says in retaliation. "Stella really... let her hair down."

I can't help but laugh.

"What she's trying to say is that almost everything you'll hear today that's ultimately come from Teagan's vapid mouth is true. I'm a shameless whore."

Emmie shrugs as she washes her hands, her eyes meeting mine in the mirror.

"Sounds like I missed a good night. Count me in for the next one."

The bell rings out around us and we all move toward the door. A wave of apprehension washes through me as I wonder what the rest of my day might hold.

I soon get an indication, because the second I step out of the bathroom, my eyes find a very dark pair loitering at the other end of the hallway.

Even with the distance between us, tension and chemistry crackle and all the hairs on my body stand on end.

He winks before pushing from the wall and slipping into the classroom beside him.

Was he waiting for me?

CHAPTER TWENTY-NINE

Sebastian

"I heard she was with all of them. In one night."

"Yeah, same. She's in my lit class. I might see if I can move seats. I'm more than happy to be part of her next harem."

My fingers tighten on the fork in my hand as I listen to the fucking dead men at the table behind me.

Looking up, my eyes collide with Alex's. He looks almost as on the edge of losing his shit as I am.

Theo's not here. Well, he was here, but he and Nico got a call from the boss halfway through our second class of the morning and they ducked out to find out what he wanted.

Toby is here somewhere, but the motherfucker seems to be avoiding all of us. He's probably sitting in his car, eating his lunch like a pussy right now.

My jaw tics as the kids behind me continue talking shit about Stella.

I knew it was going to happen. The second I threw Teagan out on Friday night, I knew there would be consequences. But we can deal with a little bit of gossip and prissy rich kids running their mouths.

I nod at Alex, reading his thoughts as I stuff another piece of chicken into my mouth.

I'm not hungry. I lost my appetite the second they started on behind me, but if I don't do something then I won't be able to wait until they leave to show them exactly what I think about them planning to get anywhere near our princess.

"You saw her last night, didn't you?"

I pause chewing and look back up at Alex.

"What makes you say that?"

"Theo said you disappeared in the middle of the night, then reappeared looking like you'd been ravaged by a lion."

I pull one shoulder up in a shrug.

"Who said it has to be her?"

"Fuck off, bro. Don't even try to convince me that anyone else is getting your cock hard these days."

"Yours too, if Saturday morning taught us anything."

His low chuckle meets my ears. "We got the message loud and clear, man. Watching her fall, though? Fucking beautiful."

"Watch it," I growl.

"Save it for the wankers behind you. They're leaving."

We wait two minutes before we follow.

The second they step foot out of the building, the two of us grab the four of them from behind. They're so fucking shocked that they don't even try to fight us as we drag them behind the boiler room and into the shadows.

"Did you want to repeat the shit you were chatting about back in the restaurant?" I bark as four pale faces stare back at the two of us.

"U-uh…" one stutters.

"Just repeating what we heard, man," another says, finding some confidence.

"So someone else was saying he was going to move closer in the hope of getting a blowy in class, were they?" Alex barks, recognising the kid as the one who was happily announcing that shit for everyone to hear.

"Um…"

"Exactly."

He grunts, doubling over in pain as my fist connects with his stomach.

"Fuck," he groans, dropping to the floor like a sack of shit.

"Anyone else need to know how it's going to feel if you so much as look in her direction again?"

Three terrified faces shake their heads at me.

"N-no. We're s-sorry."

"Sure you are. Stay out of our fucking business before we make you our business."

They stand there trembling like little punks. I half expect wet patches to emerge on their trousers, but sadly they seem to hold it together.

"Fuck off, then," I snap and watch with amusement as they dive toward their friend who's still rolling around on the ground, drag him up, and disappear around the corner.

"Shit," Alex sighs, lifting his hand to push his hair back. "That was too fucking easy."

"I barely even hit him." I crack my knuckles, needing more to rid myself of the irritation coursing through my veins at listening to their bullshit.

"Maybe you should go and find your princess. Take it out on her."

His suggestion is seriously tempting. Or it would be if I hadn't already convinced myself a good fifty times this morning that I was going to give her some space and see how long it took her to come crawling back to me, begging for a repeat of last night.

The second I looked into her eyes when she emerged from the toilets earlier, I knew I was still at the forefront of her mind.

The rest of the day is boring and uneventful. We have football practice after school, ready for our first game on Thursday night. Theo and Nico's absence pisses off Coach, but there's little he can do about it. When the boss calls, you have little choice but to jump.

Toby shows his face but barely mutters a word to either of us despite Alex's attempt to hold a conversation with him. It seems that while I might have been the one who instigated Saturday morning, he's equally as pissed at the others for letting it continue.

Theo isn't at home when Alex drops me off, so I jump in my car and head to Mum's to see if she's still somewhat sober.

To my surprise, when I let myself in I find that she's not even home.

Feeling totally lost, I end up spending the rest of the night in Theo's gym, trying to work out the frustration those pricks put there earlier as well as my burning need to go back to Stella's house and find out if she's done anything to keep me out tonight.

"What happened?" I ask Theo the next morning when I find him sitting at the breakfast bar, wearing yesterday's clothes and looking like shit.

"Ugh, don't," he groans, finishing his drink and declaring that he's going to bed.

Whatever the boss called him in for yesterday was obviously about the Italians, seeing as he was happy to put us in the middle of it on Saturday and I kinda want to know what's going on.

"Nothing. He sent us out for intel but we got nothing."

"Assuming you're not coming in today?"

His answer is to slam his door.

"I'll take that as a no then."

The first person I see when I get to school is one of the boys from yesterday.

He takes one look at me as I climb from my car and damn near breaks into a run toward the building.

Shaking my head, I meet Alex and together we make our way in.

Teag gave me the cold shoulder yesterday while she spent the day bitching about Stella to anyone who would listen. I could have done something, but I figure Stella is more than capable of dealing with a bitch like Teag herself. Honestly, I think she'll fucking love shutting the mouthy bitch up.

But today it seems I've been forgiven for my actions, because the second I step into the common room she skips up to me and rests her arms over my shoulders.

"Hey, you," she purrs.

"Uh..." I hesitate as my brain tries to catch up with her personality disorder.

Alex nodding his head to the other side of the room clues me in to why Teag is all over me like a rash once more.

Stella is watching our every move, Calli sitting right beside her, the emo chick on the other side.

"Not interested, Teag," I mutter.

After all, it's her funeral if she wants her hair ripped clean from her scalp by an angry American, because that's the vibe that Stella is giving off right now.

"Oh come on, I've missed you."

"Then you need to buy a better vibrator."

Alex snorts his amusement while Teag rears back like I just slapped her.

"You can't seriously want that fake whore over me."

Before she has time to blink, I have her pinned back against the wall with my hand around her throat.

Leaning in close enough that our noses almost brush, I hold her eyes as a ripple of awareness races down my spine.

A growl of warning rumbles up my throat and Teag trembles in my hold, her eyes quickly filling with tears.

I've never been as rough with her as I have been with Stella. I don't hate her enough. Hell, I feel almost nothing for the mouthy bitch. The only thing she's got going for her is her tight cunt, but I'm more than over that right now.

Glancing over my shoulder, I find that Stella is on her feet.

I know exactly why, and something inside me sings that she's jealous of the way I'm handling Teag. Stella literally melts beneath me when I wrap my hand around her throat, and I fucking love it.

"You need to watch your fucking mouth, Weston. You have no idea who it is you're spreading gossip about. She's capable of way more than you expect." Releasing her, I take a step back.

"She's no one," she spits, clearly finding some fight now I've let her go.

"Don't say I didn't warn you."

Turning my back on her, I march straight up to Stella, not stopping until I'm close enough that her breasts brush my chest.

My hand finds its way into her hair and she gasps in shock as I drag her head back, forcing her to keep eye contact with me.

"She's all yours, Hellion. Do your worst."

Heat crackles between us and I nearly say fuck it and slam her against the wall and fuck her right here so the entire sixth form gets front row seats to who she belongs to.

My eyes flick around her face as she stares up at me, her breaths increasing as if she's imagining the exact same thing I am.

Dipping my head, I lick up her exposed throat before sinking my teeth into her soft skin, revelling in her sweetness. I pause for a second and then release her and walk out before I end up doing something I'm not going to be able to come back from.

Like kiss her.

CHAPTER THIRTY

Stella

My heart thunders in my chest as Seb releases me and disappears from my vision.

What the actual fuck was that?

Before I know I've moved, my fingers brush the patch of skin he just bit as my body burns from head to toe.

"Girl, no wonder you're all anyone can talk about. I damn near came, just watching that," Emmie announces, thankfully dragging me out of the Seb haze I'd just lost myself in.

"What? It was nothing."

"Bet your panties don't agree."

"Uh..."

It's then that I realize the entire common room is almost silent as they stare at me.

"Everyone's waiting to see if you're gonna follow him

and fuck him wherever he comes to a stop," Emmie helpfully points out.

"Well, they're going to be disappointed."

"Either that or they're counting on a bitch fight."

Following Calli's line of sight, I find Teagan with her two puppies on either side of her as she glares daggers at me.

Oh man, she is pissed.

"Do you think her head might explode?" Emmie mutters, trying and failing to cover her amusement.

"It's possible," Calli adds.

"Come on, let's get out of here."

Threading my arms through both of theirs, I lead them out of the room before I'm the cause of any more drama.

If I don't get kicked out of this place before the term is up it'll be a freaking miracle.

"You're not just going to let her get away with that, are you?" Emmie asks.

"What? She didn't do anything to me. And I'm pretty sure being publicly humiliated by Seb was enough of a lesson for her."

"Wasn't for you," Calli mutters lightly.

"What actually happened Friday night?" Emmie asks. "And don't even think about feeding me with bullshit this time."

The bell rings, putting an end to our discussion.

"Meet us at lunch and I'll tell you all my naughty secrets. If you don't hear the gossip before then."

"Oh, I've heard it all. I just want to know which parts are actually true."

"Probably all the worst bits."

Her eyes sparkle with excitement. "That's what I was hoping for."

I'm still laughing as I walk into my morning class, although my amusement soon vanishes when every set of eyes turns toward me.

So much for starting here and just hiding in the crowd. In only a week I've made myself the target of all the guys who are desperate for some action and all the girls who need a reason to be bitches.

I've been propositioned by more guys in the past twenty-four hours than I have in my entire life. Each one makes my skin crawl that little bit more. Mostly because I know it's all my own fault.

Saturday morning might have been relatively private with only the six of us aware of what happened down in that basement. But I wasn't exactly discreet in my revenge plan on Friday night.

I slump down in my seat and fight a yawn.

I hate that I spent most of last night waiting for a midnight visitor who never appeared. When I woke from a fitful sleep full of dirty dreams involving the crazy things he does to me, my body was wound up so tightly I almost immediately reached for the vibrator in my top drawer.

I have no idea why I pulled my hand back at the last minute. I want to believe it has nothing to do with the fact that he told me he was in charge of my body, my pleasure, but I think I'm only lying to myself.

"Is this seat taken?"

Looking up, I find a zit-covered, innocent-looking boy. I have no idea how he can only be months younger than the guys, but he looks like a child compared to them.

Probably because he's never been covered in someone

else's blood and done the things they have. Whatever they might be.

"No," I say honestly, although I do shift my chair over to put some more space between the two of us.

I swear to God, if he even tries to come onto me I'm going to snap his fucking neck.

By some miracle, Teagan and her bitches actually stay out of my way for the rest of my day, but I know my peace is coming to an end unless I skip out on gymnastics this afternoon, which won't be happening.

I need the exercise, the release. And if that just so happens to come with a side of breaking Teagan's nose, then I'm all in.

"Ready for this?" Calli asks as she pushes through the door to the locker room.

"So ready," I say, dramatically cracking my knuckles and making her laugh.

"Yeah, you really need to teach me a move or two," she mutters, reminding me of our conversation the other day.

"I'll teach you everything I know," I promise her.

All eyes follow our movement across the locker room, but while Teag might stand there with her hands on her hips staring daggers at me, she doesn't say a word.

"Do you think he ripped her tongue out?" Calli whispers, clearly finding it as strange as I am.

"We can only hope."

As if Miss Peterson knows, she puts us in a different team for the afternoon so Teagan and I are always at opposite ends of the gym.

I spot her glancing between the two of us more than once, so I figure the gossip has done the rounds through the staff as well as the students.

I'm on full alert as I say goodbye to Calli after practice and make my way to the other end of the parking lot.

There are a few kids loitering around, but thankfully none of them pay me any mind as I pass them all.

Familiar voices sound out behind me, and a quick look over my shoulder tells me that Teagan and her crew are following me. Fantastic.

Dragging my bag up higher on my shoulder, I prepare for the impending fight, already wincing at the thought of her talons dragging across my face, because there's no way she's not going to fight like a girl.

With my head held high, confident that I can handle anything that she throws at me, I round the corner toward where I left my car.

But the second my baby comes into sight, it's like someone pulls the world from beneath me.

Oh no she fucking didn't.

"You fucking bitch," I bellow, turning on my heel, putting my car behind me as I fly at her.

I don't need to hear her confession. I know without her uttering a word that she's the one who organized covering my baby in red fucking paint. The guilt and smug satisfaction are written all over her face.

My fist curls, ready to slam it into her smug little face. I pull my arm back but never get to throw the punch I'm so desperate for because a strong pair of arms wraps around my waist and hauls me back.

"Get the hell off me. Look what she did." I throw my arm out in the general direction of my car as my anger bubbles over and I fight again to try to get away. I don't even bother looking back to see who's holding me—my sole focus is getting to Teagan.

The innocent smile she turns on me has me lashing out harder, but still, I can't get loose.

"I have no idea what you're talking about, honey."

An angry growl rips up my throat as she steps around us, just out of my reach.

"Oh. What a shame. It was such a pretty car as well. I hope it doesn't take too much to clean off. See you tomorrow."

Her eyes lift from mine and she winks at whoever is holding me before she slips into Lylah's car and they race out of the lot.

"You can put me down now," I seethe, wriggling once more.

The strong arms finally release me and I break free, spinning on my heels with my fists still clenched, more than ready to wail on my captor instead of Teagan.

Until my eyes find his face.

"Toby?" I sigh.

My anger subsides momentarily, but then I remember that he's done everything he can to avoid and blatantly ignore me since Saturday morning and it returns full force.

"No," I bark. "You do not get to try to protect me. To fucking protect her after what she's done."

"Her father will get you kicked out of here if you hit her, Princess."

I suck in a deep breath, my chest rising with it.

"You do not get to decide for me. If I get kicked out for knocking the dumb bitch out, then that's on me. I don't need you to get in the middle. I'm a big girl. I can make my own decisions."

His face pales at my words, his hand rubbing awkwardly at the back of his neck.

"So I've been made aware."

"What's going on with you? I've tried to reach out. I've tried to apologize but you've just blanked me. I'm sorry you didn't like what you saw, but there's not a lot I can do about it now."

Blinded by anger, I storm away from him when he doesn't respond, ripping my car door open and flooring the accelerator the second the engine turns over.

My breathing is still just as heavy when I pull up on the driveway at home.

I fly through the front door and down the stairs toward the gym. I don't bother picking up my boxing gloves as I go. I don't bother taping my hands like Calvin always insists I do. Instead, I just go full throttle at the bag, imagining it's Teagan's face.

My chest heaves, sweat dripping from me as I throw everything I have at the bag, venting all my frustration at Teagan and her bullshit prank along with all the other shit that's been keeping my muscles pulled tight over the past few days.

The only relief I've had was *his* visit the other night. That's been the only time I've been able to get out of my own head.

Damn him.

I want to hate him, but it's hard when he gives me the escape I crave.

"ARGH," I scream, throwing punch after punch at the bag.

My hair sticks to my face and neck as sweat trickles down my spine.

I lose all concept of time and eventually my muscles begin to turn to jelly, but I still don't stop. I can't.

CHAPTER THIRTY-ONE

Sebastian

"**S**he did what?" I bark into my phone, shoving my feet into my trainers and marching out of my room at Theo's only seconds after I entered.

Alex and I bolted straight after practice when his dad called and demanded his presence at home. We didn't even hang around long enough to shower, something I'm now regretting.

Toby speaks on the other end, but I hardly hear the words. I don't need to. I already know enough.

Teagan's got a fucking death wish. If Stella doesn't take her out with her pretty pink switchblade—that I might even give back just to watch her threaten Teag with—then one of us will.

Teagan should know better than this. She might not be part of the Family, but she knows damn well not to cross us. Or at least I thought she did. It seems she's dumber than she looks.

"I'll sort it," I bark down the line, hanging up and connecting my phone to my car so I can make a few more calls to get shit fixed.

By the time I pull up outside Stella's house and find her damaged Porsche sitting out the front, my knuckles are white with anger.

I don't second guess myself as I let myself into the back of the house just like I did on Sunday night.

The sound of music playing in the kitchen filters down the hallway, but I don't hear any other signs of there being anyone around.

Taking myself up to her room, I find it empty. The bathroom too.

"Shit," I bark, lifting my hand to my hair.

Where would she have gone?

It's in that moment that I realise that I don't really know anything about the girl that's taken up almost every one of my thoughts, dreams, and nightmares over the past few weeks.

The only place I can think of is the graveyard.

But would she really go back there because of this bullshit?

As I make my way back down the stairs, another noise hits my ears—a rhythmic thud coming from an open door at the other end of the hall.

Intrigued, I make my way down the stairs to find a state-of-the-art gym that rivals Damien's. And at the very far end of the vast room, I find the person I'm looking for.

Wearing a pair of black and pink leggings and a sports bra, her tiny fists are pummelling the punching bag with everything she's got.

Her skin is glistening with sweat, her hair sticking to her skin as she moves, her muscles pulling, her body twisting in the most hypnotising way as she takes all her anger out on the bag.

I lose myself watching her, and it's not until I drop her bag to the floor with a loud thud that I even really remember where I am.

I'm not the only one it startles either because Stella stills, her chest heaving before she slowly looks over her shoulder.

If I thought the sight of her venting her anger did something to me, then the sight of her face with tears streaked down her cheeks fucking wrecks me.

"Helli—"

"Don't," she snaps, her voice hard, void of any emotion. "I'm too fucking angry to deal with your bullshit."

I take a step forward and she turns to me, her eyes dropping to the bag at my feet.

"Where did you get that?"

"Toby called me. I picked it up for you."

"For me?" she asks suspiciously, her brows drawing together. "I don't even remember dropping it," she mutters to herself.

"I'm sorry she—"

"Nah, fuck that, Seb. That stupid bitch's actions have nothing to do with you."

"Really? Because I think it has everything to do with me."

I close the space between us, my heart rate beginning to increase.

"Why the fuck do you care, anyway? You hate me, remember?"

"Yeah," I mutter. "Can't fucking stand the sight of you."

My body collides with hers a beat before her back slams against the wall behind her.

Her skin is damp with sweat, her hairline wet, but hell if it doesn't make me want her more.

All the air rushes from her lungs as I surge forward, finally giving her what she's been begging for and slamming my lips down on hers, forcing my tongue into her mouth.

I kiss her like it's the only chance I'm ever going to get as I lift her from the floor, wrapping her legs around my waist.

Her body follows my lead as she loses herself in our kiss, the taste of her salty tears hitting my tongue.

Needing more, I rip my lips from hers and run my tongue up her cheek, collecting up her tears and making them my own.

"She's gonna pay for this, Hellion. I fucking promise you that."

"Seb, please," she begs. The desperation in her voice makes me forget my own fucking name as I capture her lips once more, pushing my hand inside her leggings and finding her slick for me. "Please," she whimpers again into our kiss.

As I rub circles around her clit, her head falls back against the wall and our reflection catches my eye in the mirror beside us.

Fuck, that's hot.

Licking up the column of her neck, I brush my nose around the shell of her ear, pushing my fingers lower and dipping them inside her.

"Come for me, Hellion. Let me hear you screaming my name again."

"Oh God," she whimpers, her pussy trying to drag me deeper as I rub at her sensitive walls. "Seb. Seb," she cries. Each time she repeats my name she gets louder until she finally falls over the edge.

I watch her eyes slam shut and her lips part as pleasure covers her face, her pussy dragging my fingers deeper as she loses herself.

"Fuck, you're beautiful when you come."

She stills for a beat and my heart jumps into my throat, dread washing over me.

She can't close down on me now. She just can't.

The second she opens her eyes and meets mine, I breathe a sigh of relief.

"Fuck me, Sebastian. Make me forget my own name."

"Done."

Lowering her to her feet, I drop to my knees and drag her leggings and knickers down as she kicks her trainers off, allowing me to pull the clothing free of her body.

"Bingo," I say, stuffing today's knickers into my shorts' pocket, a smirk pulling at my lips as she watches me.

"Freak."

"Yeah, and something tells me you can't get enough."

Not allowing her to argue with what we both already know, I push her toward the mirrored wall and press her front against it.

She gasps as the coolness of the glass collides with her heated skin, but she doesn't argue as I press her palms against it, take her hips in my hands and drag her backwards, exactly where I want her.

"Don't move them. And don't close your eyes. You're

going to watch as I fuck you. See exactly what I do to you and how much you love it."

Her lips part to respond, but my palm cracks against the same patch of skin on her ass cheek that I hit Sunday night.

Her skin glows red before I even move my hand. My cock jerks at the sight and it begins weeping when she arches her back, offering herself up to me.

"You gonna make good on your promise, or are you going to leave?"

"Fuck," I bark, pushing my shorts down over my arse and wrapping my hand around my hard length. "I never back down from a challenge, Hellion. I thought you'd have learned that by now."

I don't give her a chance to prepare. Instead, I find her entrance and thrust deep inside, her slick pussy allowing me to be fully seated in one quick move.

"Yes," she cries, her hot hands slipping down the mirror a little as her eyes shutter.

"Eyes, Hellion. I want your fucking eyes."

Her blue immediately collide with my dark in the mirror and I begin moving, telling her everything I hate about her through our silent connection... only at some point I fear I might be giving away a little too much.

"Come for me," I bark, my hand coming down on her arse once more, making her scream as her pussy clenches so hard I almost blow my load without warning.

I might be a cunt in many, many ways, but I'll make sure she comes first tonight even if it kills me.

Twisting my fist in her hair, I pull her head back, making her back arch so I hit her in the place I know will make her scream.

"Come, Stella. Now."

Reaching around her, I find her clit, flicking it until she shatters around me, dragging me under with her.

"Holy shit," she gasps, her harsh breaths fogging up the mirror before she hangs her head between her shoulders as she tries to get herself together.

I pull out of her and tuck myself away, taking two steps back.

After a beat, she stands and turns to me, not giving a single fuck about her nakedness. Her confidence shines through and it threatens to make my cock stand to attention once more.

She's fierce, and I fucking love it.

"Get out," she snaps, holding my eyes firmly to emphasise her seriousness.

"W-what?" I ask, feeling like she just slapped me.

"Get. The. Fuck. Out. Of. My. House."

My chin drops.

"I don't want you here."

"But—"

"Fuck off, Seb," she says with a bitter laugh. "You're only here to see me at my weakest. Well, you saw it. You took advantage. You can leave now, feeling smug that you got to witness it. And if you're fast enough, you might not even bump into my lying cunt of a father on the way out."

"W-what?"

"GET THE FUCK OUT," she screams, loud enough to make me wince.

I take a step back, a frown playing on my lips. I don't know what I expected after I fucked her, but it wasn't this.

Her chest heaves as she stares at me and her fists curl once more. My eyes drop to them, and it's only now that I register the state of her knuckles.

"Let me look at them."

Her brows furrow as she follows my line of sight.

When her eyes come back to mine, they're cold and hard, her mask completely impenetrable.

I nod, accepting that there's no other choice here than to leave.

It's right, but for some reason I don't want to acknowledge it, it's the last thing I want to do right now.

"Fine. But don't expect me to come running the next time life blows up in your face."

"Did I ask you to be here now? No. No, I fucking didn't."

Throwing my hands up in defeat, I turn my back on her and storm from the house, not once looking back or questioning my decision.

Until I'm back at Theo's and lying on my bed, staring at my ceiling.

Then I run every second of our time together through my head, trying to figure out where it all went so wrong.

CHAPTER THIRTY-TWO

Stella

I don't allow myself to feel anything until the sound of his feet running up the stairs fades away and a door somewhere on the ground floor slams.

Only then do I allow myself to drop to my knees and let the tears of anger and regret fall.

I give myself five minutes and five minutes only to fall apart. And once my time is up, I wipe my cheeks with the back of my hand and pull on my discarded clothes, wincing as Seb's cum slips down my thighs with every move I make.

Turning my back on the gym, on the sweaty, bloody handprints I know I've left on the mirror, I force my legs to move and climb up to my bedroom.

I'm numb as I strip out of my clothes and step under the shower. My knuckles burn as the hot water washes over them, but I push the pain aside in favor of feeling nothing.

It's easier to shut down and forget all this bullshit.

Teagan's spiteful smile, Toby's concerned eyes, Seb's heated touch and vicious words that I crave like nothing I've ever experienced before.

I don't notice that my curtains and one of my windows is open until I've dropped my towel and pulled on a clean tank and sleep shorts, and an engine rumbles outside, the sound of gravel crunching beneath tires hitting my ears.

Praying it's Calvin or Angie, I walk over to the window. All the air rushes from my lungs when I watch my father's car roll to a stop.

"Of course. Just how I want to end this bullshit day," I mutter to myself.

The second he gets out of his car, he walks over to mine, running his fingers over one of the biggest splats of paint on the hood.

"Here we go," I mutter as he disappears from my sight and into the house.

"Stella?" his deep voice booms, making my heart jump into my throat. "I'm home."

Usually, I'd run down the stairs to greet him after he's been away, but not now. Today he's going to get a very different kind of homecoming, because the time for keeping me in the dark is over.

It's time for some truth.

When I eventually get downstairs, Dad has already shed his suit jacket and is standing in the kitchen, nursing a glass of whisky.

"There you are, kiddo. It's so good to see you."

I don't react to his words, and he's observant enough to notice.

"W-what's wrong?"

"Aside from the state of my car?"

"Well, yes, but I'm more concerned about you than I am a car."

"Right," I mutter, not believing a word of it. If he truly felt that way then he wouldn't have lied to me every day of my freaking life. "Well, the queen bitch at school organized that little treat for me while we were doing gym practice."

"Why? You've been here a week, what could you possibly have done already?"

"I don't know, Dad. Why don't you tell me why she might not like me?"

"What's her name?" he asks, his brows pulling together.

I swallow down a million things I could say that would clue him in to what I know. But I don't want to prompt him, I just want him to own up. To be honest with me for once.

"Not important."

"So why would you think I'd know about it?"

My eyes hold his, pleading with him to just tell me. To explain who we are and why we're here.

"Where have you been?" I ask, hopping up onto a bar stool.

"Meeting clients in Manchester."

"Clients for what?"

His eyes narrow in suspicion. "What's with all the questions?"

"I just want you to tell me something. Something real.

Moving here, it's made me realize that I don't even know you."

"What? Don't be silly, sweetheart. You know me better than anyone."

"Do I?"

He studies me for a moment, concern glittering in his eyes.

He hesitates for a beat before finally giving me something. "I was meeting some businessmen who are interested in investing in something I'm a part of."

My heart pounds in my chest as I hear the honesty in his tone. I think it might be the most truthful thing he's ever said about what he's done. So the fact that it's still chock full of lies really fucking burns.

"Just tell me the truth," I whisper, hating the emotion that creeps into my voice.

"I'm sorry."

I hop off the stool and back toward the door, already having had more than enough of this.

"You can't do it, can you? Even now, even being here, you still can't tell me the damn truth."

"Stella, I don't—"

"Don't worry, Dad. The girl who did that..." I throw my arm out to indicate toward my car. "Her name isn't Greek."

I flee before he can find a comeback. I slam my door closed when I get to my room and drag my dresser in front of it. I don't want to see anyone—not Dad, and certainly not Seb if he's stupid enough to make a return appearance.

Walking over to my bed after closing my curtains, I unzip my gym bag that Seb brought with him, ignoring the little voice in my head that tries telling me what a sweet move that was. From both Toby and Seb. They clearly spoke after the event.

My breath catches when I pull back the zipper and find my pink switchblade resting on the top of my school uniform. But it's not that which really captures my attention. It's the note.

Give her hell, Princess.

I'm still sitting with his note in my hand and a giant lump in my throat when the familiar pounding of Dad's feet on the stairs gets louder.

Great.

"Stella," he booms, his fist thundering on the door.

"Go away. I don't want to talk about it now."

"Come on, sweetheart. I—"

"You had your chance. You blew it."

I let the note flutter to my bed as I flee to my bathroom.

"I didn't think. Shit—"

"No, you're right. You didn't think," I snap back before slamming the door and turning the shower on in an attempt to drown him out.

I stand with my hands on the counter and my head hanging in defeat as he continues to pound on my door. It rattles like he's trying to get inside, and my heart jumps into my throat.

I might want the truth, but not like this. I don't want to be screaming at him, forcing it from his lips.

This isn't how any of this was meant to go.

It's almost fifteen minutes later when he finally gives up and leaves. And if I thought being kept in the dark by him was bad, I have to confess that hearing him walk away fucking wrecks me.

Turning the shower off, I make my way back to my bed, pushing the bag Seb brought to the floor and curling up under my covers.

I've got homework to do, loads of it, but I forget it all as I lie there in a ball, letting my mind run wild over everything that's happened.

My cell pinging in my purse eventually drags me from my thoughts, and I reach over to pull it out.

I find a string of messages from Calli, and I can only assume she's heard what happened. But it's not her messages that I open first. It's the one from Toby that sparks my curiosity.

I was a dick to him earlier. He'd have every right to ignore me.

Toby: I hope you're okay and that I did the right thing calling him. I'm sorry :(

The sad emoji he puts at the end tugs at my heartstrings, and I can't help but respond.

Stella: I'm sorry too.

When he doesn't immediately reply, I read Calli's messages and lose myself in a conversation with her about the whole event before I turn my light off way earlier than I usually would and without having any dinner, forcing myself to block it all out and go to sleep.

When I wake the next morning and risk a look out of my curtains, I find my car sitting there as perfect as the day she was delivered. I assume it was Dad's way of trying to make things right.

Little did he know that it was going to take a hell of a lot more than that.

I discover that he's gone again when I finally emerge from my room. Irritation flows through me as Angie explains that he won't be back until late.

It tells me everything I need to know about where his loyalties lie. He really is a Cirillo man through and through. And me... I don't even know where I stand right now in his line of priorities.

Maybe I should have just stayed in Rosewood.

This place has been nothing but a headache. I had a life there. I had friends.

Although I have Calli, and Emmie even, although she keeps herself just as closed off as I do, I don't feel at home here. Everyone else hates me and wants me gone.

I let out a heavy sigh.

"Penny for your thoughts," Angie says softly.

"I just... I don't think I belong here," I confess.

Stopping at the counter before me, she reaches across for my hand.

"Things will get easier, sweetie. This is where both you and your dad need to be."

"Why? Tell me why this is where I should be and maybe I'll let it go."

Sympathy covers her face.

"You've got to trust him," she soothes.

"I'm trying," I snap, jumping from my stool and storming from the house without my morning coffee or any food, again.

I stop off at a takeout place on the way to Knight's Ridge and sit at the back of the parking lot to eat and wait for everyone else to start appearing for the day.

It's the last place I want to be after what went down yesterday, but I refuse to run. I refuse to allow that bitch to think I'm scared of her.

The time passes quickly, too freaking quickly, and I soon find myself inside the building and once again the subject of everyone's attention.

Although, to my surprise, Teagan and her little friends remain on the other side of the common room when I find Calli, and I don't even see the guys.

Weirdly, that's how the two and a half days play out.

Not once, even during cheer or gym practice, does Teag even try to say a word to me.

I want to say it's because she's smart, but I think we all know she's the polar opposite of that after the stunt she's pulled.

Part of me thinks that one, or more, of the guys have warned her to leave me alone. But I don't want to think about them. Any of them.

Well, aside from Toby. We've exchanged a few messages since Tuesday night, and I finally feel like we're making some progress, although even he hasn't explained their sudden absence in my life.

It's like they were there, every-freaking-where I turned, and now they've just gone. Don't get me wrong, the peace and space from their overbearing asses is nice, it's just... weird.

I guess they're all just busy after what went down over the weekend, but Calli doesn't know anything—not that I'm really surprised. She's the only person who seems to be almost as in the dark about their lives as me. I feel for her. They're all moving around her, doing their thing, and it's almost as if they forget she exists.

But that all changes during our hockey match on Friday afternoon.

I'm exhausted after the weirdest week of my life, and I hate to admit it, but I'm still not sleeping properly, expecting Seb to slip into my room at any moment.

Any rational person would have had the locks changed on the house, or even installed an extra one on their bedroom door. But that's not how I roll, and I can admit to myself at least that I kinda want him to appear in the dead of night and make me scream again.

I'm barely paying attention to the match we're playing, and instead of watching the ball, I'm loitering by the sideline, wondering if I can get away with blowing off cheer in favor of just going home to bed. So when someone starts shouting, it jolts me from my thoughts.

I glance up just in time to see Emmie throw her hockey stick across the field and march toward Teagan with her fists curled, ready to throw down.

"Back the fuck off, biker bitch," Teagan snaps back, her own shoulders squaring, ready for a fight.

"What the fuck did you just call me?" Emmie seethes, her voice dripping with venom.

Teagan looks her up and down, her lip curled in disgust. "Biker bitch."

Emmie flies at her, Teagan's nose taking the brunt of the hit with a satisfying crunch.

The only thing that would be better about the whole thing would be if I were the one who threw the punch.

"Girls, that's enough," Miss Peterson squeals, suddenly noticing that something is wrong from where she was flirting with one of the male teachers.

She starts moving, but she's not quick enough—nor am I as Teagan retaliates, hitting Emmie across the face before they both really start going at it.

As much as I want to stand there and cheer Emmie on —hell, what am I saying? I want to get in the fucking middle and get involved. But I know I can't, and the second I reach them, I wrap my arms around Emmie and drag her back from a very pissed-off Teagan.

The sight of the blood pouring from her nose satisfies something inside me.

"Good hit, girl."

"I'm going to fucking kill her," Emmie seethes, fighting to get out of my hold as Miss Peterson hauls Teagan up from the ground.

"Go and get cleaned up," she hisses at Emmie. "I'll deal with you in a minute."

A rush of air falls from Emmie, her body going limp in my arms as she admits defeat.

"Come on, let's go and get sorted."

"Fine. But this isn't over," Emmie warns, her words directed at Teagan, much to Miss Peterson's irritation.

"Too fucking right it's not. She's got a lot worse coming her way."

"Girls," Miss P barks, forcing us to move.

It's not until we're halfway back to the building that I realize we've got a little audience.

Theo, Alex and Daemon are all standing on the edge of the football pitch, watching us. Alex and Daemon just look amused, full smirks cover their faces. But Theo? He just looks horny as fuck. It irritates me that I know exactly how he looks when he's turned on, but I force that thought down.

"What?" I bark. "Never watched a proper bitch fight before?"

None of them say anything as we storm past, but their eyes never leave us.

Assholes.

"Are you okay?" I ask, leading Emmie to the sinks in the locker room and wetting some tissue to clean up the blood pouring from her eyebrow.

She doesn't respond beyond an angry growl that rumbles up her throat.

We're still trying to stem the blood when Miss P appears with a murderous look on her usually pretty face.

"Emmie," she barks, coming to stop in front of us with her hands on her hips.

"I shouldn't have hit her, I know. Spare me the lecture, Miss. She's been mouthing off all week. She deserved it."

I narrow my eyes at Emmie. She hadn't said anything about Teagan and her bitches giving her shit. If I knew that on top of what she's done to me, I might not have kept a lid on my anger for so long.

Maybe that's exactly why she didn't say anything.

"Fighting is never the answer," Miss P says back.

"Right. Sure thing. Are we done here?" Emmie hops down from the counter, ensuring the tissue I had pressed to her brow falls to the floor, fresh blood almost instantly beginning to run down her face once more.

"No, I don't think—" But it's too late, Emmie's gone. "Great," Miss P mutters under her breath.

"You know she's right. Teagan deserves that and then some."

Miss P stares at me for a beat before letting out a sigh and walking away.

Oh yeah, she totally agrees.

I turn up at Calli's house an hour early on Saturday morning to help her get ready for her big date with Ant.

I expect her to be the one to answer when I ring the bell, seeing as I warned her I was coming, but when the door opens, I find a shirtless, exhausted Nico staring back at me.

"Princess," he growls, rubbing the back of his neck, a move which makes his abs jump, dragging my eyes way lower than they should be.

"H-hey, um... I'm meeting Calli."

"Damn, and here I was thinking you were here for me." He smirks, teasing.

I take a step closer to him and look up through my lashes.

"You know, it's tempting, but you're too pretty to have your face bashed in by Seb." I pat him on the cheek patronisingly before slipping past him and into the house.

"Like he could do anything about it," he sulks, following me up the stairs, despite the fact that he lives in the basement.

"I can feel you staring," I snap.

"That's because I am." I huff in frustration and he continues. "I know what's hiding under that cheeky little skirt, Princess. I wouldn't be a man if I didn't imagine it."

"You're a dog. Now fuck off, unless you want me to do your hair, too."

I'm about to reach for Calli's door when his hand wraps around my arm, stopping my progress.

"I love my sister, Princess," he warns, his voice low

and deadly. "But she's not made for this kind of life. I won't let you drag her into it."

I rear back as if he's slapped me.

"Fuck you, Nico. Your sister is a big girl. She's smart enough to make her own decisions."

Without another word, I rip my arm from his grip and storm into her room.

"What's wrong?" Calli asks the second I swing the door closed behind me, ensuring the interfering asshole won't follow to continue his lecture.

"Run-in with your brother."

"Ugh," she moans. "He's been like a bear with a sore head all week."

Dumping my purse on her bed, I walk over and stand beside her in front of her wardrobe.

"I don't know what to wear," she moans.

"We're just meeting in a diner, right? So jeans and a shirt. Keep it simple. Cute."

"I don't want to be cute. I feel like that's what I've been my entire life. I don't want to be sweet and gentle Calli. I want to be Calli Cirillo."

I glance over at her, knowing exactly what she means.

"Go sit down. I've got this."

She does as she's told, and I rummage through her wardrobe until I find something I think will be perfect.

"Don't you think it's a little short?" Calli asks, looking at herself in the mirror an hour later. "I'm pretty sure I got this for my twelfth birthday."

"It's perfect. I promise. Just don't... you know, bend over." I smother a laugh at the look of horror on her face. "You've got panties on, right?"

"Oh my God, I'm changing. I should have just gone with the jeans."

"No, you are not. You look hot, and Ant's eyes will pop out when he sees you. Come on. We need to sneak out. We're fucked if Nico or any of the guys catch us."

"Well, that's not reassuring."

I pause in front of her, placing my hands on her shoulders.

"I thought you wanted to leave that Calli behind?"

"I do," she says, and I watch as she finds some confidence and holds her head higher. "I am. Let's go."

With a nod, I step away, pull her door open and gesture for her to go first.

She looks hella hot as she marches past me in her studded boots, black skirt and grey slash neck sweater. She isn't showing off that much skin, but I guess when you're used to hiding it can seem like a lot. Her hair is in soft waves and her makeup is a little heavier than she'd usually wear, giving her an edgy look.

I'm sure of one thing. If Nico or any of the guys catch us, we're in trouble.

"What is this place?" I ask when I slow outside the address Calli punched into my GPS.

"Just a diner. I've been here a few times. It's good."

"Fair enough." I pull up into a space a little down the street and climb out of my car.

"They're already inside," Calli says nervously, dropping her cell back into her purse.

"Let's go then."

Threading my arms through hers, I tug her in the direction of Marco's.

The second we push through the door, two guys stand from a booth at the back of the diner and Calli trembles beside me. I instantly feel at home in the red, white and black American-style diner. But I don't get a chance to enjoy it. Calli's nerves are too intense.

"Chill the hell out," I whisper. "Look how excited he is to see you."

I'm not lying. I was right when I told her Ant's eyes would practically pop out of his head.

"Come on."

We walk over with smiles on our faces as both of the guys eat us up.

"Hey," Ant says to Calli. "You look incredible. I love the hair."

"Thanks," she says, reaching up to touch it nervously. "It was a spur of the moment thing."

He gestures for her to sit beside him, so I slide in with Enzo, who's smiling at me like the cat who just got the cream.

"They make a cute couple, huh?" I say, reaching for the menu and doing my best to show him just how uninterested I am in him. "So, what's good here?"

I jolt when his fingers brush my shoulder.

"It's good to see you again, Stella. I've thought a lot about you this week."

Oh God. I swallow nervously and force myself to look up at him.

"We danced for like, ten minutes. You barely know me."

"Maybe not. But I'd really like to get to know you. And looking at those two, I might just get my wish."

Glancing at Calli, I find that she's already lost herself in conversation with Ant as if they're long-lost friends.

It's cute, and I'm really happy for her that she's found something outside of her overbearing family. But hell, I wish I didn't have to babysit the guy's friend while she finds herself.

"We'll see," I mutter, pulling the menu forward again once more.

We all order when the server comes over and Enzo continues to drag me into conversation while the other two barely come up for air.

"So, what are your plans for tonight?" he asks, sliding a little closer.

I'm right on the end of the bench thanks to the last few times he's attempted the same move. I'm screwed now unless I want to end up on the floor.

"I'm just going to visit the bathroom." I excuse myself and hop up. "Calli, you coming?"

"Uh..." She looks between me and Ant, torn.

"We'll still be here when you get back," Ant assures, and she stands, following me through the doorway to the bathroom.

"Oh my God," she squeals the second we're out of sight. "He's amazing. Like, totally amazing. Don't you think?"

"Uh... he seems to really like you," I say. I hardly have an opinion on him, seeing as he's spoken no more than five words to me since we arrived.

"Oh my God," she squeals again. "Thank you." She throws herself at me, hugging me tight.

"You're welcome," I say with a laugh. "Enzo wants to know if we wanted to go watch a movie after this," I say reluctantly. I really don't want to sit in a movie theater with Mr. Handsy, but I'll do it for Calli. She's gonna owe me big for this.

"We're going, right? Say yes. Please, say yes," she begs.

"Whatever you want. You're in charge today. It's going to cost you though," I add as we both walk into the stalls.

"Enzo is cute. You should just go for it."

"He is," I agree honestly. He just... doesn't affect me in any way. Dancing with him was fun, but it was nothing like having my body pressed against a certain someone else's.

"Do not tell me this has anything to do with Seb," she warns.

"What? No, of course not. I hate him."

"Yeah," she laughs. "That's how you feel about him."

"It doesn't really matter. I can hardly get close to anyone right now while I've got his fucking initials carved into my thigh," I hiss.

"That's gonna heal and like... vanish, right?" she asks a beat before her toilet flushes, so I hold my reply until I meet her at the sinks.

"I really fucking hope so. I'm not living the rest of my life with his name on me."

Calli winces.

"Or I'll just have to get it tattooed over or something."

"It'll be fine. I'm sure of it."

"We'll see."

"So yes to the movie, and you'll make an effort with Enzo? That doesn't have to involve him..." Her eyes drop to my crotch.

"Sure. Sounds like fun."

We make our way back to the table, much to the delight of both of the guys waiting for us.

Enzo hasn't moved an inch, so when I sit back down, we're basically shoulder to shoulder.

I shouldn't care. The old me would have been all up for whatever he had to offer.

Fucking Sebastian. He's in my head, and he needs to fuck right off.

Thirty minutes later, the four of us are walking inside the movie theater. I leave all the decisions to Calli, which is something I instantly regret when I discover that she's opted for the new rom-com that's recently released. What was wrong with a thriller, or at least something with a decent gun fight and car chase?

With a sigh, I follow the happy couple to the darkened back row of the theater and flop down between Calli and Enzo.

As has been our afternoon, Ant immediately monopolizes Calli's attention, so I'm forced to humor Enzo some more.

The movie is dull. It's all ridiculous jokes and sickly-sweet romance, something that Ant seems to get the benefit of because right here at the back of the movie theater, Calli gives him her first real kiss and the two of them spend almost the whole movie making out.

It's sweet. And I'm not at all jealous. Nope. Not a bit.

It seems Enzo might just have been feeling a little left out too, because his fingers that were content on brushing my shoulder and hand in the diner have managed to find their way to my thigh.

"We're going to a party tonight," he whispers in my ear, his lips entirely too close to my body. "You should both come."

"I think I'm busy tonight."

"Damn shame. We could have had some real fun."

"I'm sure," I agree, pushing his hand from my leg for what must now be at least the fourth time.

Get a fucking clue, dickhead.

Enzo's wandering hands aside, it's been a fairly good afternoon. And I'm more than happy that Calli's managed to enjoy herself without her brother and his dumb friends breathing down her neck.

I've long relaxed and forgotten about the possibility of seeing them by the time we emerge from the building to the warm afternoon sun.

Ant pulls Calli aside and pushes her up against the frosted windows while Enzo throws his arm over my shoulder, pulling me into his side.

"I wish you could come tonight," Ant says, wrapping his hand around her neck.

"Maybe another time." She smiles at him, and I can't miss the disappointment in her voice.

I'm just about to cave and tell her we can go when Ant crashes into the two of us, his face exploding with blood.

"What the—"

"Nico, what the hell?" Calli screams, rushing toward Ant, but she doesn't get anywhere near because her brother wraps his arms around her waist and hauls her back against his body.

"What the—" I start when I'm pulled back and damn near thrown into the building as three hyped up, angry guys descend on Ant and Enzo.

"What the fuck are you doing? Get the hell off them," I scream, reaching for Seb's arm when he slams Enzo against the windows with his fist in his shirt. "Seb, stop it."

But he's too lost to his anger. He pulls his arm back without thinking, and I'm not quick enough to move. His elbow connects with my eye socket and I cry out as he swings, landing a solid punch to Enzo's face.

I back away from the scene, sirens blaring in the distance, there's nothing I can do to help. Hell, they don't even deserve me trying to stop them. They deserve to get caught for this.

"Stella," Seb calls as realization dawns on him.

"No," I bark. "You're a fucking asshole. Whatever this is," I gesture between the two of us, "it is so fucking done. I don't want you anywhere near me ever again."

His chin drops as the devastation continues to play out behind him, Theo and Alex taking the reins of ensuring both Ant and Enzo are in no fit state to touch either of us.

With one more look into his dark and haunted eyes, I all but run to my car to get the hell away from him and his poisonous soul.

I don't stop to think about how much my eye freaking hurts, or where Nico disappeared with Calli, I just start my car and floor the accelerator to get away from them —from him.

Pulling up outside my house, I note that my dad is here and groan. I really don't have the kind of patience to deal with him right now. I've managed to avoid him almost as successfully as Seb has me for the past few days, and I'm more than happy for it to continue.

Slamming my car door closed, I race for the house. I'm almost at the door when someone calls my name.

I pause, recognizing it, and look over my shoulder.

"What happened?" Toby asks, rushing toward me, concern pulling his brows together as he takes in the state of my face.

"Ask your friends. Although they'll probably need bailing out of jail first," I mutter continuing inside the house. The fact that I don't slam the door in his face is a freaking miracle.

"Stella, wait," he says softly, and my body follows orders, too exhausted to even think about arguing with him. "Are you okay?"

I take a step back, colliding with the wall. My knees almost give out and I think he senses it because he's in front of me in a flash.

He stares into my eyes and tears fill mine faster than I'm able to comprehend.

"Shit. What's going on? Tell me how to help."

I suck in a ragged breath as his hand lands on my waist, his support, his presence almost enough to send me crashing into the realms of emotional breakdowns.

"I-I don't... I just want to forget it all," I whisper.

His eyes drop from mine and to my lips as I speak, and my heart rate picks up. When they come back up, the blue is significantly darker than a few seconds ago, telling me everything he's thinking about right now.

My chest heaves as I wait for him to win whatever internal battle he's fighting, and when he does, my entire body sags in relief as his lips meet mine.

I barely register the thundering footsteps heading our way as he presses the length of his hard body against mine, pinning me deliciously between him and the wall, but I sure as shit hear the panic in my dad's roaring voice.

"Stella, no."

One second Toby is there giving me everything I need, and the next, he's gone.

When I open my eyes, I find his arm in my father's grasp, the confusion on his face rivalling my own.

"N-no, you can't," Dad repeats, his words coming out

between heaving breaths as if he just ran a freaking marathon.

This isn't the first time he's caught me with a boy, far from it actually, yet he's never freaked out like this before.

"Why? It's not like you usually care what I get up to," I spit.

"This... this is different. You can't be with Toby." The fact that he knows exactly who it is when he's only seen the back of him is weird, but it's nothing compared to the words that fall from his lips a second later.

"He's your brother."

All the air rushes from my lungs as I push from the wall.

"He's fucking what?" I bark, convinced that this must be a fucking joke.

Toby's face is deathly pale as he stares at me with wide, horrified eyes.

Looks like everyone's been lying to him, too.

"T-Toby's your brother," Dad repeats as if I didn't hear it perfectly fucking clearly the first time.

"Fuck this," I bark. "Fuck all of this. I'm so fucking done."

I run through the front door right as a car speeds into the driveway. A fucking Maserati. Of course.

But Seb's not quick enough.

I'm already past the car and heading toward the street when the passenger door flies open.

My feet pick up pace as I run, my lungs already screaming at me to drag in the air I need. I'm not sure I've actually breathed since Dad dropped that earth-shattering bomb.

I don't look where I'm going. My only focus is to get

away. Voices boom from behind me, forcing me to go faster, to push myself harder.

My legs pump, my feet pound against the ground. I'm praying that it's enough when I run into something akin to a brick wall.

"I'm so—What?"

I look just in time to see the glint of my pink switchblade before it sinks into my stomach and pain explodes through my body.

I glance up just in time to see a masked figure inches from me before everything goes dark and I'm thrown into the back of a vehicle.

Something hits me in the arm after I crash to the floor. I kick my legs out to fight, pain shooting from my stomach before everything goes black and finally the world and all its bullshit fades away from me.

Stella and Seb's story continues in
WICKED PRINCESS.
Coming 18th November 2021

Meet Stella before she moved to Knight's Ridge in my Rosewood High series.
DOWNLOAD THORN
now or continue reading for a sample.

THORN

CHAPTER ONE
Amalie

"I think you'll really enjoy your time here," Principal Hartmann says. He tries to sound cheerful about it, but he's got sympathy oozing from his wrinkled, tired eyes.

This shouldn't have been part of my life. I should be in London starting university, yet here I am at the beginning of what is apparently my junior year at an American high school I have no idea about aside from its name and the fact my mum attended many years ago. A lump climbs up my throat as thoughts of my parents hit me without warning.

"I know things are going to be different and you might feel that you're going backward, but I can assure you it's the right thing to do. It will give you the time you need to... adjust and to put some serious thought into what you want to do once you graduate."

Time to adjust. I'm not sure any amount of time will be enough to learn to live without my parents and being shipped across the Pacific to start a new life in America.

"I'm sure it'll be great." Plastering a fake smile on my face, I take the timetable from the principal's hand and stare down at it. The butterflies that were already fluttering around in my stomach erupt to the point I might just throw up over his chipped Formica desk.

Math, English lit, biology, gym, my hands tremble until I see something that instantly relaxes me, *art and film studies.* At least I got my own way with something.

"I've arranged for someone to show you around. Chelsea is the captain of the cheer squad, what she doesn't know about the school isn't worth knowing. If you need anything, Amalie, my door is always open."

Nodding at him, I rise from my chair just as a soft knock sounds out and a cheery brunette bounces into the room. My knowledge of American high schools comes courtesy of the hours of films I used to spend my evenings watching, and she fits the stereotype of captain to a tee.

"You wanted something, Mr. Hartmann?" she sings so sweetly it makes even my teeth shiver.

"Chelsea, this is Amalie. It's her first day starting junior year. I trust you'll be able to show her around. Here's a copy of her schedule."

"Consider it done, sir."

"I assured Amalie that she's in safe hands."

I want to say it's my imagination but when she turns her big chocolate eyes on me, the light in them diminishes a little.

"Lead the way." My voice is lacking any kind of

enthusiasm and from the narrowing of her eyes, I don't think she misses it.

I follow her out of the room with a little less bounce in my step. Once we're in the hallway, she turns her eyes on me. She's really quite pretty with thick brown hair, large eyes, and full lips. She's shorter than me, but then at five foot eight, you'll be hard pushed to find many other teenage girls who can look me in the eye.

Tilting her head so she can look at me, I fight my smile. "Let's make this quick. It's my first day of senior year and I've got shit to be doing."

Spinning on her heels, she takes off and I rush to catch up with her. "Cafeteria, library." She points then looks down at her copy of my timetable. "Looks like your locker is down there." She waves her hand down a hallway full of students who are all staring our way, before gesturing in the general direction of my different subjects.

"Okay, that should do it. Have a great day." Her smile is faker than mine's been all morning, which really is saying something. She goes to walk away, but at the last minute turns back to me. "Oh, I forgot. That over there." I follow her finger as she points to a large group of people outside the open double doors sitting around a bunch of tables. "That's *my* group. I should probably warn you now that you won't fit in there."

I hear her warning loud and clear, but it didn't really need saying. I've no intention of befriending the cheerleaders, that kind of thing's not really my scene. I'm much happier hiding behind my camera and slinking into the background.

Chelsea flounces off and I can't help my eyes from following her out toward *her* group. I can see from here that it consists of her squad and the football team. I can also see the longing in other student's eyes as they walk past them. They either want to be them or want to be part of their stupid little gang.

Jesus, this place is even more stereotypical than I was expecting.

Unfortunately, my first class of the day is in the direction Chelsea just went. I pull my bag up higher on my shoulder and hold the couple of books I have tighter to my chest as I walk out of the doors.

I've not taken two steps out of the building when my skin tingles with awareness. I tell myself to keep my head down. I've no interest in being their entertainment but my eyes defy me, and I find myself looking up as Chelsea points at me and laughs. I knew my sudden arrival in the town wasn't a secret. My mum's legacy is still strong, so when they heard the news, I'm sure it was hot gossip.

Heat spreads from my cheeks and down my neck. I go to look away when a pair of blue eyes catch my attention. While everyone else's look intrigued, like they've got a new pet to play with, his are haunted and angry. Our stare holds, his eyes narrow as if he's trying to warn me of something before he menacingly shakes his head.

Confused by his actions, I manage to rip my eyes from his and turn toward where I think I should be going.

I only manage three steps at the most before I crash into something—or somebody.

"Shit, I'm sorry. Are you okay?" a deep voice asks. When I look into the kind green eyes of the guy in front of me, I almost sigh with relief. I was starting to wonder if I'd find anyone who wasn't just going to glare at me. I know I'm the new girl but shit. They must experience new kids on a weekly basis, I can't be that unusual.

"I'm fine, thank you."

"You're the new British girl. Emily, right?"

"It's Amalie, and yeah... that's me."

"I'm so sorry about your parents. Mom said she was friends with yours." Tears burn my eyes. Today is hard enough without the constant reminder of everything I've lost. "Shit, I'm sorry. I shouldn't have—"

"It's fine," I lie.

"What's your first class?"

Handing over my timetable, he quickly runs his eyes over it. "English lit, I'm heading that way. Can I walk you?"

"Yes." His smile grows at my eagerness and for the first time today my returning one is almost sincere.

"I'm Shane, by the way." I look over and smile at him, thankfully the hallway is too noisy for us to continue any kind of conversation.

He seems like a sweet guy but my head's spinning and just the thought of trying to hold a serious conversation right now is exhausting.

Student's stares follow my every move. My skin prickles as more and more notice me as I walk beside Shane. Some give me smiles but most just nod in my direction, pointing me out to their friends. Some are just downright rude and physically point at me like I'm some fucking zoo animal awoken from its slumber.

In reality, I'm just an eighteen-year-old girl who's starting somewhere new, and desperate to blend into the crowd. I know that with who I am—or more who my parents were—that it's not going to be all that easy, but I'd at least like a chance to try to be normal. Although I fear I might have lost that the day I lost my parents.

"This is you." Shane's voice breaks through my

thoughts and when I drag my head up from avoiding everyone else around me, I see he's holding the door open.

Thankfully the classroom's only half full, but still, every single set of eyes turn to me.

Ignoring their attention, I keep my head down and find an empty desk toward the back of the room.

Once I'm settled, I risk looking up. My breath catches when I find Shane still standing in the doorway, forcing the students entering to squeeze past him. He nods his head. I know it's his way of asking if I'm okay. Forcing a smile onto my lips, I nod in return and after a few seconds, he turns to leave.

THORN and the rest of the ROSEWOOD series are now LIVE.

DOWNLOAD TO CONTINUE READING

ABOUT THE AUTHOR

Tracy Lorraine is a *USA Today* and *Wall Street Journal* bestselling new adult and contemporary romance author. Tracy has recently turned thirty and lives in a cute Cotswold village in England with her husband, baby girl and lovable but slightly crazy dog. Having always been a bookaholic with her head stuck in her Kindle, Tracy decided to try her hand at a story idea she dreamt up and hasn't looked back since.

Be the first to find out about new releases and offers. Sign up to my newsletter here.

If you want to know what I'm up to and see teasers and snippets of what I'm working on, then you need to be in my Facebook group. Join Tracy's Angels here.

Keep up to date with Tracy's books at
www.tracylorraine.com

ALSO BY TRACY LORRAINE

Falling Series

Falling for Ryan: Part One #1

Falling for Ryan: Part Two #2

Falling for Jax #3

Falling for Daniel (A Falling Series Novella)

Falling for Ruben #4

Falling for Fin #5

Falling for Lucas #6

Falling for Caleb #7

Falling for Declan #8

Falling For Liam #9

Forbidden Series

Falling for the Forbidden #1

Losing the Forbidden #2

Fighting for the Forbidden #3

Craving Redemption #4

Demanding Redemption #5

Avoiding Temptation #6

Chasing Temptation #7

Rebel Ink Series

Hate You #1

Trick You #2

Defy You #3

Play You #4

Inked (A Rebel Ink/Driven Crossover)

Rosewood High Series

Thorn #1

Paine #2

Savage #3

Fierce #4

Hunter #5

Faze (#6 Prequel)

Fury #6

Legend #7

Maddison Kings University Series

TMYM: Prequel

TRYS #1

TDYW #2

TBYS #3

TVYC #4

TDYD #5

TDYR #6

TRYD #7

Knight's Ridge Empire Series

Wicked Summer Knight: Prequel

Wicked Knight #1

Wicked Princess #2

Wicked Empire #3

Ruined Series

Ruined Plans #1

Ruined by Lies #2

Ruined Promises #3

Never Forget Series

Never Forget Him #1

Never Forget Us #2

Everywhere & Nowhere #3

Chasing Series

Chasing Logan

The Cocktail Girls

His Manhattan

Her Kensington